The
Farm Girl's
Dream

FLOWERS OF SCOTLAND

Eileen Ramsay

The Farm Girl's Dream

FLOWERS OF SCOTLAND

ZAFFRE

First published in 1997 in the United Kingdom by Little, Brown as *Walnut Shell Days*

This edition published in Great Britain in 2017 by
Zaffre Publishing
80–81 Wimpole St, London W1G 9RE
www.zaffrebooks.co.uk

A CIP catalogue record for this book is available from the British Library.

Paperback ISBN: 978-1-785-76229-1

Also available as an ebook

3 5 7 9 10 8 6 4 2

Typeset by IDSUK (Data Connection) Ltd
Printed and bound by Clays Ltd, St Ives Plc

Zaffre Publishing is an imprint of Bonnier Zaffre,
a Bonnier Publishing company
www.bonnierzaffre.co.uk
www.bonnierpublishing.co.uk

For Ian Sommerville

Acknowledgements

Thank you to all the writers who share so much, especially Hugh Rae, Sheila Lewis and Elizabeth Sutherland.

Prologue

Paris, 24th May 1900

HE HAD LEFT THE WINDOW open and the sound of the fruit sellers' carts, as they rattled along the cobblestones, woke him. The early-morning scents of Paris – baking bread and cold, damp, sickly sweet river water – drifted through the windows and mixed with Genevieve's perfume, the bouquet of the remainder of that second bottle of very good claret and the pleasing, masculine smell of an excellent cigar.

He smiled and stretched, remembering the assorted pleasures of the night. France was a most civilized country. Great food, fine wine, wonderfully seductive and enchanting women; too much to expect the cigars to be French. He should buy a box or two before he caught the boat train: couldn't get tobacco like that at home.

Genevieve woke, her glorious eyes focusing slowly.

'Jean,' she breathed, in that so French way she had of caressing his very ordinary Scottish name, the way that turned his legs to water. 'Jean,' she said again, and she stretched out her white hand with the scarlet fingernails towards him and he almost yielded.

'Must go, my darling,' he said, kissing her lightly but keeping out of the way of those nails, nails that could caress so softly but could scratch so deeply. 'I have to catch the steamer train.'

'Oh no,' she said, her hands gripping him. 'You said two whole days in Paris.'

He laughed. 'It *has* been two days, *ma belle*, the most beautiful two days . . .'

'Of our lives, my Jean.'

She was so desirable; he had never met a woman like her. He groaned and forced himself to move away from the rumpled bed. How easy it would be, and how very, very pleasurable, to slip back into the warm bed, into Genevieve's arms. 'I have something to attend to in Scotland, Genevieve. I'll come back just as soon as I can.'

Genevieve was not a woman to beg. She shrugged a shoulder in a very French way. *Très bien*, her shoulders said. Who cares? I am just as content if you go. What does it matter?

For a moment he looked down at her creamy back and toyed with the idea of making her change her mind. He could do it. They were all the same, *n'est-ce pas*? And then he remembered Scotland and his responsibilities. He echoed her shrug and began to dress.

Less than half an hour later, he was whistling merrily as he sauntered down the plushly carpeted staircase to the foyer, where two maids were already angrily scrubbing and polishing unseen dirt. He strolled past them and reached the door.

'Monsieur, Monsieur, the bill?'

John Cameron tipped his hat lightly back on his handsome head. He stared boldly at the hotel manager out of his grey-blue eyes and laughed.

'Don't fret, my man. Madame will take care of it.' And, once more whistling gaily, he was gone.

Priory Farm, Angus, 24th May 1900

Pain gripped Catriona. It tore at her angrily, as if punishing her for some unknown crime. Sweat broke out on her forehead and she tried desperately not to scream. She had never believed it would be like this, never. Was she not the daughter of farmers? Had she not seen birth a dozen times a year – a thing done privately, causing as little trouble as possible.

'Ach, lassie, let it out. There's no one to hear but me and auld Jock out there and he'd bear it for you, if he could.' The voice was that of Maggie, employed by Jock Cameron as dairy maid and now midwife.

Catriona's scream tore through the air and died to a gasping whimper. Maggie held her hand and, outside, Jock stopped his pacing and listened.

'Dear God, help the lassie, as I've never been able to help.'

She was quiet. Was that it? Was it over? Was he a grand-father?

There was another scream, cut short by the simple expedi-ent of biting as hard as Catriona could on the rolled-up towel that old Maggie had put into her open mouth. Catriona's eyes rolled in agony; there was a name she wanted to call out, but she would not. She would not beg and she would not hurt the old man any more by having him hear it.

The pain receded and she took the towel away. 'It's cold for May, Maggie, so cold.'

The midwife looked at the girl for a moment. Cold? It was a perfect May day. This morning the sweat had been rolling down between her ample breasts as she had sat milking in the parlour, and now her newly washed cot-ton frock was damp with perspiration. But the lassie was cold. 'Dear Lord, shock.' She ran to the airing cupboard for clean, warm blankets. Everything was to hand, meticu-lously prepared by Catriona herself.

'Let me wrap you up a bit more, lassie: you've lost a wheen too much blood but it'll soon be over. In a moment, the next push will bring us the head and your bonnie wee bairn will slip out like a boat being launched into the Tay.'

Catriona could hear Maggie's voice but she could not make out the words. She seemed to be floating. It was such a lovely feeling. She had been so cold, and now she was wrapped up the way her own mother had bundled her up against the cold of an Angus winter. So safe, so secure. Nothing hurt, nothing mattered – nothing, nothing. She would drift away, oh so slowly, like a leaf tossed into a quiet stream.

But Maggie would not let her slip away into that peace and contentment. She shook the girl, she cajoled, she wheedled. 'Catriona, Catriona, fight, lassie, fight. The bairn's crowning. He's coming, lass. I can see his head. What a crown of dark hair, just like his daddy.'

His daddy. John. John with his grey-blue eyes, his devastating smile, his hands that could . . . For a moment she struggled but no, it was so warm here, so peaceful – no pain, no tears, no wondering why. She would stay here where it was warm, where nothing hurt, where sound was blurred and hazy and soft. 'Oh, John, why?' Had she said the words or just thought them? She had no time to wonder, for the pain struck again and instinct took over her exhausted body.

'Work with the pains, lassie, dinnae fight them. That's it, that's it. Just a wee breath there, a wee rest to get ready for the next one.'

In the passageway outside, Jock Cameron paced as he waited. It was his fault, all of it. That lassie had been in there for fourteen hours trying to birth her baby, and the man who should have been here, either by himself or marching side by side with Jock, was God alone knew where.

'I spoilt him, Mattie,' he told his long-dead wife. 'He was that bonnie though, and always minded me of you. I couldnae hit you, Mattie, that's what it would have felt like and he knew it, the wee rascal, but he's a grown man now, Mattie. I'll never forgive him for this and if the good Lord spares me my daughter-in-law and my grandchild, I'll make it up to them.'

He walked on, backwards and forwards, sometimes praying to the Almighty, at other times justifying himself to his Mattie. Then he would work out how best to reward Catriona for her patience, her friendliness, her charm. He would bypass John, hurt him in his pocket – that would teach him. He would see the lawyer fellow and write the babe in and John out.

The door of the best bedroom opened and Maggie stood there, drying her hands on one of Catriona's best towels. She was smiling – well, as near as auld Maggie could get to a smile for a man. 'You can stop your tramping, Jock Cameron. You've near worn a hole in that good rug and it's the mistress will have to be on her knees darning it, and her with more than enough to do.'

'Catriona? The bairn?' He could barely speak, so anxious was he.

'Mistress Cameron's fine. A bit tired, and who's to wonder at that after what she's been through. The bairn's bonnie. She'll lead you a dance, you auld fool.'

'A lassie?' The relief was so great that he felt his knees buckle and he forced them to stay straight. A wee girl. What a comfort to an auld man a wee lassie would be. He felt humble and grateful.

'Can I see them?' he asked.

She stood back to let him enter the dark, low-roofed room. Catriona, her face pale in the cloud of her red hair, was lying back against the pillows, but she opened her eyes as if she sensed his presence and smiled tiredly at him. In her arms rested a tiny shawl-wrapped bundle, no bigger, he thought, than one of her own dumplings.

'I'm sorry it's no a laddie, Faither.'

'A laddie?' His heart swelled within him with love and he put out a hard, calloused, work-worn finger and gently touched the bundle. 'Ach, Catriona Cameron, was it not a lassie like you and my Mattie that this house needed?'

The baby lay snug in her mother's arms, and as her grandfather leaned over she yawned heartily in his face. Then she opened her eyes and stared at him measuringly, as if she found him wanting. He was captivated.

'You'll have thought of a name, lass.'

Catriona was quiet, as if summoning up her strength. She had been through so much, one way and another, in the past nine months. At last she said, 'I prayed for a boy, another John.'

Mattie, he thought, it should be Mattie. Then he turned from his study of the baby's face and looked at the serene expression of his daughter-in-law, after all she had been through. Women were amazing creatures. He would never understand them.

'Do you know what day it is today, lass? It's the auld Queen's birthday. Can you believe she's eighty-one years old and most of that spent on the throne? Victoria. Is that no a name for a bonnie bairn?'

'Victoria. It's perfect. Welcome, Victoria Cameron.'

Miss Cameron yawned again and thus dismissed her court.

'I'll leave you to sleep, lass. I'm sorry my son's no at your side where he belongs, Catriona. If I could change him I would, but I promise you this, lass. Everything I have is yours and the bairn's and I'll no allow John to give you any more pain.'

She tried to argue, to talk, to tell him that a halfpenny-worth of love from John Cameron was worth more to her than anything.

'It has to be my fault,' she tried to say. But how can you tell your father-in-law that in some essential way you must have failed his son? Otherwise John would be here, wouldn't he? She knew well that they did no real business in France. John's business trips to see stock, to see crops – she forced herself to admit that he had to be seeing other women. 'But, dear God, dear God, I have no pride. I want him. I need him.'

She closed her eyes and the old man tiptoed out and left her to sleep.

John Cameron arrived home from his latest business trip in France to be met by the barrel of his father's shotgun.

'You shouldnae have dismissed your cabbie, lad. It's a long walk to the town in your fancy shoes.'

'Father, are you crazy, man? It's me, John.' He made to move closer to the house, but the rock-steady hands of the old man gestured backwards with the gun – the gun that John knew could be used to deadly effect against foxes and other predators. Jock Cameron never wasted a shot. He would not waste any now.

'I know fine who you are. Isn't it me that's ashamed of fathering you.'

'Come on, Father, it was business. Wasn't I looking at French cattle? I want to see my wife and my bairn. You cannae deny me my own child. A boy it'll be – a grand, healthy John Cameron to carry on the farm.'

'And what do you care about the child or the farm? What were you doing the night your wife lay in there near bleeding to death to bring your daughter into the world?

You're nae good, John. You never were, and for your mother's sake I wouldnae let myself admit what I saw, but that's over. I should have belted you years ago, and as God's my witness, you come one step nearer this house and I'll blow yer head aff and swing fer you.'

John started to shout then. 'Ye crazy auld fool. I'll get the bobbies in. Catriona, Catriona, come out here and tell that auld devil to let me in my own house.'

'It's my house, John Cameron,' Old Jock said, 'and one day it'll be the lassie's. Take yourself back to your French whore, and see if she'll keep ye warm when she finds out the landed gentleman has lost his land. Not a penny more do you get from me. I'll be at Boatman's office first thing in the morning to change my will.'

He wouldn't shoot him, he wouldn't. John moved closer and the gun spoke. John jumped as the dust flew from the ground exactly in front of his right foot.

'You're crazy, you old fool.' He was crying with fear and anger, and with fatigue. 'Catriona,' he called out desperately, 'Catriona.' But he did not see the weeping figure at the window, and he turned from the gun and stumbled blindly into the night.

1

1910

IT HAS BEEN SAID BEFORE, and will, no doubt, be said again, that the time before the Great War was very special.

Certainly it was for Victoria Cameron. She was a most important small person, at least in the eyes of Grampa, for whom she could do no wrong. Mamma was firmer, but that was the way, Victoria knew, of both mothers and grandfathers. She loved them both fiercely, and she loved the old stone farmhouse with its magic kingdom of the walled farmyard, where Grampa would groom the Clydesdales. There were always six huge, broad, gentle beasts with noble names – Scottish Maid, Glentanar, Thermopylae, Stornoway, Queensberry and, of course, the Cutty Sark. Grampa never used these grand names; to him the horses were always 'hen', 'lass', or 'ma wee laddie'.

To the end of her life, Victoria could recall him as he polished their coats before hitching them up to the carriages, which local children took on their annual Sunday school picnics.

'That's it, hen, good lass. Aye, that's ma own good lass.'

Sometimes he would hoist Victoria up and put her on the broad back of a large horse. She would clutch the mane with her little hands and look down, down from the broad, gleaming shoulders of the horse to the ground so far, so very far below; and she would look into Jock's whiskered face and she would laugh. Fear? She did not know the meaning of the word, not with Grampa there, with his strong brown hands.

Did the sun always shine in the years before the war? There must have been rain and snow, but Victoria's memories were full of sun-filled days, days when she would wander out of the farmyard and follow one of the drystane dykes to the burn. There were two stiles between the house and the burn. Years later she could still feel the sense of adventure that she experienced each time she climbed a stile and wandered farther away from her mother. She never went too far, though, for in later years she recalled that she had always been able to see the house.

Her mother worked the whole day long. Everything in the house, including Victoria, was scrubbed to within an inch of its life. Like the linens, Victoria was also starched and ironed.

Mamma baked, preserved, cured and dressed, and in the evenings she sewed and mended, knitted beautiful woollens for the three of them and somehow found time to do exquisite embroidery.

Her day of rest was Sunday, and so Sunday was Victoria's favourite day of the week. Jock would hitch two of the Clydesdales to the carriage, and everyone, masters and maids, stiff and starched in their Sunday best, would set off for their beautiful little country church.

But it was the time after the traditional huge Sunday midday dinner that Victoria relished. It was then that she and Grampa would escape. For this truancy they had a beautiful little phaeton, which was always pulled by the Scottish Maid, the lightest of the Clydesdales, and off they would go, Grampa in his black frock-coat and hat and the child stiff and starched in her pinafore and best Leghorn hat.

There was not a nook or cranny in Angus that they left undiscovered. The old man was never loquacious, but their silences were companionable. Every now and again he would say, 'Whoa, maid. Whoa, ma lass,' and together old man and young child would sit and drink in the view. Wherever it was, there were always trees somewhere in the landscape.

'Breathe deep, Victoria,' he would say, 'there's no air in the world to match this. It's a perfect walnut shell day.'

The little girl looked up at him with those clear, grey-blue eyes – Mattie's eyes. It was bearable to think of them as Mattie's eyes.

'What's a walnut shell day, Grampa?'

'A day that's beautiful because you're with the person you love most in all the world. Everything is so perfect that you want to keep it for ever, so you put it in a walnut shell and save it for the days when nothing is good. Then, my wee Victoria, you take it out and all the joy and peace is there just as you remembered it. Oh, my wee Victoria, is life not hard at times, and does that not make these walnut shell days a' the mair precious?'

He looked gently down at the much-loved child and knew that she did not really understand.

Momentarily his heart sank – for Jock Cameron knew that, in time, God love her, she would know only too well what he meant.

'Let there be plenty of walnut shell days for her, Lord,' he prayed, and for months afterwards he would save walnut shells for Victoria to attempt to fill.

Memories of past picnics were enclosed in them. Wrapped in a clean, white linen napkin would be their shivery bite. They would sit on their tartan rug in the shadow of a ruined abbey and eat their scones and talk of the holy men who had lived there, and of how they must have enjoyed just the same trees, 'but, never the same scones, Victoria.' Grampa would laugh, for everyone in Angus knew that there was no finer baker than Catriona Cameron.

* * *

Victoria Cameron was so used to being the centre of attention that it came as rather a shock to find herself ostracized at the local primary school. Only the other social outcast, Nellie Bains, who wore ragged clothes, smelled and had a constantly dripping nose, wanted to play with her. And Victoria, who had been brought up to know her own worth, did not want to be anywhere near a dirty, ragged child like Nellie Bains. When she was small, Victoria saw only the rags, the tangled hair, the runny nose. She did not see the smile of pure friendship; she was too young and self-centred to glimpse the reflection of a loving heart.

'Nobody plays with me, Mamma,' Victoria complained. She did not mention Nellie, who was a nobody and therefore did not exist.

Catriona's eyes filled with tears. How dare they make her child suffer? She hugged her daughter so hard that the little girl pushed herself away. She put her balled-up handkerchief into the front pocket of her hand-embroidered apron and tossed back her dark hair.

'Nellie Bains said a bad word, a really, really bad word. She said I was one and none of the nice girls is allowed to play with me.' She leaned towards her mother and whispered the offending word so quietly into her ear that Catriona, taken by surprise, asked her to repeat it, and was then both shocked and mortified that her little daughter had ever uttered such a word.

'You are not,' said Catriona angrily. 'Shallow minds, with not enough to do but make up stories. Just never you mind, Victoria. Some day a really nice little girl will want to play with you.'

'Why some day? And what does that bad word mean, Mamma?'

But Catriona refused to tell her, saying that well-brought-up children should not know such words. Victoria was looking both upset and slightly mutinous. Catriona desperately tried to find a solution and then she found one, but one that frightened her, for she was not used to confrontation. 'I know, Victoria. I'll come into the school and have a word with Miss Spencer.'

But the word with Miss Spencer did not mend matters, for Miss Spencer looked down her educated nose and told Catriona that it was all highly irregular and she could not control what the children learned in their own homes.

Catriona had never disliked anyone in her entire life. Even her philandering husband had received no criticism from her, but this was different: this concerned her child.

Narrow spinster, thought Catriona angrily. No wonder no man's wanted her. Thirty years old, if she's a day, and trying to look like a lassie.

But she was no match for the contempt of the other woman. Besides, Catriona had been brought up to think teachers superior to ordinary mortals. Were they not full of book learning? Some had even been to a place called the university. That inbred feeling of inferiority, however, was warring with her own very justifiable anger.

'Just make sure you control what they learn here, miss,' she said furiously and, head up in defeat, she walked away.

And then Nellie, angry that her offers of friendship were constantly being spurned, took matters into her own rather grubby little hands and told Victoria exactly what the bad word meant.

'You've no pa, you stuck-up wee child, and your ma's no better than she should be.'

Victoria looked at Nellie, at her dirty face and her snotty nose. She was not quite sure what Nellie was saying, but she recognized the vindictiveness with which it was said. She slapped Nellie hard across her wizened wee face. Then she turned and ran crying from the playground, and she did not stop running until she reached the haven of the farmhouse.

'Where is my father?' she blurted out as soon as she could draw breath.

Catriona, who had felt the heart stop beating in her body as her distraught daughter almost fell in through the door, sat down on a kitchen chair, something she seldom did during the day. She took a deep breath and tried to steady the wild clamour of her heart. It had to come, of course. Father had warned her that she should have spoken of John, so that the bairn could grow up accepting his absence. But it was hard, so hard, to admit her failure. She took the angry, distressed child on her lap.

'Your father was not a very good . . . not a very dependable family-type of man, Victoria, not like Grampa; but I loved him very much . . . Maybe I still do,' she added sadly. 'He had charm, you see, like Grampa, but he was never meant to be a farmer – more a man of the world. He has gone away: he went away before you were even born. He was Grampa's son, but we don't speak of him.'

'Where is he? Didn't he like me? Grampa likes me.'

Catriona looked at her daughter. Which question to answer? The memory of that awful evening when John had turned up at the farmhouse, only to find the door barred and his father standing there with a double-barrelled shotgun in his hands, made her wince. She could almost hear the angry voices. At first John had cajoled, in the way he usually did, to worm his way back into his wife's or his father's affections.

'Father,' Catriona had begged. 'He's sorry. He's Victoria's father. I cannot deny my bairn her father.'

'I'll see Boatman about more than my will the morn, Catriona. Lassie, you cannot still love him after the way he's treated you.'

'I don't know. Sometimes I hate him . . . sometimes . . .'

Jock had looked down at her compassionately. 'That goes, lassie, believe me. You're better off without John. He'll break yer heart.' He had turned back to the window and pushed the barrel of the shotgun through the opening. The blast had shattered the silence and caused the sleeping baby to awake, screaming.

Catriona had stared at her father-in-law and the blood had receded from her cheeks. 'John,' she had gasped on the point of fainting.

'Lassie, lassie, away to the bairn. It was only a rat that was sunning itself at my very byre door. I was wanting to mind John on who it was that taught him to shoot.'

And now Catriona turned to her daughter. 'He never knew you, sweetheart. When he did come home after you were born, Grampa wouldn't let him in the house. He left us, sweetheart, but I will never leave you, never.'

Victoria had stopped sobbing. Still she shuddered, but now she was calmer.

'And I will never leave you, Mamma, never.'

There was an earnestness in the young voice that almost frightened Catriona as the child added, 'That's a really truly promise, Mamma.'

2

1913

THE SEASONS CONTINUED IN ALL their varying splendour and the world moved just as steadily towards madness. Victoria finished at the little local school and went, every day, in the horse bus to the Harris Academy in nearby Dundee.

Grampa and Catriona, but not Victoria, had had many discussions about the form that the young girl's further education should take. It was a momentous decision to make. After all, no one on either side of the family had ever gone beyond an elementary education.

'Our lassie has a brain, Catriona,' murmured Grampa in awe. He himself had had to leave school, where he had not been known for perfect attendance, just after his twelfth birthday. 'Third prize and a special certificate for music. Clever *and* musical.'

Catriona was not sure that an ability to thump out marching tunes for the Boys' Brigade on the old upright piano in the parlour could be classed as musical, but she, as well as her father-in-law, was quietly pleased with Victoria's achievements.

She was, however, full of doubts about this new stage in her daughter's development. 'I wouldn't want to push, Father. Victoria's never talked about staying on at school. It's not as if she's always said she wanted to be a teacher, or a missionary or anything. Just happy to spend her days reading books and walking around the farm.'

'I'm talking about a university education for my wee lassie, Catriona. So it'll be the Harris Academy. I've met some fine people that got their schooling there. We don't want to send her to the high school. I've walked by there some days when I'm in at the bank and, I'm sorry, but some of those bairns get a bit above theirselves. I wouldn't want anything rubbing off on our wee lassie, but you're her mother. If you want her at the high school, I'll be more than happy to find the money, you know that, and I'll rely on your good sense to keep her feet on the ground.'

Privately, Catriona thought there would be obstreperous children in every school, but Victoria herself had shuddered at the idea of going all the way into the city centre to Dundee High School. One or two of the friends she had eventually made at Birkie would be at the Harris. She wanted to be with them.

As it happened, her best friend at the Harris Academy was to be a girl she met on her first day. Elsie Morrison was the only girl in a large family and she fascinated Victoria. Her life, surrounded by parents and grandparents, brothers, aunts and uncles and cousins, was so different from Victoria's own rather narrow existence. Every spare minute that the girls had they spent together, for while Victoria loved being exposed to the rough and tumble of Elsie's overcrowded life, Elsie loved the peace and quiet of Priory Farm. In the evenings they would sit in the comfortably upholstered farm parlour (or sitting room, as Elsie insisted on calling it) and play the piano and sing, or wind up the old Victrola, put on a record and dance. Elsie knew all the latest dance steps; she had seven brothers, after all.

On Sundays after church, when Grampa was too tired or too busy, Victoria and Elsie would go rambling all over the countryside. Sometimes they took a tram and then walked to a well-known beauty spot, or they would pack a picnic tea into their saddle-bags and venture farther afield on their bicycles. It was during one of these rambles that Victoria met Robert.

It was one of those September days when the world was warm and golden. The trees were just beginning to turn, and green, yellow, scarlet and brown leaves danced, it seemed, on the same branches; brambles hung fat and juicy on the hedgerows, and rowans and rosehips vied with each other in colour and number; the friendly smell of wood smoke from a hundred cottage gardens hung on the air. It was a walnut shell day.

The girls, like countless other Dundonians, took the ferry across the Tay to the village of Newport, in the Kingdom of Fife. They left the others happy to laze on the Newport Braes, those pleasant grassy slopes, and were soon deep in woods near the estuary of the great river. Rowan, oak, pine, birch, beeches – everything that was beautiful – was growing in those woods and the girls were going to sketch them. At least Elsie was. Victoria played with her charcoal and then wandered off.

She sat down on a mossy bank, trying to memorize the colours and, as always, feeling inadequate. She could not possibly paint the autumnal tints, let alone the sighs that the boughs made when a breeze moved them or the rustle, like golden coins, as they fell.

'Quite something,' said a voice beside her.

His voice was what Grampa termed 'county'. It belonged to the crested carriages that occasionally came to the wee village church. Normally Victoria would have curtsied quickly and moved away, but there was a power in the golden day that made her stay.

'Quite lovely,' she agreed, and looked up at him as he stood silhouetted against the pale autumn sun.

Her heart seemed to stop beating. He was the most beautiful boy she had ever seen – tall and slender; an aquiline profile with deep blue eyes and hair the colour of a raven's wing, blue where the sun struck it. And how the sun was shining that day in September 1913.

She was suddenly breathless, and fought for control of her heart, which was beating so rapidly that her blood seemed to be rushing around her veins in the strangest, and yet most pleasant, way. 'I was trying to sketch it,' she managed at last, holding up her sketchpad with its virgin pages.

He looked at it measuringly, as once she had seen her art teacher do when the First Year Art Appreciation class had walked into the Dundee Art Gallery to view its masterpieces. 'You sketch as well as I do,' he said laughing, and they laughed together.

He helped her up, and at the touch of his hand her whole body seemed to burst into flame. She was afraid that her normally pale skin had turned red – so unattractive – but he appeared not to have noticed, and she turned away to pick up her drawing materials. Somehow it seemed right that he should stay beside her as she continued her walk. They talked easily of the beauty of the woods. The splendid boy (what was his name? Oh surely, surely, Hector or Lysander – something poetic) pointed out some especially fine specimens and Victoria wondered at a boy who could speak so easily and serenely about nature. Grampa might say that he liked flowers, but he was old. She could not imagine Elsie's brothers admitting to a fondness for flowers.

They talked too of the ugliness of war, for the boy said that his father knew someone who said that there were evil people in the world, who would stop at nothing to force their views on others. Then, too soon, because the tides of the River Tay wait for no man, and certainly for no wee lassie who has just met her Sir Lancelot, it was time for Victoria to go home.

He watched her walk off through the great bushes of rhododendrons and then, as she reached the turning that would take her out of sight, he called, 'What's your name?' She turned and saw him again, outlined against the sun as if he were not quite real, and she knew that this moment and this boy were important and had changed her for ever. She called back, 'Victoria.'

'I'm Robert.'

'Robert.' Not the name of a knight in a picture book. 'Robert.' Such an ordinary name for such an extraordinary boy. No, it was right, perfect. She had never met anyone who wore their name so well. She whispered *Robert* over and over again on the long journey back to Dundee. She wondered where he lived, and where he went to school, and whether she would ever see him again. For Robert's face was the one she had given every knight and hero she had ever read about, and Robert's slenderness and grace were theirs too. She did not say 'I am in love' because she was only thirteen years old, but wherever she went after that she looked for Robert, and each time she returned to the enchanted woods she felt a dull ache of disappointment that Robert was not there.

*

Not, that is, until Easter 1914. Victoria and Elsie were looking for spring flowers, and Robert's woods were full of them. Elsie sat on a fallen log, happily sketching primroses while Victoria wandered off, as usual.

'Hello, Victoria,' said a voice, and there he was.

He was taller and thinner and even more beautiful than she remembered.

'Hello,' she said as calmly as possible, for her heart was beating so loudly that she felt he must hear it.

'No sketching today?'

She gestured back to where Elsie was sitting. 'I was, but I'm no better at sketching now than I was in September, so I decided to walk a little.'

He fell in beside her and they began to pick up where they had left off in that golden autumn.

'There will be real trouble soon, Victoria, you'll see,' said Robert. 'Lots of chaps at school are joining up. I wish I were old enough. I'd go, and we'd soon rout those Huns.'

The Huns. Everyone talked about them, but no one talked with relish, not in the the way Robert was talking, as if what was happening was a great game. Tam Menmuir, Grampa's best worker, had sons, and Victoria had heard them talk about these people called Huns. They talked with sorrow, with anger, with despair. They worried that if these Huns were not controlled, there would be trouble. Then they went on to talk about record harvests and yields, and about the things that really mattered.

Suddenly Victoria felt older than Robert, older than Catriona, older than Grampa. 'How old are you, Robert?' she asked.

'Sixteen – almost – but I'm tall enough for sixteen, don't you think?'

He grabbed her hands and whirled her round in a mad dance. 'That's what I'll do. I'll lie about my age.'

How could he look so happy at the prospect of going to war? Victoria fought down a rush of fear. She hated the very idea.

Her scarf had slipped down from her neck and he bent to retrieve it from the carpet of leaves.

'I shall keep this, Victoria, as a favour from a lady. Perhaps I shall tie it round my rifle.'

Again he bent, but this time he picked two perfect primroses. 'Take these in exchange.'

'These are private grounds. It's against the law to pick flowers here,' said Victoria primly, although she took them.

Robert laughed. What a joyous laugh he had. 'They'll forgive a knight going off to the Crusades.'

Perhaps many of the boys and men who went to the carnage that was the Great War thought of themselves as Crusaders – knights in shining armour, fighting evil. Right was on their side and they would win. But at what cost?

'I must get back to my friend,' Victoria replied conscientiously, instead of expressing all the sensible things she wanted to say about the futility of war.

'Wait,' he said. 'Victoria, may I write, if I get in, I mean? And you could write to me, about home fires and all that rot. Here,' he snatched her sketchpad and tore a sheet from it. 'Write your name and address and I'll write mine.'

She scribbled them down, then they swapped papers and she blushed furiously when she saw his name. Of course he could pick the primroses on his own father's land.

'*Au revoir*, Victoire,' he said grandly, and, taking her hand, he raised it, in what she thought of as a very Gallic gesture, to his lips.

'Goodbye, Robert,' she answered softly and another blush swept over her cheeks.

She returned to Elsie and very carefully put the primroses between the pages of her sketchpad. Later that night she gently pressed them between the pages of *Mansfield Park*. Her Bible, she thought, would have been a worthier repository, but she used it often and the primroses would have been sure to fall out.

*

Europe went mad and the glorious harvests of 1914 and 1915 were obliterated by marching feet and tanks, and by all the other implements of mass destruction. Not in the Angus glens, though, where Jock Cameron stood sucking his empty pipe contentedly, as he watched the final gathering of his most successful harvest. Victoria, her hat falling from her tangled hair and her skirts kirtled up about her legs – best make sure Catriona did not catch her ewe lamb looking like that – waved to him from Glentanar's back.

'I've eaten all the brambles I was supposed to collect for jam, Grampa.'

He laughed. She had no need to tell him. Were her lips not stained with the evidence?

'Best slip down and tidy yourself afore your mother catches you, young lady,' he said in mock seriousness, but Victoria did as she was bid.

When she had dismounted from the gentle giant she ran to his side, shaking down her dress. 'Oh, Grampa, was there ever such a walnut shell day. It's the best ever.'

For a moment she almost took that back, for was not yesterday the best day ever, because a scrap of paper had arrived from *Somewhere on the Front*.

No, she could not share that even with Grampa. It was too new, too precious, too achingly sweet.

They went back to the farmhouse. Catriona took one look at her hoyden of a daughter and began to fill a bathtub with boiling water from the kettles on the gleaming range.

'I do not know which of the two of you is the greater child, Father,' she said crossly. 'I'll never get her fit for the harvest dance.'

But she did, and three hours later a model of propriety stood with tapping foot beside her grandfather. Catriona and Bessie Menmuir, wife of Grampa's senior stockman, had laboured for hours the previous night, after Victoria had gone to bed, to finish a dress fit for this first dance. No couturier ballgown this, but still a hand-sewn work of art. Where had they found the material? The dress was, in fact, made from tartan tablecloths that Jock's wife, Mattie, had made long before the turn of the century, and which had been discovered in a trunk in the attic. The neck was cut lower than Catriona could permit, so she had ripped cream-coloured lace from her late mother-in-law's one and only evening-gown and filled the neck with that. There were lace bows at the cuffs of the sleeves, which sat just below the girl's sun-browned, dimpled elbows, and more lace disguised the hem of the swirling skirt, where one tablecloth had had to be tacked to the other.

Conscious that she had the most beautiful dress in the room, Victoria sparkled with a young girl's joy as she waited impatiently while her grandfather welcomed neighbours and workers alike to his home. Oh, if only there was some way to capture her image in her lovely dress and send it to *Somewhere on the Front* to warm the heart of a soldier boy. Victoria smiled and looked at the tables sagging under the weight of the pies that Catriona and her helpers had spent days preparing. When the dancing started, whisky and ale would flow more readily than the water in the parched Tay. Would it be in poor taste to write a description to Robert, who was existing 'somewhere' on meagre rations?

It was the most joyous evening. Victoria danced with everyone, young and old alike: Tam Menmuir, Davie (his oldest son, home on leave from the war), ploughmen and cattlemen, Bessie, Catriona, Elsie, and finally she forced her Grampa away from his whisky and his cronies.

'A dance, Grampa, come on. Sandy's away to play "Strip the Willow".'

Surely only a man with shoes nailed to the floor could have resisted the fiddle that night. Jock Cameron whirled his granddaughter round as if she were no heavier than the small treasure he held tight between his gnarled fingers. One of Elsie's brothers, the only one of the seven not already in the Forces, his eyes almost blinded by the mad sweep of Victoria's lacy petticoats as she whirled past him in her grandfather's arms, stood waiting to snatch the girl for the next dance.

Suddenly Jock stopped his mad dervish whirl. He looked across the smoke- and dust-filled room at his daughter-in-law.

'Forgive me, Catriona,' he said. 'I always meant to put it in the lassie's name,' and he fell forward. The walnut shell he had been clasping slipped from his fingers and rolled to the feet of the girl, who stood like a statue frozen in stone. It was then that she screamed.

Jock would have enjoyed his funeral – the biggest in Angus for many a long day. Crested carriages and farm carts jostled for room and, even in her grief, Victoria could see how much he had been loved. Although her eyes were swollen and red, she did not cry in public. Nor did her mother and yet her grief was as great as, if not greater than, the girl's. And to that grief was added worry for the future, for in her head were echoing the words: 'I always meant to put it in the lassie's name.'

A few weeks after the funeral, Victoria came back from school to find an unfamiliar pony and trap in the farmyard. Old Tam had been watching for her and he came out of the stable, comb in hand.

'Away to the scullery for your tea, Victoria. The mistress has a lawyer fella with her.'

In the scullery, perched on a scrubbed stool, Victoria ate scones with jam and drank hot, sweet tea and tried to taste them. 'The best baker in Angus.' Was that not what Grampa had said about her mother? Grampa? She felt again the hot tears squeezing up and she struggled to force them back. Would she ever, ever be able to think of him without crying?

'Oh, Grampa, Grampa,' she sobbed to herself. 'Why did you leave me?'

Later, Catriona came into the scullery while Victoria was at her homework, and sat down at the table beside her.

'Victoria, my dear,' she said. 'The time has come to talk, a little, about your father.'

Victoria looked at her expectantly, but with misgivings. Her father? She cared nothing about her father. It was Grampa she cared about.

Catriona understood what was going through her daughter's mind and ached to be able to spare her pain. She began to speak in a clipped, almost cold voice – emotionless. How else could she cope?

'Your father, my husband, was . . . is, as you know, your grandfather's son. I . . . I . . . divorced him ten years ago.' Once again Catriona thought with gratitude of the love and care of the old man, who had insisted that she be freed from his own son. Thank heaven, he had always said, that Scots law was light years ahead of English law. All Catriona had had to do was prove that John had deserted her. And since he had never been seen in Angus since the day that his father had thrown him out, desertion had been cited as the *just cause*. She had found out later about the fees old Jock had had to pay, first to Arbuthnott Boatman and then to the very competent Edinburgh advocate, whom the canny Scots lawyer had recommended to handle the case. But, however much it had cost, he had paid them willingly.

Catriona continued. 'Since then I have been house-keeper here for Grampa. He always meant to make a new will, in your favour, Victoria, but he never got round to it. However, he – without my knowledge, needless to say – has paid me an extremely generous wage all these years, and it has accumulated at a good rate of interest. We will be able to cope, but we must leave the farm. It now belongs to . . . Grampa's son. As yet we do not know where he is, but Mr Boatman will find him. Lawyers are very clever, Victoria. Anyway, I want to leave as quickly as possible. I will not be here when . . . It is better to make a clean break. Do you understand, Victoria? Mr Boatman is arranging to buy a house in Dundee for us, on Blackness Road.' She stopped, and in her mind's eye she saw once again the house she intended to buy. So different, so very different. She went on, 'It's a respectable area. You will be able to continue at the Harris Academy, Victoria, and so all your friends will remain the same.'

She stopped and looked at her daughter expectantly but, in the depths of her own grief, Victoria was too numb to think. Nothing registered, but that awful moment of silence when Grampa had stood there staring at Catriona, clutching at his heart, his voice gasping. What had he said? What did it matter? He was dead.

'I don't care where we live,' she said and Catriona winced, but she knew the child was putting up her defence mechanisms just as she, with her cold, unfeeling voice, had done.

Victoria always wondered how her mother managed to be out of the farmhouse within the three days that followed the signing of the contracts between Catriona and the lawyers of the late owner. She must surely have stayed up all night, for the following Saturday found them ready to leave Priory Farm.

Had the farm ever looked lovelier as it sat nestled among its carefully tended gardens? Redcurrants that Catriona had been unable to put up were still hanging like rubies on the bushes. The sun sparkled on the early-morning spider's webs strewn across the hedges. Already, smoke from the fires in the tied cottages was drifting out of the chimneypots and Victoria could tell which of Grampa's workers were already up and ready for the day.

I can't bear the pain, thought Victoria. I can't leave here. I'll die, away from this air, these scents.

She said nothing of her agonies as they spent the day carrying out their last duties, for Catriona was determined that the new owner would find no trace of the previous occupants. At last it was time to eat one final meal and, for the very last time, climb into the old phaeton that Victoria and Grampa had used for their forays. She could still, she was sure, smell his familiar, much-loved presence. She did not look round as Tam bowled them out of the farm and along the road to Dundee.

'It's a nice area, Victoria,' said Catriona desperately. 'Near Elsie and the Harris. We'll make it work.'

Victoria said nothing as they raced along the road, past Templeton Woods and into Dundee. Had the river ever looked more beautiful, stretching for miles like a long, silver ribbon? Had the sun ever burnished the leaves on the trees to such splendour? No one in the phaeton noticed the beauty of the road; no one cared.

'Keep going, keep going for ever and ever until we run off the edge of the world,' Victoria silently told the horse.

But eventually it stopped and the two passengers looked at what was to be their new home.

'Ach, mistress,' Tam said, before he remembered that he was only a servant, 'you cannot live here. It's nae better nor a slum.'

Victoria looked up and saw a three-storey stone house almost buried beneath its overgrown garden. The gate was hanging on its hinges and all the ground-floor windows were broken.

'It's not as bad as it looks, Victoria,' said Catriona, desperately trying to reach inside the unblinking statue that her daughter had become.

Victoria climbed like an old woman from the phaeton. She helped Tam unload, much against his wishes, since he had strict ideas about what was right for masters and what was expected of men, and she carried some baskets into the house. Catriona had gone ahead to light some lamps and set a match to the fire she had laid earlier in the week. She did not light all the lamps – lamplight is flattering and welcoming, but better perhaps to keep the real state of their new home from Victoria until the girl had slept.

Victoria said nothing as she put baskets in the kitchen and wicker hampers of clothes in the bedrooms. Catriona carried a small leather steamer-trunk, which really belonged to John, but which he had given her for their wedding trip. Most of the labels had peeled off over the years, but one still said Hôtel St-Etienne, Paris. Had she realized it was there, Catriona would have scraped it off too.

'We'll make some cocoa afore you go back, Tam,' she said as he put down the biggest and heaviest of the boxes.

'Mistress, come on back tae the Priory. We'll think on something. This is no right, and it's no what he would have wanted. We can talk to the new boss.'

'I've made my bed and I mun lie on it, Tam. We'll be fine, Victoria and me. We'll manage, you'll see. What was it Jock used to say, when we complained about anything? *Pull yourself together, laddie. Ye've never died a winter yet.* Well, we're not going to die this winter either, Tam. We're going to manage.'

Victoria stood at the dirty window and looked out on to the darkened street. How strange to see houses, side by side, some with soft lamplight glowing, most in darkness.

'Oh, dear Grampa,' she whispered, 'definitely not a walnut shell day.'

3

AN ARTIST WAS BUSY OUTSIDE her bedroom window. The huge beech trees were just struggling into their green spring coats – how many tints and shades there were. Mother Nature never ceased to astound her. Soft green shoots were bravely pushing up their heads, like so many watchful sentinels, out of the ground, away from the weakening grip of winter and towards the young sun. She could see two – no, three – of Jock's beloved Clydesdales in the far field, their heads bent as they grazed. Suddenly one, his particular favourite, The Cutty Sark, threw up her tail and her heels and went skittering away across the field. Catriona peered to see what had excited the horse.

It was Jock, his hands full of carrots, his pockets full of apples. He looked up, but his face disappeared and in its place Catriona saw . . . horror! She woke up with a start, and at her anguished cry the rat that had been chewing the wainscotting in the corner whisked out of sight behind the wardrobe.

Victoria, beside her mother in the big bed, moaned softly in her sleep. Catriona leaned over, as she had done so many times over the years, to soothe her child.

Victoria fell quiet and Catriona lay back again and tried, as she had always done before rising, to make a list of all the tasks she hoped to accomplish during the day. First thing was to light a fire. At least Victoria would be warm. She slipped out of bed, pulled on her dressing gown and crept quietly down to the kitchen.

The table was a seething mass of mice. They were everywhere. Already they had eaten their way into the bags of flour and sugar, the packages of good farm butter, the loaves of yesterday's bread. Some of them jumped from the table at Catriona's arrival, but the bigger and bolder ones looked at her with their malevolent, beady eyes and went on chewing.

It was too much . . . to be brought to this. All her life, every day, every moment, Catriona had worked and cleaned, and tried to keep up the standards instilled in her by her mother. Now . . . to come to this.

I always meant to put it in the lassie's name.

Dear God, would the words always be there to haunt her, to poison her love for the old man, to tarnish his memory? She could bear no more. For the first time since

Jock's sudden death, Catriona began to cry. Great choking sobs were wrenched from her and scalding tears chased one another down her cheeks.

'Oh, why, Father, why? I cannot bear this; I cannot deal with such dirt and damp, and neglect.'

A mouse, startled by her cry, ran across her foot on its way to its hole and the delicate touch was the final straw. Catriona screamed and screamed and screamed. The vermin ran to their holes and Victoria, terrified out of her sleep by her mother's distress; jumped from the big double bed and, without waiting to put on dressing gown or slippers, rushed down the stairs and into the kitchen.

She was nearly fifteen years old and suddenly she grew up. She threw her arms around the wailing woman and Catriona felt their strength.

'It's all right, Mother,' soothed the girl. Never before, no matter what had happened, even on that dreadful night when Grampa had died at her very feet, had Victoria seen her mother unable to cope. She held her mother and was no longer a child; she would never again be a child. At the sight of her mother's distress Victoria had stopped thinking only of herself. She had grown up. She felt a million years old. 'We'll cope. We will. We'll make it work, together. I'll help. Don't cry, don't cry.'

She pushed her mother down into the chair beside the range and, putting her arms around Catriona's waist, laid

her head in her mother's lap, but still she was the com-
forter, not the comforted.

'We'll cope, Mother. A cup of tea. I'll make you a nice
hot cup of tea and then we'll start.' She looked around and
repressed a shudder. 'It's only dirt. Dirt has no respect for
anyone, rich or poor, but boiling water and good carbolic
soap'll sort it. You'll see. You won't recognize this place
when we're finished with it.'

She looked fearfully at the wainscotting and observed
the tell-tale holes. She had seen the mice rushing away
from her mother's screams. No mouse or rat had dared
to disturb the peace of Priory Farm. Had they done so,
they would have met a timely end. Victoria took a deep
breath.

'We need a good mouser and we'll get one, but first we
need tea. That was what Grampa used to say, Mother, do
you remember? 'I can handle anything, if I get a decent
cup of tea. None of your holy water here.' Do you remember, Mother, how he loved his tea?'

She got up and Catriona, calmed by her daughter's
strength, watched her at work. The set of the head on the
thin, young shoulders was John's; the flashing grey-blue
eyes that had vowed to do battle with dirt and poverty
were John's; but, oh dear God, thank you, the courage and
character were Jock's. That they were also hers did not
occur to Catriona Cameron.

'Tam will tell us how to deal with vermin, Mother,' said Victoria later, as she held the teacup so that her shaking mother could drink the reviving brew. Oh, so nearly had she said, 'Grampa will tell us.' Sometimes her grandfather seemed still to be alive. She could almost hear his voice, almost smell his pipe. But here she could smell only damp and a strange, rotting smell that had to be the mice. Tam would know how to deal with mice. And might there be rats too? Victoria shuddered and tried to smile at her mother. Had Grampa still been alive, of course, there would have been no need to learn how to cope with such horrors.

'Now, Mother,' said Victoria as Catriona made no move, 'have some more tea and I will find something for us to eat.'

Catriona retched. 'No, child, there were mice in everything. Everything's contaminated. We can't eat.' Her voice rose hysterically and Victoria heard the warning signs of distress and tried to deal with them.

'We *must* eat, Mother. We have a great deal of work to do. See, the eggs are untouched. Wasn't that nice? The mice left the eggs to have as their second course and now they've lost them. I'll make something nourishing. You go upstairs and wash and dress. Here, there is water in the kettle. We'll get this range cleaned and then it will stay lit twenty-four hours a day and there will be water, lovely hot water. And in two shakes of a lamb's tail there won't be a germ anywhere.'

To Victoria's delight, her mother tried to smile.

'I'm fine now, lass. It was just—'

'I know, but we'll survive, Mamma, and we'll do more than that. Just think. It's the two of us against the world. Does the world have a chance? No.'

Victoria found a bag of flour that the mice – she refused to think any more about the possibility of rats – had left inviolate and soon there were scones browning on the griddle iron.

'I'm making up the whole bag,' she said as Catriona, washed and dressed, re-entered the kitchen. 'I hope I remembered your recipe properly. I should, since I've watched you bake often enough. We'll have scrambled eggs and scones for breakfast, and boiled eggs and scones for dinner. We have plenty of vegetables for soup, and you can make that, Mother, while I start cleaning. Unfortunately, we've no bone for stock.'

'There's a wee grocer's just round the corner.'

'No.' Victoria was in control. 'We'll be pioneers today and use only what we have. There isn't time to go to the shops, and by the look of this place we'll be too dirty to go anywhere. Here, Mother, doesn't a scrambled egg scone taste wonderful?' Catriona had to agree that it did.

After breakfast Victoria went to dress while Catriona washed their few dishes, and then they started to clean. Everything the vermin had contaminated was taken out into the back garden and burned. The dirty paper that had lined all the shelves in the kitchen followed the foodstuffs onto the fire. The floors were swept and scrubbed, and after the floors came the walls and the shelves, even the doors. Soon the smell of dirt and decay was replaced by the healthy and not too unpleasant smell of carbolic.

'Once we start polishing there'll be a fresh smell of lemon in here and then we'll get some apple logs for the fire. Won't that be nice?'

'I'll do the privy,' offered Catriona, anxious to make up for her weakness of the morning, 'and you can get started on the front room.'

Victoria dropped into a chair by the fire. 'The front room? Mercy, Mother. Would you look at the time. It's nearly four and we've been at it since before nine this morning. If I don't eat I . . . I . . . don't know what I'll do.'

'You're right, lass. Look, I'll start making the soup and it can be simmering while we finish. I'm glad we brought these oil lamps from the farm. They're homely, aren't they?'

Victoria turned away. She was not ready for talk of the farm, and certainly not ready for odious comparison. 'I'll boil these last two eggs, Mother, to go with our soup. Or will it just be mixed vegetables, since there's no stock for flavour? Doesn't matter. Tomorrow we'll investigate the wee shop.'

Did Arbuthnott Boatman deliberately choose an extremely wet day on which to take the new owner of Priory Farm around his property?

John Cameron had spent the night very comfortably at the nearby Birkhill Inn. His handsome face and figure and the cut of his London clothes had endeared him to the barmaid, and his generous tip had won the heart of the groom who was to convey Mr Cameron the two miles to the farm. Sammy Taylor was not the brightest employee of the inn, but he knew horses and he knew farms. He looked at the hand-made leather shoes, at the polish and the fine tooling with something approaching anguish.

'Ye'll no hae a pair o' galoshes, maister?'

John shuddered at the thought of squeezing his beautiful shoes into a pair of ugly, but no doubt practical, galoshes. 'Wore my last pair some years ago.'

'There'll be a puckle mud at the fairm.'

'Which I shall be more than happy to wipe from my feet, laddie,' said John grandly.

He would go, as his father's lawyer wished, to the farm and he would see the inventory, and then he would take the wind from Arbuthnott Boatman's sails by telling him to sell up. He could hardly wait to change that pained, prune-faced look to one of surprise.

Arbuthnott Boatman, in a sensible hooded driving cape and with his best-quality rubber galoshes pulled carefully over his second-best pair of shoes, waited at the once sparkling mullioned windows of the front room of Priory Farm. Catriona had been gone only a few days but already the house seemed to sag into itself, as if ashamed that it was not as immaculate as it had always been. Boatman saw, with some pleasure, the look of irritation on his new client's face as he stepped from his cab into a puddle, which immediately oozed over the top of his shoes and ran down inside his silk-socked ankles. He hid his smile and walked out briskly, an expression of welcome painted on his face.

'Mr Cameron, I'd have known you anywhere. You have the look of your father about you.'

John avoided the outstretched hand. There was no need for pretence with this man. They did not like one another, but what did that matter? He, John Cameron, owned every mucky inch of this place, every wisp of hay, every hen – even, he supposed, every mouse that lurked in the warm barns. His father could hardly have shot them all, he decided with a quick flash of irritation. The other man was his employee. It was a good feeling.

'It was always dinned into me that I resembled my mother,' John said coldly. 'Now, if you don't mind, can we sign whatever we have to sign? I'm thinking of heading for Mexico. This damned war has ruined France, but with the proceeds from the sale of this little lot I should be able to live like a king in Baja California. And there's America just over the border, if I feel the need for what passes there as civilization. Ever been to France, Boatman?' He did not wait for an answer. 'France is the country, Boatman. Such wine, such women, such food. I'll miss French wines, but Mexican *señoritas* and excellent cigars should compensate. And they say there's the odd vineyard, and lobsters, of course, jumping straight out of the sea into the pot.'

'Sounds delightful,' said Boatman drily. 'But what of the farm? And, by the way, Cameron,' he added, knowing full well that it was not only unprofessional, but none of his business, 'you haven't forgotten that you still have a daughter?'

Did John flinch for a second at the word 'daughter'? Had he missed holding his own child? Did he regret not hearing her first, lisping words?

'Neither means a damn thing. The farm never has: sometimes I even wondered if I was my father's son. As for the girl, I came back from business – important business – in Paris at considerable discomfort to be there within hours of her birth and they turfed me out. Never even saw her. I owe the girl nothing.'

'I take it you want me to find a suitable tenant?' The lawyer's mind was working furiously. Could Catriona lease the farm? With Tam to help, really to run the place . . .

John looked at him, his face a caricature of incredulity. 'A tenant? You must be out of your mind, man. When I shed the mud from these shoes, I want to do it in every way possible. There's a war on, in case you hadn't noticed. I don't intend to stay guarding the ancestral acres while waiting to be conscripted. Mind you, if all else failed, I'd be a farmer before I'd be gun-fodder, and I suppose if I made a show of farming, they'd give me a dispensation.' He thought for a minute, obviously weighing up the advantages of a safe haven for the rest of the damned war against the lure of exotic places. Mexico. What did he know of it? He looked over at the barn and saw the short, broad shape of Bessie Menmuir carrying peelings to the chickens. He could find nothing alluring in the sight. But Spanish *señoritas*. Sunshine . . . 'Show me where to sign. Sell, and sell now.' He looked around him at the carefully tended farmsteading. 'It should make a nice tidy sum.'

The two men looked at one another and, for once, the lawyer's guard dropped and his dislike of his client showed in his eyes. John Cameron blushed with embarrassment. *Well, let them all hate me. What do I care? I am going to sell.*

'Shall I quote you the full legal terms of your father's will, which is essentially the same as his father's, or do you want it in plain English?' Boatman waited, childishly and unprofessionally relishing the other man's discomfort. How had a son of the soil like Jock Cameron ever fathered a wastrel like this?

'Get on with it, man. Spit out your legal jargon.'

'The farm can't be sold, Mr Cameron. It's yours for your lifetime, Cameron, and then it goes to Victoria.'

'Victoria?'

'Your daughter.'

'My daughter? You mean he left the farm to the girl? A girl I've never laid eyes on.'

'She is your child.'

John laughed. 'Either that or an immaculate conception, man. You wouldn't catch Catriona in the barn with the ploughman. More's the pity,' he added under his breath. 'She might have been more fun.'

Boatman looked at him dispassionately.

'Your late father made his will when you married in 1899. He left everything to you for your lifetime. Anything except the house and the land can be disposed of as you see fit, but it wouldn't be wise to dispose of animals or machinery; you'll get little rent for a farm without them. The farmhouse and the land become the property of your surviving legitimate children on your death. Victoria's.'

'What's she like, the girl?'

Arbuthnott Boatman considered both the question and his answer. Had John asked because he had a man's normal interest in a child he had fathered? Perhaps there was a nice John Cameron under all the antagonism. 'She's a pretty wee thing. Very like you,' he added honestly.

John tried to picture a girl with his hair and eyes, his features, but all he could conjure up was a picture of himself just after his mother had died. He saw a pale, drawn face, shadowed blue-grey eyes that were used to smiling and were now wet with tears that he would not shed. He supposed the girl must be pretty.

'Well, she'll catch herself a man in no time, if she plays her cards right. Let's hope she can keep him. Depends what her mother has taught her. There's more to marriage than well-cooked meals, Boatman.'

'Indeed, and as the Merry Monarch, Charles the Second, told us, there's more to marriage than four legs in a bed.'

John turned away in anger. What was the dratted lawyer trying to say, with his Charles II nonsense? All John knew was that, even in death, his father had thwarted him. He had tied him to this damned place. Well, he would *not* be tied.

I'm off to Mexico, he thought. They can send me the money there. 'Get the best rent you can for the place, Boatman. Shouldn't be difficult in wartime, with people anxious for security and the government keen to make the country as self-sufficient as possible. I'm sure there's an account at the bank that I'll be able to draw on from overseas. Your firm must be big enough to have overseas clients. My grandfather dealt with your grandfather, or so my father was always fond of telling me. Old, established firm. Anyway, he had some way of making sure that I was always able to get funds in France.'

'Of course.' Boatman would not say 'Mr Cameron'. 'We have several agreements with the Bank of Scotland and

I'm sure we can have the necessary paperwork drawn up before you leave. Have you a sailing date?'

'Need to get myself a tenant first. How long should all this take?'

'Who knows? I'll advertise locally and nationally. Or maybe one of your father's men would like the opportunity? They're good workers and they know the land, the animals and the people. Perhaps Mrs Cameron . . .' he began tentatively.

John did not even have to think before rejecting that hare-brained idea. Catriona, his former wife, living in his home. 'Don't talk rubbish, man. What would a woman know about running a farm? She'd ruin it, and me, within a year. Besides, it's poetic justice, isn't it? She threw me out. Now the boot is on the other foot.'

John looked down at his hand-made shoes and did not see the look of dislike thrown at him by Boatman. His anger still simmering, he ignored his ruined shoes and walked boldly through the mud away from the lawyer. 'Do what you can, as quickly as you can,' he shouted. 'There's more than the mud of Angus that I want to brush from my shoes.'

'Good day to you,' said Arbuthnott Boatman, but the words went unheard – or ignored.

4

IT WAS THE FIRST TIME in her life that Victoria Cameron had ever walked to the kirk. Every Sunday, for as long as she could remember, she had gone in a carriage with Grampa and the folk from the farm. Summer or winter, rain or shine, he had insisted on using his own father's carriage, and Victoria had sat squeezed between him and the window and had looked across at the unfamiliar Sunday face of her mother. Catriona, her red hair firmly pinned down under her hat – which was anchored, but surely not to her scalp, with huge pins ending in improbable diamonds – her ruffled blouse buttoned up to and beyond her chin, had sat unsmiling as she in turn had examined her daughter for any speck of dirt or dust that had gone undetected.

But their world had changed. Now there was a new church in a new town and they were alone, just the two of them. When the minister raised his hand for the final blessing, Victoria's hand sought her mother's and she squeezed the leather-gloved fingers gently. With God's blessing and their own hard work, they would manage.

The minister welcomed them at the door, introduced himself and said that he would call on them. He knew, as well as they, what a visit from the minister of the established kirk would do for their standing in the community.

'You've taken on quite a job with old Mrs Thomson's house, Mistress Cameron. It stood empty quite a while. Family wrangling, I believe, and no doubt a bit of legal wrangling, too. There'll be a job of work to get it in order, I expect, but there was always a nice garden there – some grand gooseberry bushes at the bottom, if I remember properly.'

Catriona had had little leisure in which to inspect the garden. All her time was taken up with making the house a fit place in which to live.

'We had hoped soap and water and some new windows would cure its ills, Mr Brown, but I'm afraid neglect and some vandalism have caused major problems.'

The minister shook his head in disbelief. 'Vandalism. . . on Blackness Road, and you not too far from that nice private hospital for women. What is the world coming to? It's the war, of course, not the militant suffragettes, I'm happy to say. Everything that is going wrong can now be laid at the feet of this unholy war.'

'So no doubt everything that went wrong in Dundee before the war was caused by the suffragettes.' Thus Victoria dispensed with the militant women. What is a holy war? she thought. The two words don't seem to go together. Surely all war is unholy. But she hid her thoughts and smiled at the minister.

'Well, if there's anything I can do,' he said, and he meant it, 'you have only to ask. And I shall certainly drop in to see you both later this week. You'll have met your neighbours – such good people, pillars of the kirk and the community.'

Catriona mumbled something innocuous and they moved on.

'Good neighbours who have done nothing but inspect us through their lace curtains, Mother,' said Victoria as they walked off together.

'Aye, but Mr Brown visiting can only help us, Victoria, and he knows that.'

The streets of Dundee were quiet, the only people abroad being those on their way to or from their local church. Catriona and Victoria, chastely buttoned up to their chins in their best Sunday black, nodded and bowed to the people they passed, but no one stopped to chat to them, no one dropped into step beside them as they walked home.

'It'll be different when we know people, Mother,' consoled Victoria, 'when we're accepted.'

Catriona noted again the use of the formal 'Mother' and sighed for Victoria's lost childhood, but she said nothing. They walked along, admiring the trees and talking of how lovely they would be in the spring. Suddenly Catriona stopped in the middle of the pavement and her heart, dead with grief for the past few weeks, began to swell and burst with renewed love and hope.

'Look, Victoria, oh look.'

The road outside their house was awash with people, and with carts laden with tools. Victoria, forgetting her new-found adulthood, kirtled up her skirts and ran, calling as she did, 'Tam, Nellie, Bessie,' and then, 'Flash.' It was Jock's collie, who had stayed at the farm with Tam Menmuir.

Tears of happiness were in Catriona's eyes as she greeted her former servants – now, in her eyes at least, her equals.

'We'd have come before, mistress, but we had to wait for a free day,' said Bessie Menmuir. 'We're here to give a hand, like.'

'But it's Sunday, Bessie.'

'Did the auld minister, bless his heart, not hold an early service the day, and he'll be here himself as soon as he's had his soup. Martha Livingstone wouldn't let him out of the manse without he had his dinner. Noo, you and wee Victoria go and get out of your kirk finery, and in two shakes of a ram's tail we'll have this place tidied up. The laddies are in the garden. You'll no mind that they took the liberty. Our Davie's no a lad for wasting his time and he's off to his regiment again the morn. Tam'll get to your roof – it's no looking sound – and I'll put some soup on and some tatties. We brought you some tatties and some neeps for your pantry. They'll rot in this rain if we do not use them up.'

An hour later, Catriona went out to call in the Menmuir 'laddies' – grown men all. The wilderness at the back of the house was beginning to resemble a garden.

'It was no that much work, mistress,' said Davie Menmuir, a tall, strapping Black Watch sergeant, just finishing his leave from the Front. Married and widowed in the same year as Catriona's own marriage, he had become quiet and introspective, but never surly. 'The beds had been well laid out and a good gardener had known fine what he was doing. We had nothing to do, like, but just tidy up and get it under control a bit.'

Catriona looked at what had, a few hours before, been an impenetrable jungle. 'Oh, Davie, it's like a different place. Thank you.' She said nothing about the gooseberries that might or might not be growing at the bottom of the wilderness.

Davie blushed with the embarrassment of the countryman who sees no need for thanks for giving a little help to a neighbour. Had not Catriona Cameron spent near sixteen years at Priory Farm helping its workers in a hundred different ways?

'I'll leave my brothers to finish off here, mistress, and I'll fix those windows afore we go. Sam has gone to cut glass for them. You should be watertight afore night.'

The tears once again threatened to overwhelm Catriona and she turned from him and stumbled back to the kitchen. At least she could help Bessie dish up hearty plates of the good broth she had brought with her and had heated up on the iron range.

'I don't know how to thank you all, Bessie,' she began.

'Ach, mistress, is friendship no like the land? You only get out of it what ye've put in. Now, if you take that meat out of the soup pot we can serve it with tatties and neeps, and then I've a tart we can enjoy with a good cup of tea afore we get back to work. Where's wee Victoria? She was supposed to be setting the table.'

Victoria had finished the table. The last time she had helped to set a table for so many had been the night of the harvest dance and she was determined not to cry at the memory, but to rejoice in once more being with her people. But it was too hard, and she could not keep back the choking tears. She heard a footstep outside and, so as not to be caught crying, whisked herself under the table. Davie Menmuir caught a glimpse of woollen tartan skirt as he entered. He knelt down beside the table and fished a little bundle out from inside his shirt.

'Ma was thinking that you'd take this wee fellow, Miss Victoria,' he said to the skirts of the tablecloth. 'He's his mother's son and already jumping on anything that moves. Father'll take care of the holes and he's put some stuff down for . . . well, anything that shouldnae be here. But when this fellow grows he'll make sure there's nothing living in this house that you and your mam don't invite. Father's leaving you Flash as well.' Davie stopped and smiled as he heard the excited rush of indrawn breath. 'He's an auld dog, too old to take to a new master, and deserving a bit of retirement. A grand house-dog for the people he knows well. There's nobody will cross this threshold without an invitation.'

The tablecloth moved, a tear-stained face smiled up at Davie and a hand reached for the kitten.

Victoria looked into the kitten's soft little face. 'I should call him Ginger, Davie, but maybe there's too many ginger toms around. I'll call him Priory.' She held the mewing bundle against her cheek. 'He's a bit of it, after all.'

She crawled out from under the table. 'Don't tell Mother I was crying. It just all reminded me of Grampa.'

'But that's good, lass. Enjoy your memories of him.'

'He always told me to remember good days, Davie, and to put the memories in walnut shells for the bad days.' She laughed and removed the kitten, who had shown his adventurous spirit by digging his little claws into the fabric of her dress as he climbed up on to her shoulder. 'I think this is a good day.'

Davie thought with some trepidation of what the morrow would bring for him. 'It's the season for walnuts, lassie. Maybe I'll take one with me.'

She looked up at him, suddenly remembering that Davie Menmuir had been a soldier for almost as long as she had known him.

'I have . . . a friend . . . at the Front, Davie. He's in the Black Watch too. He's only sixteen. His name is Robert.'

Davie looked at her. Had his wife lived, had the bairn had a chance to grow and develop in her womb, he too might have had a daughter exactly this child's age. Already she was walking out, was she? A lad in the Black Watch, somewhere on the Front. Thank God she obviously had no idea of what the word 'Front' meant. 'If I come across him, lassie, I'll try to mind him for you. Now, let's tell your mam we can have our dinner.'

Much, much later Catriona and Victoria sat before a roaring fire, with Flash curled up on the rag rug, one that Catriona had made and brought from the farm, and Priory asleep in Victoria's lap. For once there were no scuffling, scuttling sounds and the curtains no longer moved with the winds that battled furiously outside, unable to gain entrance.

'Our friends are coming back next Sunday to help repaint the house,' said Catriona. 'What a fine, good man

Davie Menmuir is. Your grandfather aye liked him the best of all the Menmuir laddies, and they're all grand men. He'd have made a good farmer if he hadn't joined the army to get away from all his memories. I was that surprised to see him today, working away.'

Good, thought Victoria. This was perfect, a natural lead in to what had been on her mind for some time.

'Mother, talking about helping . . . We can't depend on the Menmuirs and the others too much. We are going to have to earn some money.'

'I know, lassie, and I have it all thought out. Listen, Victoria, it's not what either of us was brought up to, but once the inside is painted I'll make some nice new curtains and I'll find some decent bits of furniture from a roup-sale, then . . .' Catriona stopped. How on earth would her daughter accept what she was going to say? She finished off in a rush, 'I'm going to take in some boarders.'

Victoria's answer surprised her and showed her that the girl had been doing her own heart-searching and thinking over the past few weeks.

'Good, Mother, you'll be wonderful at that. But in the meantime I think I should look for a job.'

'Oh, no, lassie. You have such a good brain, Victoria. Grampa was so proud when you won the scholarship to the Harris. Do you know he even said to me once at a prize-giving, "I wouldn't be a bit surprised if our Victoria

61

was the first Cameron ever to go to the university." Think of that, lass.'

Victoria *had* thought. She had dreamed of a university education; she had seen it within her grasp. She had discussed it with Elsie, who was to go to a training college for teachers. She had even written about it to Robert, who talked grandly of *going up to Oxford when this little show is over*. But in the cold light of day Victoria was clever enough to see that there was no way she could remain a financial burden to her mother for the next seven to ten years. With the optimism of youth, she rewrote the scenario. She would work for a while at any job she could find, then, when the house was as habitable as its neighbours', Catriona would take in lodgers and, relieved of her burden, Victoria could pick up her education where she had left off. This wasn't the Middle Ages, after all. Heavens, it was the twentieth century. There were night schools where one could learn secretarial skills. Nothing should spoil this walnut shell day. From now on, life was going to get better.

The next morning, full of enthusiasm, Victoria took the tram into town. She had taken the tram to the Harris when they had lived at the farm, and she had had to hold her nose against the overwhelming smell of jute. The jute workers rode the trams, loud and raucous in the mornings as they saw old friends not seen since the night before, quiet and white with fatigue in the evenings as they headed home for their bacon busters, their chips and their good hot soup. Deliberately, Victoria now took her handkerchief with its delicate edging of white lace away from her face. She would get used to the smell of jute: she was going to be a part of it, and there was no time like the present to start.

There was a crowd outside the factory gates. Baxter's were hiring. Jute had always been a job for women. Men demanded too much money: better by far that they should stay at home and mind the bairns, while their wives worked for half the money that the owners would have had to pay the men. Now both women and men were finding well-paid jobs due to the insatiable appetite of the war machine.

Victoria had scoured the employment columns in the *Courier and Advertiser*. Good, plain cooks were wanted. Strong, willing boys were wanted. Message boys ... girl to work in dairy ... Nothing for which Victoria Cameron was suited. Grampa had never let her soil her hands with farmwork and Catriona had taught Victoria few domestic skills, preferring her to devote her time to academic study. But the hungry maw of the jute mills would not care that Victoria could write a tolerable essay or could tot up a column of figures faster than any boy in her class.

A voice hailed her from the open door of the factory.

'Victoria? It's never you, Victoria Cameron.'

Victoria looked at the grey figure in front of her. She could tell it was a woman because of the skirts, but as for her age, she had no idea. The woman could have been anything between fourteen and fifty, so pale and drawn was her face, so thin her body, so grey with dust her indiscriminate hair. Only the eyes shone out as merrily and cheeky as ever.

'Nellie, Nellie Bains?'

'Aye, it's me. What are you doing here? I haven't seen you since I left the school at Liff.'

'I need a job, Nellie.'

Nellie looked at her in disbelief. 'Victoria Cameron at a jute mill. You'll be going into the office as a secretary.'

'No. I have no skills, Nellie. It's the mill for me too.'

Nellie looked at her compassionately. She saw well-tended skin and hair, good well-cut clothes carefully cleaned and pressed. She could bet the nails hidden by those gloves were well manicured, and certainly not bitten to the quick like her own.

'Ye'll never manage it, lassie. It's back-breaking work. The jute gets in yer eyes and yer mouth, and up yer nose. And you cannae dress like that and be a mill lassie; it's only the weavers that wear a hat and gloves to work, to show that they're better than anybody. Ye'll get the claes pulled from your back and the hat and the hair from your head. I wouldn't wish the mills on my worst enemy and you were never that. A wee bit stuck up, with yer bonnie frocks and ribbons, but you and yer ma always gave good parcels to the Bains.'

Victoria thought with shame of the many times she had refused to sit beside Nellie because she smelled. It was easy to give away outgrown clothes and extra food from a well-stocked larder. Real kindness was harder. Nellie obviously had it. Victoria resolved to try for more of that virtue.

'That was nothing, Nellie,' she said seriously. 'And now I need a job and I'd be grateful if you would tell me what to do. And if I do look a bit odd to the rest of the workers, they'll get used to me.' She tried to laugh and managed a half-smile. 'I dare say, if I don't tell my mother, I can stop wearing a hat and gloves.'

'My lad's a tenter, Victoria. Most of them are right bastards – they're fell important, you see – but Tam's a decent laddie and will maybe give you a job. I cannot see anybody else takin you on.'

Victoria had no idea what Nellie was talking about, and Nellie saw the incomprehension and she sighed. 'Tenters recruit workers. They look after about twenty machines each and every machine needs its workers. You'll maybe get a job as a shifter, and God in heaven I hope you're strong enough for it. All you have to do is take the filled bobbin off the frame and put an empty one there. You'll get so many machines to look after and, since they'll all run out at different times, you'll aye be chasing your tail. You have to watch out for the shifting mistress; the auld bitch has a strap, but I think she'll no use it on you, just on the weans – the half-timers, ye ken.'

'That's children who work part-time and go to school part-time?'

'Right. Now come on, I've just missed my breakfast with talking to you, but I'll take you to Tam afore you get thrown out. I'm a weaver's apprentice – informal like, but it beats shifting, and I'll get my own machine one day, especially since my lad's the gaffer.'

*

Two hours later, Victoria stood with Nellie before a frighteningly huge machine that deafened her with its noise and blinded her with the bits of flying ooze from the jute. Wordlessly she did as she was told, over and over again. The noise beat her head and body, the incessant rattle of the enormous machines made the very teeth in her head shake. She would never get used to it, never. Where now the scholarship-winner to the Harris Academy? Here she was the lowest of the low – a shifter, not even a spinner, and certainly not a lordly weaver. At last, when she thought she would fall down from exhaustion, a hooter sounded and they all poured out into the yard to eat their lunch. Victoria was incapable of thought. She stood wordlessly while the others walked and talked around her. Inside the mills a sign-language had developed, for no word at all could be heard above the machines, and now the women (for it was mostly women) talked as if they would never stop, would never tire of hearing the sound of a human voice. Not so Victoria. She just wanted to lie down and sleep.

'I thought it was time to go home,' she almost sobbed to Nellie.

'We're barely started, Victoria. We was late starting this morning, with having to learn you everything.'

Humbled, Victoria tried to swallow the bread she had brought with her, but it stuck in her dry throat and refused to go down.

'It'll get better, hen,' said Nellie, putting a callused hand on Victoria's soft white hands.

The hooter deafened them yet again.

'I hate that sound,' said Victoria.

'Ach, it's only in the morning when I'm warm in my wee bed that I cannae cope with it, Victoria. Just think, the next time ye hear it, ye'll be on yer way home to yer ma.' She stopped awkwardly, as if unsure about whether or not to proceed. 'We heard . . . about you and yer ma gettin thrown out. We're a sorry. Ye'll tell yer ma.'

Victoria looked at her. This was much, much worse than she had imagined. To be the subject of talk among the likes of the Bains . . . 'Thank you, Nellie. It was kind of your family to worry. We're fine.'

Five hours later she stumbled back to the tram stop with an undaunted Nellie.

'Ach, don't let it bother you, Victoria. You'll get the hang of it in no time. I'm away tae the pictures with Tam when I've had my to. The one and only Charlie Chaplin in *Charlie at the Bank*. Want to come?'

Victoria did not have the strength to tell her that all she wanted to do for the rest of her life was sleep. She fell fast asleep on the tram and overshot her stop and had to walk back through the dark, unknown streets. Catriona had been out with an old lamp from the farm several times to look for her and was so relieved to see her exhausted daughter stumbling along that she managed not to scold her until she was safe in the big chair by the fire, a mug of soup in her hands, with Priory in her lap and Flash on the floor at her feet.

'You're not to go back, Victoria. I always wanted better for you even than I had. Your grampa wanted to see you a teacher, maybe a doctor even.' She shook that ridiculous thought away. 'Well, at least a teacher. Never, never the mills, Victoria. That's for, for—'

'People who are desperate to feed their families, Mother,' answered Victoria more fiercely than she had meant to.

'But you have a good brain,' Catriona almost wept.

'And so do too many of the women in that mill, Mother, and in other mills all over Dundee.' She sat up, revived by the soup. 'And I'm learning there. We've always taken the mills for granted, but it's quite exciting being there.' She crossed her fingers in her lap, hoping that God would forgive her for that dreadful lie. There was nothing exciting; it was soul-destroying. She went on, 'It's hard work and the noise is almost unbearable, but the jute itself comes all the way from India, halfway across the world. Women in India break their backs to pick it and we break our backs spinning and weaving it. We're connected, Mother, a girl near Calcutta and me. Maybe one day . . .' She stopped for a minute and her pale face was suddenly aflame with enthusiasm and the glow from the fire. 'Wouldn't it be wonderful to go to India, Mother, to see the Rajahs on their golden thrones, with emeralds as big as eggs for buttons, to walk along the banks of the Hooghli and see those graceful Indian girls.'

She laughed at the expression on her mother's face. 'Life is what you make it, Mother, and if I have to work in a mill, I'm going to learn as much as I can while I'm there.'

'Come to the table and eat your tea. I'm not having you sit at the fire, like . . . some I could mention. We'll keep up our standards, Victoria, and you'll get out of that mill just as soon as it can be managed.'

But it was the evidence of Victoria's growing wander-lust that was terrifying Catriona. Was that why John had not stayed beside her? Had he too felt the call of exotic places? Was there more of him in his daughter than she, Catriona, wanted there to be? She had to get the girl out of that mill, and the first step was to finish the house so that her way to becoming a landlady was clear.

It took a whole year, a year that saw Victoria change from a fresh-faced country girl to a thin, grey-faced town woman. There was little enthusiasm left for learning of the wonders of the mysterious East after a day in a jute mill. All Victoria wanted to do was lie on her bed in her clean, quiet room and look at the trees from her window and pretend that she was at the Priory. She had no energy even to write to Robert and had forgotten who had written the last letter. Sometimes those few hours with him in the woods seemed like a dream, a fairytale to tell to children. The Prince had come, had awakened the Princess with a kiss, but her wak-ing eyes now saw only dirt and oil, and noisy machines that invaded her mind as the jute invaded her body. When she did manage to think of Robert, she could not keep him in the beauty of the woods: he refused to stay there but stood, with her scarf around his rifle in a mud-filled hole, which was even noisier and more horrifying than the one into which she had so willingly flung herself.

Catriona watched her daughter grow old and redoubled her efforts to restore the house. Priory grew from playful kitten chasing his own or Flash's tail into the terror of four-footed vermin. Elsie, preparing for her own safe studies in Edinburgh, had taken one look at the house on Blackness Road, at Victoria's once-immaculate fingernails, and had decided that 'pressure of academic work' meant that she could not visit – 'just until my exams are over, Victoria.'

*

In the autumn of 1916 two advertisements appeared on the same day in the Dundee *Courier and Advertiser*. One was for a 'Deplenish Sale of House Goods from the Home of a Lady' and the other stated 'Parlour and Bedroom wanted by Professional Lady'. Catriona went to the first and answered the second, and the result was that in October of that year Miss 'Doctor' Currie moved into the newly decorated front parlour and best bedroom of the scoured, mended and repainted house on Blackness Road. She had liked the comfortable settee in the parlour and the highly polished oak table, which was just the right height for her work. If she had known they had come from the home of a 'lady' and been purchased at a bargain price through Catriona's haggling, she would have said, 'Well done.' She had frightened the life out of Catriona by arriving in a very noisy and unbelievably fast little car, driven by herself. Never in her life had Catriona been so close to someone so elegant and, as soon as the doctor spoke, Catriona realized that Dr Currie was not only a woman but was herself a 'lady'.

What was someone who had so obviously been born with all the advantages of life doing working for a living and in such a profession? Grampa might have thought doctoring suitable for his beloved grandchild, but he had known nothing at all about the daily grind of a doctor's life and had in his mind an idealized picture of an immaculately dressed, starched Florence Nightingale. What would he have made of Dr Currie, who was even now stubbing out a cigarette in the ashtray of her motor car?

Dr Currie had correctly interpreted Catriona's look of shock. Had she not seen it a thousand times before? 'I'm Gynae, Mrs Cameron,' she had explained, 'and you can't tell an unborn baby to wait for the number twenty-seven bus. Now, I like the rooms and – not that it's important – I like you. I'll arrange to have a telephone put in, but don't worry, I'll pay for everything myself. You'll find it a boon, believe me. What a great time the twentieth century is.'

Although Dr Currie was supposed to look after herself, Catriona soon found herself setting an extra place at the table for her and, although the doctor paid extra for her meals, it would have been worthwhile just to have her there to help Victoria. She brought a gale of educated fact and opinion into the house, and her very presence seemed to have medicinal value. She also gave some interesting unmedical advice.

'Buy a bottle of Abdine, Mrs Cameron, and give Victoria a restoring glass every morning. Good for the stomach and very good for the complexion. At least, she'll think it's good for her – the advertisements tell her so – and therefore it will be.'

To Dr Currie, who occasionally gave her a lift into Dundee, Victoria revealed all about Robert and her hopes for further education.

'I thought I could go to night school after the mill, doctor, but I'm too tired. My friend Nellie had a baby . . . without being married,' she added delicately, 'and she laughed and said it was the easiest way out of the mill, and she's only sixteen. Her . . . friend, the baby's father, left to join the army. He gets lots more money and he sends her some regularly. She has a room up the Hilltown.'

Dr Currie sighed. 'She's changed one life of drudgery for another, Victoria, but at least she'll have a little love.'

Love. Victoria was rather shocked at the easy way in which the doctor spoke of something that normal people never mentioned in the course of conversation. She was heady with excitement, with the car, the conversation, this amazing woman in a man's world.

'May I ask what brought you to Dundee, Dr Currie?'

Flora Currie inhaled deeply and then blew the smoke out into the confined space, but Victoria was used to filling her lungs with jute. The tobacco smoke she found more pleasant.

'The war,' said Dr Currie. 'Surgeons and doctors are being begged to enlist. That left jobs for second-class citizens. Women, my dear,' she explained. 'I had to work in Africa for two years and I got home as fast as I could when the war started.'

Victoria gasped in awe. 'You've been to Africa?' She wanted this journey and this conversation to go on and on. Unfortunately they had reached the turn-off to the infirmary and Victoria had to get out and walk the last part – her mind, for once, full of adventure: Africa ... King Solomon's mines ... diamonds and lions ... the Victoria Falls.

I know very little about Africa, Victoria castigated herself. Mary Slessor, David Livingstone, I presume. I'll get books from the library and I'll try to talk to Dr Currie.

She walked happily to the mill, her footsteps light.

At home, Catriona was awaiting a second lodger. A Mr Dundas was to call and Catriona had spring-cleaned the already spruce best back bedroom and had opened the windows to let the cold, fresh air sweep any stale air away. It would be nice to have a man about, for safety's sake.

Flash was grand, and Dr Currie added even more security, but there was a war on and there were, according to Tam Menmuir, unsavoury characters in plenty who would be only too willing to take advantage of lone women.

She put a shepherd's pie, top-heavy with potatoes, into the oven for Victoria's supper and went to answer the demanding doorbell.

She looked up and her welcoming smile froze. Her heart plummeted into the pit of her stomach and for a second she felt faint. Then she stiffened her backbone.

'What are you doing here?'

Her visitor swept the hat from his still-black locks and bowed to her mockingly. 'I find myself in need of temporary accommodation, and I must confess that after all these years I was curious. May I come in?'

'There's no welcome for you here.' Catriona tried to close the door, but he had already stepped part-way into the hall.

He smiled, the smile that had so easily charmed the heart from her body. Was it working now, still?

'My God, but you're a handsome woman, Catriona, and by the smell of supper, as good a cook as ever you were.' He pushed her easily aside and closed the door, thereby confining them together in the tiny hallway. 'A man could do a lot worse. Come on, lass, let's give one another mutual aid. And then, of course, there's my daughter . . .'

She slapped him as hard as she could across the face and he shouted with anger and grabbed her arms. He did not hit her but just held her, unable to move, to breathe, in his arms. Then he bent his head and kissed her. She stood unmoving and, slightly embarrassed, he let her go.

'You threw me out, Catriona, you and my sanctimonious, self-righteous father, so don't accuse me of having no interest in the girl.'

'You managed to pull yourself out of some French . . .' She could not bring herself to say the word which sat on the edge of her tongue. Aware of her difficulty, he laughed again.

'Trollop's bed, were you going to say, Mistress Cameron?'

'You knew our baby was coming – *our* baby, John Cameron – and you left me for her. I near died giving birth to *my* daughter and then, bold as brass, you turn up. I needed you, John. I cried for you, and who was there? Your father. *He* walked the floor, not you. He held my hand, not you. He heard Victoria's first cry, not you. And did you once write to ask forgiveness? Did you once try to make amends? No. You waited like a vulture till he was dead, and now you come back for what you can get.'

'It's mine. He left it to me.'

'He meant to leave it to Victoria,' she said vindictively. Oh, she wanted to hurt him, as he had hurt her. To let him know that his father had intended to change the will, but just had not found the time or energy to do so. 'Those were his last words, John. *I always meant to put it in the lassie's name.* So enjoy your inheritance, but you won't enjoy it here. Anyway, why should you want to? The farm is yours.'

'Like Hell it is. It's tied up and pays me almost nothing. At the moment I find I'm a little short of cash: just until the next quarter-day. Come on, Catriona. Let me stay. I'll pay my way, and maybe I can get to know the girl and you again, and we can make our peace. At least give me a chance. You were always fair, lass.'

'Aye, and where did my fairness get me?'

At that very moment they heard someone at the front gate and Victoria, still keyed-up and excited by her talk that morning with Dr Currie, hurried up the pathway and opened the door. She stopped short, aware of the tension, of unease. Her mother and Mr Dundas, she assumed, were standing so close, so very close together.

'Mother? Hello, Mr Dundas. Do you like the room?' She looked at him with interest. He reminded her of someone. Who? She smiled at him. 'Next to Miss Dr Currie's, it's the best in the house.'

He smiled at her, sensing easy prey. 'Oh, I'm sure I'll love it, my dear. Why don't you show it to me? Your mother was just about to do so.'

He looked at Catriona. His eyes, so like her daughter's, gazed so charmingly, so straightly into hers. She had fought so hard to get him out of her heart. Had it all been for nothing? I will not be soft-talked again, she thought. I must remember, I must remember that this man is a swine.

'Victoria, this is not Mr Dundas, and he is not—'

'Catriona, my dear, let me introduce myself to this beautiful young woman.'

John turned away from Catriona and smiled his melting smile at Victoria, who, immediately captivated by his charm and his strange familiarity, smiled back. 'Let me take your coat, my dear, and hang it up for you. There must be a lobby-press. Your mother was always proud of her lobby-press. Every boot and shoe in its appointed place.'

Victoria stared at him, mesmerized, and he smiled again. 'My name is Cameron, Vicky, John Cameron, and I'm your long-lost father.'

5

IT WAS NOTHING LIKE HIS dreams of glory. It was dirt and squalor, and blood and fear – and more: it was smells, the sickly smell of earth soaked by rain and blood, the palpable smell of raw terror, but even worse, above everything else, it was noise. Shrieks, from men and machines, the booming or cracking of guns, whinnies or squeals from wounded horses, shouted orders, muttered prayers to God, to the generals, to mothers – and somewhere, at all times of the day or night, the sound of sobbing. Robert Fotheringham pulled one foot out of the clinging mud that invaded everything and then, with an almost unbearable effort, the other foot, and turned round so that he could lean his head against the wall of the trench. Tomorrow, just a few hours away, there was to be a big offensive, but first there was something he had to do. Yes, he wanted to write to Victoria. If he tried hard he could just remember what she looked like, and if he tried really hard he could smell her – clean, sweet, fresh – although that lovely scent made him hungry for something that he did not really understand and was becoming more and more elusive. It could not cope here: it was too lovely, too innocent, too pure to exist in this charnel-house. He looked out across the no-man's-land where death and destruction waited in hungry anticipation and he saw not miles of smoke-blackened French farmland that had once been fertile, but his home, his beloved Inchmarnock, and red rowan berries blazing on the trees and great copper beeches raising their mighty arms to the skies above the Kingdom of Fife, and below them drifts of purple autumn crocuses and among them Victoria, her empty sketchbook in her hand. She raised it to him and she laughed.

'I was trying to sketch it,' she said, and the autumn sun shone on her dark hair and Robert reached out to touch her, to put her between him and the insanity to which he had willingly, happily, proudly bondaged himself – but she was not there.

He felt in the pocket of his battle-dress and pulled out the little gold pencil that Pa had given him for his fourteenth birthday. Paper? What could he write on? Pa's letter was there, with its message of fondest love from Ma. Ma? He saw her too easily. He sighed. He would write on the back of Pa's letter.

My dearest Victoria,

Tomorrow we're going over the top. Isn't that a silly expression for a major offensive? But a humble private, even one with an honourable stuck in front of his name, doesn't tell the High Command what he thinks. He just does.

It's not as I saw it . . .

No, he could not tell her what it was really like. He could not say, 'It's so awful that grown men are blubbing like babies and I am so scared, not that I will die, but that I will be hurt so badly that I will cry too, and I just couldn't bear to lose face like that.' He could not say, 'I have never been hurt before,' because only the people one loves are capable of inflicting real pain.

It's different, it's real. I find that if I remember the woods and you, and the way the sun makes your hair shine, and how stern you were when I picked Pa's primroses, then somehow I remember why I am here, why I must stay and do the right thing, why we must never, ever allow this monstrous insanity to happen again . . .

'Fotheringham, stop mooning there, laddie. Did ye no hear the pipes?'

The pipes. Pipes, bugles, shouted orders. Fall in, fall out, fall in, fall out. How in the name of God were they expected to fall in when this ghastly mud gripped the boots so that merely to lift them was an effort? He folded up the letter, scribbled Victoria's name and address on the grimy envelope and stuffed it back into his pocket. His rifle – oh, dear Lord, where was his rifle? The sergeant would kill him if he'd let it slip into the mud. Kill him, that was funny. Robert Fotheringham was laughing as he followed his platoon over the top. But he was not laughing while utter chaos and bedlam broke out all around him, when he could see nothing but smoke and occasional flashes of fire. Where was the sergeant? Where was the enemy? They were everywhere and they were nowhere. He could see and hear nothing that made any sense, so he was certainly not laughing when the shell exploded and sent his cloth bonnet flying into the air like a partridge; sent him, bleeding, back down into the welcoming embrace of the mud.

'France, the only civilized country in the world, Victoria. I loved it there.' John Cameron stopped walking and turned to look at his daughter. She was his flesh and blood, good lines there – peasant stock no doubt, the aristos would say, but good stock for all that. 'We should go there, together. A decent dress, your hair . . . Wait till you see the restaurants, the little sidewalk cafés. Every woman looks like one of those mannequins in the tea-room at Draffen's: such elegance. And the countryside.' He kissed his fingers with a very Gallic *moue* and Victoria laughed up at him.

'You are funny, Father,' she said and she smiled, because really, did any girl in Dundee have a more handsome, elegant and cosmopolitan father than hers? He even spoke some French, learned, he explained, on business trips.

'Like the one I was on when you were expected, lass. I rushed from Paris – rushed, Victoria – to get home and what happened? They turfed me out. My own wife in league with my father against me, as if I were responsible for the vagaries of French timetables, for the appalling weather in the English Channel.'

'It was May,' said Victoria shortly. How often had she heard that soft May discussed and described: never better blossoms on the flowering cherries, never a finer crop of spring flowers.

'Aha. There speaks the non-sailor. The English Channel, my dear, is like a woman and has a mind of its own, which it's constantly changing, and always without warning.'

She smiled. She wanted to believe him. It would just be so wonderful if he and Catriona could make up, but even though Victoria had persuaded her mother to give 'Mr Dundas' a temporary welcome, she saw no thinning of her mother's antagonism, even though Victoria had explained that the 'Mr Dundas' charade was so clever really, if only one was prepared to listen. 'He wanted to see you, Mother, and me. Isn't that romantic?'

Now Victoria said, 'It's a shame Mother couldn't rent the Priory, Father. I wish you would live in it. I'm so glad you didn't sell.'

'Sell? Victoria! Would I sell my only child's birthright?' His eyes were wide-open and honest.

'Mother would have made a good farmer.'

'Your mother is a grand housekeeper, lass, always was, but the truth is she couldn't run a business. The men would have taken advantage of her.' He stopped, sensing that Victoria felt allegiance to the farm for and he didn't want to alienate her, not when the next ent from the farm was six months away. Besides, Catriona was a good cook, almost as good as some French women he'd known. And she was attractive. If Menmuir wasn't so old and doddery, John might have thought there was something besides fellowship in his constant 'dropping in wi some tatties'. *My* tatties, thought John, although he could hardly complain, since they were being given to his wife – ex-wife – and his daughter, and he himself ate one or two. That potato soufflé she'd made last night, for example . . .

'When this blasted war is over, Victoria, I'll take you to France. We'll go and see some of those marvellous *châteaux*, and Paris. The sights, the sounds, the smells . . .'

'But I like all the sounds and sights and smells here, Father,' said Victoria, sweeping out her arm to encompass the view, which stretched across acres of fertile farmland to the banks of the great River Tay. 'Grampa and I used to explore every nook and cranny of the farm and then, when I was bigger, we would go out into the countryside. We'd take scones wrapped up in cloths to eat, and a jug of sweet milk to drink, and he'd tell me about all the people who had lived here, and why our farm is called the Priory. It's built from stones from an old abbey. Did you know that?'

John forgot that when he was a child his father had been a working farmer with no time for stories. 'No, he was always on at me about lessons and chores. No wonder I hated farming – muck and glaur from morning to night. Do you know what glaur is, Victoria? It's mud that seeps everywhere and won't let you get yourself clean.'

Victoria recognized the bitterness in his voice and was distressed. She fished in the pocket of her dress. 'Look, Father.' She held up two perfect halves of a walnut shell.

He took the shells from her with a pitying look. 'No, don't tell me, that nonsense about the walnut shell. "Put your nice day in here, wee John, and when the cold wind blows, bring it out and it'll warm ye." Silly notion, Victoria. It's good hot coal and fine foods and wines that warm ye, and coats and boots with fur linings. And you won't get those by struggling away in this patch of mud, till they cart you off dead to throw you into more Angus mud.'

Desperately she tried to repair the day. 'No, Father, it's a lovely idea. This could be our first walnut shell day – yours and mine. We're here together; we have had our picnic.' She looked up at him with those eyes so like his own and smiled shyly at him. She really was a fetching wee thing. 'I always wanted to know you, you know. I used to worry so much that you didn't want me. Maybe,' she began tentatively, 'we could really get to know one another.'

He smiled at her, his well-practised, devastating smile that never failed. It didn't fail him now. She tucked her arm into his and sighed happily.

'Don't hang on to idle dreams, lass. Life is tough and you have to fight for what you want. Come on, we had better be getting back. I'm out of cigarettes. Eight pence they asked me for ten State Express yesterday. I had to have Black Cat at fourpence-halfpenny.'

Without thinking he stopped and swung his arm, and Victoria saw her grandfather's walnut shell sail in an arc through the air and land far out in the silvery waters of the Tay. She choked back a sob. She guessed that he would not appreciate tears. Tears were for babies, not modern young women. It wasn't his fault. She had not told him that that particular shell had actually been given to her by her beloved grandfather. He didn't understand, but she would make him understand. Like so many women before her, Victoria forgave him. She stifled her fears and vowed to change him. She could do it, she just knew she could, and how happy Catriona would be.

That same afternoon Dr Currie threw her car through the wonderful wrought-iron gates of Professor Dobson's home on Perth Road, narrowly missing two Italian flower-pots, a gardener, who swore under his breath with amazing fluency, and two of Dundee's matrons, who had had to walk to the soirée and were therefore doubly annoyed.

They could not, of course, let their ire show. Not only was Dr Currie Dundee's leading female medical practitioner but, gossip had it, she was related to several of the finest families, not in Scotland – insular, surely – but in England, and her little eccentricities like motoring and smoking cigarettes were therefore to be tolerated. The good doctor knew exactly what was going on in their minds and despised them for it, while at the same time she admired such virtues as they undoubtedly possessed.

'Got more than enough patients, Maudie,' she yelled to Mrs Lionel Brewster, who was in jam. 'Never hit anyone I didn't want to yet,' she added to Mrs Samuel Taylor, who was in jute. She forced the car to a halt just the right side of her host's prized rose garden, jumped out with an amazing show of well-shaped and expensively stockinged leg and swept the bewildered ladies before her down the fairly steep driveway to the door, where several attendants waited to take their wraps.

'Price of sugar must be playing hell with jam-making,' she went on for no apparent reason, except perhaps to add to their shock with her use of the common word for the Kingdom of Beelzebub. The huge entrance hall was already full of all the local dignitaries, whom the university's professor of music and his wife, Jessie, had gathered together at an extortionate two shillings a head to drink tea and listen to a little music, all in aid of the Boxes for Jocks campaign.

'I hope to God if I have to listen to music, Archie,' said Dr Currie as she kissed her old friend, 'that it's you playing the piano and not some ghastly soprano screeching away.'

'Both, except that she doesn't screech.'

'Spare me, Archie, you old liar. Every soprano screeches – the only bearable human voice is a basso profundo. Well, I'll park myself in the back row so that I can escape if it's unbearable. Being a doctor does have some advantages. If I leave, no one will know whether I'm on an errand of mercy or merely bored out of my tiny mind.' She knew perfectly well that her host would not be insulted by her pre-performance criticism of his entertainment and turned to his wife. 'You've done wonders with this hall, Jessie, and those stained-glass windows are a delight.'

She moved away and joined a group of local business-men and their wives, who were all bemoaning the atro-cious rise in prices.

'Do you know, I told Jessie I would make her some egg salad sandwiches. Three shillings a dozen for local eggs. Can you believe it? Still, I've done my bit.'

'It's not just the prices,' said Alistair Smart, owner of a local jute mill. 'It's the shortage of manpower. I can't get an office boy for love nor money. Three weeks I've advertised in the *Courier*, but nothing but the halt, the lame and the lazy have turned up. And no, don't tell me I shouldn't turn away someone who's lame – the poor man didn't have any of the skills I need. I did give him a chance, but every time he added up a row of figures, and it took him all day, he got a different answer and none of them right.'

Dr Currie moved closer. 'What else does your office boy have to do, Alistair?' she asked.

'Well, adding up accurately is vital. Then he mustn't be afraid of the new telephone system – up-to-the-minute my firm is – a neat hand, of course, and an ability to look a customer in the eye without being shy or bold. Impos-sible to find.' He looked at her hopefully. 'Don't tell me you know a boy with all those talents, Flora?'

Dr Currie smiled at him and slipped her arm through his. 'I may just have the answer to your prayers, Alistair. Let's slip out before the singing . . .'

They wandered out into the lovely garden, which sloped down towards the Tay. Flora led her reluctant escort down to a seat under some gnarled old apple trees.

'This had better be good, Flora. Archie and Jessie always have the best musicians.'

'It's a soprano, Alistair,' replied Dr Currie, as if that explained everything. 'Don't fret. We'll hear her down here and with less damage to our eardrums. Now, this job. I just happen to know someone who is young, smart, intelligent, able to use the telephone, very good at figures and with a fine, legible hand.'

'And why isn't this paragon in the army?'

Flora Currie held up her cigarette for him to light and gave him a straight answer. 'Because she's a girl.'

'A girl. I've never heard of an office girl. How old is she?'

'Sixteen. She's my landlady's daughter – really university material, but the family fell on hard times. Give her a chance. I think the only thing she can't do is make tea.'

He laughed. 'Miss Jessop makes my tea. It will be hard enough having another female around the place, without having one who might usurp her rights.'

'Good. Come on, there's your soprano. I'm going to stay down here to smoke. When may I bring Victoria in?'

'Just an interview: I'm not promising. If Miss Jessop objects . . . Very well. Tell her to come tomorrow at eleven.'

Dr Currie smiled and lit her cigarette. She had done her part. It was up to Victoria to win round the formidable tea-making Miss Jessop.

Victoria was too tired to eat that night when she came home from the mill. Catriona had made a rabbit stew, with two rabbits that Tam Menmuir had brought her, together with some carrots that 'will nae last the winter, missus' and an earthenware bowl containing eggs that had been preserved in glass water. Catriona had wept over the simple goodness of her friends, who had little themselves but were always ready to share. But even the enticing smell of the stew could not tempt Victoria's appetite.

Catriona looked at her. The girl was too thin. My bairn is fading away in front of my very eyes, she thought. She's gone from wee lassie to auld woman, and what can I do to stop it?

She heard the sound of the front door opening. Dr Currie was home. That should encourage Victoria to make a pretence of eating.

The doctor came in. 'Come along, Catriona,' she ordered, as she saw the state of apathy in which the girl sat. 'Major surgery required. Put that wonderful stew to the back of the boiler, pour me a cup of tea to hold me and then – we are going to give Madame Victoria here a bath.'

Victoria jumped up. It was years since she had had to be bathed. She looked at her mother in alarm, but Catriona looked just as puzzled as she.

'I'm clean, Dr Currie. I'll have a bath on Saturday night for the kirk.'

'You'll have a bath tonight, my dear, for the office.'

She laughed at their expressions and told them of Victoria's opportunity and, as she had known, Victoria brightened up and, her fatigue forgotten, became once again an excited sixteen-year-old.

'Now, you haven't got the job yet, but he's fairly desperate. Gosh, how rude! I didn't mean that to come out the way it sounded, but Mr Smart has a secretary, a formidable elderly spinster, whom he inherited from his father, and she's the hurdle over which you, my dear, will have to jump. As far as I can gather, she won't mind how much office work you do, just so long as you don't run round after Mr Smart. She likes to do that herself. She is also unbelievably efficient and may make you wish you were back in the mill. She is, although you are to pretend you don't know, a teeny weeny bit afraid of the telephone.'

Victoria clasped her thin, reddened hands together. 'And I'm not, thanks to you, Dr Currie.'

'If I needed an office girl, I would hire you myself, Victoria. But now we need to get the smell and stour of jute out of that lovely hair of yours, and out from under your fingernails.'

'And out of my nose, Dr Currie. Oh, just think, Mamma, if I get this job, I may never sneeze again. Did you know, Dr Currie, that lots of the mill lasses take snuff to clear their nostrils?'

'Well, it's a blessing that's a bad habit you never developed.'

An hour later a very sweet-smelling, happy girl with a rediscovered appetite sat down to eat. Victoria looked at her mother and at their lodger, who in such a short time had become such a part of their family. What could she say? What could she do to let them know how much they meant to her?

Dr Currie looked at her and smiled softly. 'Don't fret, Victoria. Words aren't always necessary between people who care for one another.'

6

THE BRITISH ARMY LOST 60,000 men in 1916, 19,000 on the first day of the Battle of the Somme. Almost everyone had someone 'out there' or knew someone whose brother, uncle, father or sometimes, God forbid, all three were there. Davie Menmuir came back to Angus with lungs blackened by smoke and his mother told Catriona a little of the horrors he had experienced. Catriona listened with sympathy and patience, but tried to shoo Victoria away. She had the same argument with herself over Dr Currie's vast learning and was in a quandary – on one hand approving of the pursuit of knowledge, but on the other disapproving of most of the knowledge that the lady doctor had.

'It's not fitting that Victoria should hear such things,' she had explained diffidently at the dinner table, and now she certainly did not want her daughter to hear, almost at first hand, of the horrors of war.

But Victoria was fascinated, for Robert was out there, wasn't he? She had told him of her new job. He had said in one of his letters that it was so wonderful to hear of everyday things. She had told him of her interview with Mr Smart, and of the much more frightening Miss Jessop.

But I got the job, probably because there was no one else, and there is so much work and I love every minute. Miss Jessop is really very sweet and thinks I should go to a business college to learn shorthand . . .

But Robert did not write back to say how pleased he was that she was out of the mill – he had hated, he had written in one letter, to think of her in a jute mill, but her being there had helped him, in a way, to be accepted by the rank and file. With his accent, his education and that honourable before his name (which a sergeant had discovered and used, not unkindly, but in fun) Robert should have been an officer and at first the men hadn't accepted him. But his girl worked in a mill – everybody's girl worked in a mill – so Robert became one of the boys. But he did not write, although Victoria refused to believe that anything was wrong. She wrote again, telling him that she had actually written a letter to Calcutta, India.

And then, in late April, when she had almost given up hope, there came a letter of beautiful parchment quality, so stiff that it crackled in her hands.

'It's from London,' she breathed in awe, looking at the envelope and the postmark but making no attempt to open the letter. 'Who do I know in London?'

'Open it and find out, girl,' said Dr Currie with her usual cool common sense, and Victoria did so. A small blood-stained piece of paper fell out as she withdrew the letter from its beautiful envelope. She bent to pick it up and then, recognizing the almost indecipherable spidery writing, held it against her breast as she read the other letter.

Dear Miss Cameron,

The enclosed letter was found in my son's battle-dress at the military hospital in France some time ago, but I only now find myself able to deal with it. The news of course was so appalling that, if you can understand a mother's love, I was quite unable to cope . . .

'It's from Robert's mother,' Victoria whispered, lifting a white, drained face to Dr Currie. Her mind leaped swiftly to the obvious conclusion. 'He's dead,' she moaned, as the awful reality of the dried blood forced itself on her consciousness, 'killed, in France.'

'Oh, my dear,' said Dr Currie, but Victoria had gone back to the letter. She read on.

'I don't understand. No, wait . . .'

The sight of my beautiful baby, his face swathed in bandages, his sensitive hands smashed . . . I can't bear to see him and, for his sake as well as my own, I have left him with his father at the hospital at Craiglockhart in Edinburgh. I felt, although I am at a loss to understand how you can even have met one another, that a visit from you might cheer him up. I enclose, together with his letter to you, a banker's draft to cover any expenses you might incur.

Julia, Lady Inchmarnock

Victoria sat in a crumpled heap in the chair by the fire, where Dr Currie had unceremoniously planted her with her head between her knees, and she handed Dr Currie the letter. The blood-stained paper she kept to herself to read later on, if she could decipher the words. Had he been writing to her when he was hit? Had he been carrying the letter when they had gone into action? It did not matter. Recently, when she had almost believed that he had forgotten her, Robert had been thinking of her and writing to her.

'Well, you'll go, Victoria?'

To Edinburgh? Going to Fife was an adventure. Victoria tried to remember what Robert looked like. How often had she met him? How often had they written? She still clutched the blood-stained piece of paper with the half-written letter. She took a deep breath. 'Yes, of course I'll go. But, oh, Dr Currie, I'll be so scared.'

'We'll go together.' Dr Currie also made instant decisions but, unlike Victoria, she had years of experience of doing so. 'I'd quite like to see how they're handling things at Craiglockhart – should be jolly interesting. It was a spa, you know, before the war, a fearfully expensive watering hole for the idle rich who ate or drank too much. We'll stay the night, Victoria, and make a holiday of it. I have a cousin who'll put us up. We'll have an adventure. I wonder if your mother would come . . . a ladies' day out? Afternoon tea at The George. We all deserve some fun. Work, work, work – ruins more than just your lily-white hands, Victoria.

By the time Dr Currie had finished talking, Victoria no longer looked as if she was going to be violently ill. 'He's alive, Dr Currie. Robert's alive.'

'Yes, dear,' was all the doctor said.

Catriona could not possibly go to Edinburgh. With two of them out of the house, it would be a good chance for a thorough spring-clean. The house pleased her now: she no longer felt as if she did not belong and, although everything was in pristine condition, she would enjoy re-establishing her old tradition. The Priory had been spring-cleaned every year. It would be the same with

Blackness Road. Catriona smiled quietly to herself at the thought of the pleasures in store.

She tried not to show her hurt that Victoria had been corresponding with a young man and had never even told her own mother. 'It is the twentieth century,' she reminded herself. 'Things are different from how they were in my young day.'

Instead of scolding Victoria for deceit, she did everything in her power to make sure that her daughter enjoyed this first exciting train journey as much as possible. Even though Catriona was quite sure that sandwiches made with her own bread would be infinitely superior to anything the railway company could manage, she gave in to Dr Currie's plea that Victoria should be allowed to be her guest for the day. The banker's draft had been sent back to London, with a short note signifying that it might better be used for one of the many war charities – Catriona was embarrassed and angry that anyone should think her daughter could not afford to travel.

Victoria slept not a wink the night before the impending journey. She took out her few letters from Robert and read them, desperately trying to remember him. They had been children, and it had all been so long ago. When she did conjure up a picture of him, he appeared dressed in silver armour like an illustration by Alma-Tadema, and with a halo of light around his beautiful head.

It was a groggy Victoria who boarded the Edinburgh train the next morning. Even the lovely new Border tweed costume that Catriona had bought for her from D. M. Brown's in Dundee, at the unforgivable price of five whole carefully saved guineas, failed to cheer her. She had never been in a hospital; she had never seen anyone hurt or injured; and the lovely old spa was said to be full of terribly injured young men. What would she do if she started to cry, or ran screaming from the place at her first sight of horror or pain? More terrifying still was the nightmare thought: what if she did not recognize Robert? She had met him only twice, and his mother had said that his head was bandaged.

'You merely ask the nurse, dear,' said Dr Currie calmly, and then she smiled an absolutely devastating smile, which included more than a hint of wickedness. 'Besides . . . I know his father.'

Victoria could not eat, but drank three cups of hot, sweet tea between Dundee and Edinburgh, which meant an embarrassed muttering to Dr Currie before they got a taxicab. She saw the solid bulk of the castle and tried to fix it in her mind to describe to Catriona, for she knew that later her mother would be thrilled that she had seen it. In spite of her tension, she marvelled at the city's skyline as they bumped and jolted their way up Lothian Road, around Tollcross and out to Craiglockhart.

They got out of the taxi and looked up at the massive stone building, with its welcoming open doors. Several young men, some with slings or crutches, were draped picturesquely on park benches, on the lawn itself and on the wide stone steps that led down to the grass tennis courts. Victoria cheered up. They didn't look too awful. One even shouted, 'Looking for me, darling?' She laughed and waved.

And then they were inside, and the atmosphere changed. It was cool and quiet, and everything in sight was clinically scrubbed and polished. A nurse in a starched blue dress, and with starched white wings flying from her head, directed them up the wide marble staircase to the second floor. Robert was in a little room that held nothing but an iron bed, a chair and a small wardrobe. There was a lovely watercolour on the wall, of an old-fashioned boy with softly waving, long blond hair, a brown smock and blue stockings, standing in a wood full of bluebells. It imprinted itself on Victoria's mind and never left her. A tall, slender, distinguished-looking man was sitting by the bed reading a book, and he got up when they entered. His face went quite white as Dr Currie held out her hands, which he gripped painfully.

'By Jove, Flora, what a sight for sore eyes,' he said and hugged her to him.

Victoria took all this in and then her attention focused on the bed. There was a long, painfully thin body lying under the white sheet and rough grey blanket, but whether it was that of a man or a woman . . .

'Robert?' she whispered and reached for the bandaged hands. The thing lying on the bed winced and drew them painfully away.

'I'm sorry,' she whispered, aware that somewhere behind her Dr Currie (Flora – strange to realize that Dr Currie had a first name) and Robert's father were talking softly, happily, like old friends.

There were slits in the bandages and she could see his eyes staring at her, alight as if with fever.

'Victoria?' It came from the grotesque slit that allowed his father to spoon soup into him and the nurses to administer oral medication. 'Victoria,' he said again, and this time the voice was more human, less tortured. 'I prayed you'd come. They thought I was going to die, but I knew, Victoria, if I could get back to you, to the woods . . . I'll get well in our woods, Victoria, won't I?'

'Yes,' she whispered while the tears ran unchecked down her face. She could say no more.

Dr Currie was at her side, lifting her up. 'Victoria, I think that's enough for now: speaking tires him.' She turned back to Lord Inchmarnock, who had moved to the other side of the bed and had one hand resting gently on

Robert's shoulder. 'I'll take her to Charlie's flat, Sandy, to freshen up. Then we'll come back after tea.'

Victoria must have shaken hands with Robert's father, for ever afterwards she had the memory of a very kind face, but she felt nothing and cried helplessly all the way to Dr Currie's cousin's flat in Heriot Row. Even the fact that Charlie was an unmarried man who lived alone did not occur to her until they were on their way back to Dundee, and Catriona's questions. She did recover though, after a bath and a lovely meal in the most beautiful room she had ever seen in her entire life. Charlie had been introduced – a gentle, stooping, scholarly man – but Victoria could not remember his name and afterwards she could not even remember his face. He had been solicitous during the meal, a charming and generous host, and then he had left them.

'Not leaving to smoke, my dear,' he had said to Victoria. 'Cousin Flora has all the bad habits in our family. She smokes, as no doubt you know, but I like neither cigarettes nor coffee, both of which you will be offered now.'

He excused himself and Victoria sat back in the beautiful chair and relaxed. 'This is class, isn't it, Dr Currie,' she said, looking at the light furniture, the Chinese rugs, the etchings, the exquisite lamps.

'Well, it's good taste, dear, which isn't always the same thing. Old Tam Menmuir has class – a real gentleman.

Sandy has it and so does Charlie, who also has good taste. I think that Grampa of yours probably had it too.'

Victoria smiled. 'You mean class is more what a person's like inside?'

'Exactly. Never pay attention to labels, Victoria. Examine the merchandise for yourself.'

'Is Robert going to get well?' Victoria asked abruptly.

'It's too early to tell. We'll go back for another visit.'

Victoria rested by the fire and drew strength from the atmosphere of peace and beauty in the lovely room. Then, when Dr Currie felt that Victoria was ready, they returned to Craiglockhart.

Robert was alone. His eyes were closed and his body was very still. Victoria looked down at him and in her heart she heard his laugh, as he had picked the primroses. The knight had gone to the Crusades and had come home battered, while the battles still raged. An overwhelming anger filled her and, as if he felt her passion, his eyes opened and slowly focused on her. They crinkled as if, under those bandages, he was trying to smile.

'I thought you were a dream,' he whispered. 'I kept seeing you among the trees, and sometimes there were primroses and sometimes autumn colours. But when I tried to touch you, you dissolved, like a will-o'-the-wisp.'

'No, I'm very real.'

'Never leave me, Victoria. Promise you'll never leave me.'

Again she heard an echo from the past – a little girl's voice saying, *I will never leave you, Mamma, never.*

'Promise.'

'I promise, Robert. I'll never leave you.'

She sat beside the bed, his bandaged hand resting in hers, until Dr Currie told her that he was asleep.

'Write him a letter, Victoria, to say that we'll come back just as soon as we can. Sandy will read it to him.'

'I promised him. I said I'd stay.'

'No, you said you wouldn't leave him, dear. That's not the same thing. His father will stay by his side. We have responsibilities in Dundee. Our work. Your mother.'

In Dundee, Catriona had finished her labours and had made herself a nice pot of tea. Wickedly she spread real butter on the heel of a loaf. She had worked so hard cleaning the rooms. Even John had been out all day. Where he got to she did not know, nor what he did with his time, and, she told herself, she did not care to know what he did. But today he hadn't even come in for tea, so the fish pie could be heated up tomorrow. It was hard to get a nice bit of fish and she'd managed to fill this one out with some dried eggs.

Oh, the taste of real butter. Imagine, some children born in the past few years had never eaten anything but margarine. Well, Maypole wasn't bad, and only eleven-pence a pound, but butter . . .

Catriona was almost content. She lay back on the settee and looked around her, her eye catching the Wally Dug that Tam and Bessie had brought on their last visit. She really didn't care for china animals, but it made her think of the farm and it cheered Victoria. Thanks to Dr Currie, Victoria had that lovely office job at Smart's, and Mr Smart was talking about sending her for secretarial classes one day a week. If she could just get rid of John . . . But, honestly, did she want to get rid of him? Yes. No. She didn't know.

'Goodness,' Catriona laughed at her fancies and put another log on the fire. What strange roads eating a pat of precious butter sent one down. She caught a glimpse of herself in the mirror before sitting down again. She was quite a well-looking woman, considering, and although she had become scrawny and haggard after Jock's death, she was beginning to relax and fill out again. And this scrape of butter will help that along, she thought and then she sighed. Where had she gone wrong? What had she not been able to give John that would have kept him beside her? By rights they should be out there at the Priory – solid Angus farmers, with a brood of children round the table of an evening. In the early days it had all been so wonderful.

Alone now, she allowed herself to indulge in happy memories. She had hardly been able to believe it when

John first asked her to walk out with him. Her father was a farm labourer, but John's father actually owned his land. John could have had any woman in the district, and the talk was that he had had many of them. But he had wooed her honourably, and their first days of marriage had been everything that any young bride could have dreamed about – sun-filled days of hard work, and nights . . . oh, the nights, of learning, seeking, loving. She arched her back slowly and stretched, yearning, remembering. 'Oh, John, where did it all go wrong?' Did she ask the question out loud?

She looked up out of memory-filled eyes and he was standing there on the rug in front of her. She had been so busy with her thoughts and, oh yes, her achingly sweet memories that she had not heard him come in. She had not lit the gas, and the firelight flickered, sending shadows over his handsome face. He knelt down beside her and she tensed, but he turned sideways so that he was looking at the fire and held his hands to the flames, as if for warmth. She relaxed again. For some time they were quiet, enjoying the peace and the warmth.

'You're still a fine-looking woman, Catriona,' John said into the fire. 'I came back to you, you know. I left her in Paris and came back to you and the lassie, to the blasted farm.'

So he had been with a woman. But how good, how noble of him to admit it, after all these years. She had known and had forgiven him long since.

When had he turned to imprison her work-worn hands? His head was on her knee: she could feel the warmth of his mouth against the thin stuff of her dress. She wanted to move, to break the spell, but she dared not, could not. His mouth, warm and soft, still against her thigh, his hands moving softly, gently, teasingly. Oh God, oh God, how sweet, how achingly sweet.

'Do you remember yon Hallowe'en sociable, Catriona?' His voice was as gentle and loving as his hands. 'You had a yellow dress and a ribbon to match threaded through your curls.' He could feel her relaxing and he smiled inwardly and let his hands continue to do their work. 'You were as light as thistledown on your feet and I wanted to imprison you in my hands, in case someone else stole you away. I could hardly bear to wait for you until we were wed. You didn't know your own power, did you, lass? You still have it, Catriona.'

He was up and beside her on the settee.

How good his arms felt. It had been so long. She allowed him to rest her head against him and to stroke her hair and cheek. The flames danced before her eyes and it was so warm and cosy. She sighed and his hands strayed lower, and she tensed again, but he knew the ways to make the old magic work and she gave herself up to him.

'Catriona,' he moaned softly and kissed her very gently on her lips. 'Catriona,' he said again, and he pushed her back against the cushions and his hands moved and his lips demanded. His hands were inside her blouse; they found her nipples, swollen and erect.

Dear God, what was she doing? With all her strength she pushed him away. Had she gone mad? This man had left her and her unborn child to spend his money on some floozie. For months now he had been playing with Victoria's innocence, watching Catriona struggle out of the gutter that he had landed her in – and now this. No, no, no! She came back from the brink of insanity, or whatever this feeling was, and fought him with all the strength she possessed. And she begged.

'No, John, please, I don't want this. No.'

But if he heard, he paid no attention. Catriona struggled and cried out, but she was no match for him. Behind them the fire burned fiercely, like John's passion, and then died low in the well-blackened grate.

Eventually John too was still. He lay heavy on top of her for a few moments, then he stood up and righted his clothing.

'Christ, you never were any bloody good in bed. I must have been desperate for it. At least you were cheaper than the Dock Street whores, Catriona, but not nearly so much fun.'

She did not hear the words; she was barely aware that he had moved away from her. She did not hear the door close or the front door slam. She lay where he had discarded her and then, as the fire died and the room became cold, cold as her heart, she pulled herself up and sat rocking herself as she wept.

7

DR CURRIE DROPPED VICTORIA AT the door of Smart's
office and drove on to the Blackness Road house. She had
enjoyed her short break; if she was honest with herself, she
would admit that it had been especially good to see Sandy
Inchmarnock again. He was one of those men who look
better as they age, unlike his son, who had been a particularly lovely boy. She refused to admit to any feelings
at all, besides pity, for her old friend. It would be a long
time, if ever, before the boy recovered and there was obviously no consolation to be found for either Lord or Lady
Inchmarnock in their marriage. The thought: What if he
had married me, as everyone expected him to do? popped
briefly into her head and she snorted in a most unfeminine fashion. All those years ago, none of their set had
been able to see anyone else when Julia was in the room. It
had been a competition, and Sandy had won the prize. Dr
Currie banished the images of privileged Victorian youth
and turned her attention to her driving.

It was she who had suggested that Victoria go into the office to begin catching up with the work that would have accumulated during their two days in Edinburgh. The girl had been quiet on the train, withdrawn and worried. Now that she was away from the boy, she had time to realize what she had seen in the last few days, to wonder about what she was expected to do now and to pray that she could cope.

'Go to the office for the afternoon, Victoria. Mr Smart isn't expecting you until tomorrow but he'll be delighted to have you.' She did not add, 'Hard work will take your mind off your young man and his troubles.'

She thought about Victoria and young Robert, and about the conversations she had had with Lord Inchmarnock and the doctors attending the boy, all the way home. Her mood was as melancholy as Victoria's as she stepped out of her little car and into the lovely May sunshine. What a delightful month it was in Dundee, with some trees still in glorious blossom and others unfurling their fragile green leaves tentatively to the sun.

The curtains at the house on Blackness Road were still drawn. How unlike Catriona, the most fastidious and conscientious of housewives, not to have the blinds drawn up and the windows open to allow the wind to blow away the bad night air. The doctor trod firmly, but without undue speed, up the path and opened the unlocked front door.

She heard Flash barking from Victoria's room, where he and Priory had no doubt decided to sleep during their mistress's absence. She called out reassuringly to him and the dog fell quiet. So too was the rest of the house – deathly quiet. Dr Currie began to feel the first twinge of unease. At this time of day Catriona should have been cooking or ironing, and she could smell neither activity.

She found Catriona huddled on the settee in the living room. Her hair had escaped from its neat pins and her dress was torn and disarranged. Her knees were drawn up, she had her arms wrapped round them, and she was rocking herself back and forward and moaning, moaning, moaning. Dr Currie, who had seen such sights too often before and who realized without asking the cause of Catriona's distress, went over to her quickly.

'It's all right, Catriona. I'm here. Everything is going to be all right.'

'Victoria?' It was a tortured, pleading gasp.

'I sent her to work.'

The mother relaxed and allowed the doctor to help her from the room and upstairs.

Quickly and methodically Dr Currie stripped and examined her landlady, now so horrifyingly her patient. There was little external damage. The scratches and slight bruising would heal quickly. The real wounds, which were internal, would take time to mend.

An unforgivable invasion of her self, thought the doctor angrily as she worked.

Later, her patient finally sleeping peacefully, Dr Currie went to release the animals. Flash had contained himself, but not Priory.

'If life isn't one mess, it's another,' said the doctor, disobeying Catriona's strict instructions and lighting up a cigarette before beginning her second clean-up operation.

She opened Victoria's window to allow the cigarette smoke and animal odours to drift away together, then she set the living room to rights. Only then did she make tea for herself and her patient. She forced Catriona to drink a cup of tea and to eat a little bread and butter, while she sat by the side of the bed and listened to the distressed woman going over the sordid little story again and again.

'It was my fault, doctor, my fault. He always was a . . . loving . . . man, and I led him on. I—'

'For heaven's sake,' said Dr Currie, when she had listened to the story for the umpteenth time. 'When will you stop blaming yourself for John Cameron? He's no good, Catriona – never was – and it has absolutely nothing to do with you.'

Catriona looked at her. She did not believe her. She did not really believe that an unmarried woman could possibly understand what had happened. But Catriona had been brought up to look upon doctors, ministers and teachers as almost God-like creatures, with whom one never argued. 'I don't want Victoria to know,' she said finally. 'I've sheltered her from everything sordid.'

'Catriona, Victoria has just spent two days at the bedside of a gently reared young boy who, for reasons known only to the powers that be, has spent the last several months fighting for his life in a rat-infested hell-hole known as a trench. He has been hideously disfigured and is now fighting a second, even tougher, battle. Victoria was calm and supportive. She will not see what has happened to you as the end of the world.'

'What are you talking about, Dr Currie? What has happened?' Victoria was standing in the doorway, the hat and gloves that an office girl could wear with impunity grasped unceremoniously in her hands, her eyes anxious.

They had not heard her come in.

Ignoring Catriona's protestations, Dr Currie told Victoria truthfully and simply what had happened.

Victoria went white and then red, first with shock and then with barely suppressed anger. Sex . . . Violation . . . She had never given either one much thought. Sex was something that married people did occasionally. It had to be done, of course, or there would be no children, but to think of it in terms of her mother and her new-found father. No, it could not be. There was some horrible mistake. She looked at her mother, grown old and frail again in the space of a night, and Victoria went to her and, as she had done on the very first morning in the house, took the older woman in her arms. 'How could he, how could he?' she seethed. 'It's my fault, Mamma. I forced you to take him in. I should have been here to protect you.'

'Enough,' said Dr Currie. 'What a pair for overloading yourselves with guilt and responsibility. John Cameron is responsible for this, and no one else.'

'Can we have him arrested for assault, doctor?' Victoria could see only the need to punish someone for her mother's pain. She was ready to rush to the nearest police station.

The two older women exchanged glances over her bowed head. A divorced woman who takes in her former husband as a lodger and then claims that she has been assaulted might not be dealt with too sympathetically.

Dr Currie, more sophisticated and worldly wise than Catriona, tried to answer as diplomatically as possible. 'It would be too unpleasant for your mother, Victoria. He was her husband . . .'

'They are divorced,' Victoria reminded her, and felt her mother wince even at the sound of that shameful word.

'He was living here, Victoria. Some people might find that fact . . . interesting.'

'I could explain that it was for my sake, that I wanted to get to know him, that I hoped . . .' Victoria's voice trailed off. What had she hoped? Was she a child who believed in fairy stories?

All three women were silent while unpleasant thoughts chased around in their heads.

'Where has he gone anyway?' asked Victoria at last. 'He needs money. He never paid for his lodgings and the next rent from the farm isn't due until the September quarter-day. I'll check his room.' She jumped up and hurried out.

Dr Currie leaned over her patient and adjusted her coverings. 'Excuse me for a moment too, Catriona. I'll heat up that fish pie . . . No, I'm perfectly capable of seeing that it doesn't burn.'

But the doctor did not go to the kitchen. With a heart beating faster than it had done for some time, and a feeling of disaster threatening to overcome her, she hurried downstairs to her own quarters. She closed the door behind her and leaned against it while she tried to calm her heart. He had, oh dear God, he had. Several times in the past few months she had felt that someone besides Catriona had been in her room. A ten-shilling note had been removed from her purse, but never all the money, so that a busy woman might think she had spent it; or a shilling had disappeared from the pile she kept on her dressing table for emergencies. She had decided to say nothing to Catriona, in the hope that she and Victoria would soon see the true worth of John Cameron. But now this.

Like an old woman, she stumbled to her bed and looked at the small space beside her pillow, where the exquisite gold half-hunter watch with the words *Sandy loves Flora* picked out in diamonds had kept her brave for twenty lonely years.

Oh, they could have a warrant made out for his arrest now. But would it bring back her watch, her carefree girlhood?

For the first time in those twenty years Flora Currie sat down on her bed and allowed the tears to roll down her cheeks. A few hours ago she had been remembering with pleasure the days of her girlhood, the days when young Sandy Fotheringham had spent every minute he could in her home; she had remembered fondly the excuses he had made to find himself beside her at a tennis party or a ball. Every day for twenty years she had seen the watch he had given her on her eighteenth birthday, just a few days before Julia swept through London society like a comet. And now it was gone. And to think that its sale would line the pockets of a wastrel like John Cameron. Feeling that she too had been violated, Dr Currie sniffed loudly, blew her nose soundly and, after washing her face, went back upstairs to comfort her patient.

And who is to comfort me? she thought. I cannot add to Catriona's guilt, and if I tell her she will blame herself. There must be something I can do. Or must I let him get away with it?

Nellie Bains sometimes wondered if she had been right to exchange the drudgery of the jute mills for the somewhat dubious pleasures of motherhood. Wee Jimmy was quite a handful for a lassie not yet eighteen years of age, and now that Tam was away in Flanders with the Black Watch, the cramped room and kitchen up the stairs in the Hilltown was often a lonely place.

Perhaps she should have married Tam, then at least there would have been some money coming in. He had promised to arrange things and at first there had been a few shillings regularly every week, but since he had been away, she supposed that he had been too busy marching and saluting officers to worry about his family. That was all he had done, he said, during his three-week training period. He had learned to salute his superiors, and heaven knows but it seemed that everyone was more important than eighteen-year-old Tam Sinclair; and he had learned to slope arms, whatever that meant. He had not yet seen a machine-gun and he had never fired a rifle, but now he was off defending the Empire and Nellie was left behind to look after his son. She decided to take him for a walk in the lovely June weather. They would walk down the High Street and look in the windows of all the posh shops.

Victoria saw Nellie as she left the office for her lunch break and called out to her.

Nellie was surprised, but delighted to be hailed by her one-time schoolmate. She only wished that any one of her neighbours was there to see her well-dressed friend.

'Well, Victoria, that costume definitely says: I work in a nice clean office.'

'Oh, I know, Nellie. I'm so lucky. I love the work and I go to Bruce's College one day a week for shorthand and typing. But what about you?' Victoria looked down and was rather disconcerted to find herself being grinned at by a very gummy little face. 'Is this your wee boy?'

'He's teething,' explained Nellie, wiping the child's cheeks with a far from clean handkerchief cut from an old sheet. Nellie looked at her son through the eyes of this well-fed, sophisticated friend from her childhood. 'He's a bit washed-out looking, isn't he?' she said critically but honestly. 'I wish I could get him out to Birkie, Victoria. The air was different out there, wasn't it?'

Victoria smiled. Even to think of the air of Birkhill cheered her. 'Nothing like it anywhere, Nellie. A tonic for what ails you, my grandfather used to say.' For a moment she thought of her mother, still unable to cope fully with what had happened to her barely a month ago. She smiled brightly at Nellie again. 'Can't you move in with your mother while your . . . man is at the war?'

'Move in with my ma and seven other weans, and two of them with bairns, in one room and a kitchen? You must be kidding. I have a room just for the two of us . . . and Tam, when he's home. I like my independence and my privacy.'

Victoria looked at Nellie. The snotty-nosed ragamuffin had grown into a handsome woman. Her clothes were well pressed and mended, and it was only the child's face and the over-used hankie that were dirty.

She spoke spontaneously. 'Let's take the bairn to Lamb's for coffee, Nellie. My treat.'

'Goodness, are the waitresses there no as stuck up as the clientele, Victoria? They'll no be happy to see me in there, especially wi wee Jimmy. I read in the paper once that Mrs Pankhurst – you know, *the* Mrs Pankhurst, the votes-for-women lady – she ate at Lamb's. They'll think they've come doon in the world serving me and wee Jimmy.'

'You have as much right in there as anybody else. Besides, he looks like a well-behaved wee laddie.'

Nellie hoisted her son on to her hip, where he settled contentedly. 'Oh, he's grand, just greets a bit when the pain's bad, but a wee nip of whisky soothes the gums.'

Victoria looked at Nellie in horror as she ushered her charges across the tramlines. 'The bone of a lamb chop is better, Nellie, and has nourishment in it, too . . . So the doctor that lodges with my mother tells her patients.'

'Aye, well whisky's easier to get, Victoria. My, isn't this a bonny place?'

They had arrived at Lamb's and were shown to a table that Victoria could not help but notice was hardly the best seat in the restaurant. Should I make a fuss? Am I brave enough to ask for a better table? Nellie and the baby seemed perfectly happy, so Victoria sat down. Since she had no experience of small children, she was interested to see how the boy accepted being in a different environment. He accepted it as he accepted everything. He stared around at the green plants, the tables with their starched white cloths and the waitresses in their starched white aprons, and he grinned cheerfully at anyone who looked at him.

'He's a happy baby, Nellie,' said Victoria with a tinge of jealousy in her voice.

'Och aye, he's a nice bairn, and my family is great with him. Granny, my ma, my sisters . . . everybody helps.' Nellie deposited her son on the floor at her feet, helped herself to a cream-filled cake and leaned across conspiratorially.

'You'll never guess what I did the other day? The wean had a hen: you know, we were all told to have hens and eggs to help the war effort. Well, we got this tough old hen from the Priory – don't ask how, Victoria – and we put it in a pen on the drying green. I gave it tattie peelings and scrapings from the porridge pot, and it laid three lovely brown eggs, no all on the same day, but then the thrawn old thing stopped laying and just ate me out of house and home. So, says I to myself: We'll hae a good bowl of soup. I wrang its neck, but wee Jimmy saw it before I had the thing plucked, and you'll never guess what I tellt him.' She leaned across the table, her eyes sparkling with humour and pleasure at being in such a nice place with a friend.

Victoria humoured her. 'I hardly dare think, Nellie Bains.'

'I tellt him the Germans got it. We buried it on the drying green, with a cross and everything, and when I'd put him down for a sleep, I went to dig it up to cook it.' She stopped talking and started laughing uproariously.

'Nellie,' said Victoria. 'You didn't eat the child's pet, especially after you had buried it in the ground?'

Nellie wiped her eyes with the same cloth she had been using for Jimmy's nose, and for his wet and now cream-covered cheeks, before answering. 'I would have done, but old Maggie Thomson up our close had dug it up as soon as my back was turned. I made her give me the carcase for soup.'

Nellie held no grudge towards the neighbour who had stolen her dinner: she would probably have done just the same herself. Victoria thought again how well Nellie handled hardship. Sometimes, in the years since her grandfather's death, she had felt that the Camerons had hit rock-bottom, but they had never yet had to dig up a dead hen. Nellie had nothing . . . except happiness.

'And how are you all, Victoria? Yer mam?'

'Oh, you wouldn't recognize the house, Nellie.' Victoria could not tell her the truth; she could not say that Catriona was a shadow who floated around the house or sat dully, staring into space, and who started at any sound, especially the noise of an opening door. 'We have a lady doctor living with us, but you knew that. She's wonderful. You wouldn't believe the hours she works. She has a motor car and she smokes cigarettes but, it's funny, Nellie, she's still a lady.'

'I've seen her. Don't get in her road if she's heading for the Dundee Royal,' said Nellie feelingly. 'Must be great to know a real live doctor, even if it's a woman. Dae ye get free medical care?'

Victoria thought of the care and attention her mother was receiving. 'Me, Nellie? I'm as healthy as one of Grampa's Clydesdales.'

'Oh, I loved to see him sitting up there on a Sunday in his tall hat and his frock-coat. Whae has the horses now?'

'One or two were sold off when Grampa died, but Glentanar and the Cutty Sark still work the farm. Tam Menmuir loves them just as much as my grandfather did. It's almost like seeing Grampa. He speaks to them in the same way. I'll need to go, Nellie. You wouldn't believe the demands for jute with this war going on and on. I'll be lucky if I get all the letters and bills typed in time to catch my tram.'

Victoria paid the bill, said goodbye to Nellie and hurried back to the office. She loved being there. She loved the dark wallpaper, the heavy polished wood, the feeling of usefulness and especially of accomplishment at the end of the day. If only everything in life was as easy as neatly typing a column of figures.

8

Lord inchmarnock sat beside his son's bed and waited for the surgeon. They were going to take off the bandages that had been applied after the first of many operations that they had told him Robert would have to undergo. He was not expecting much. Unlike his wife, he had sat there day after day while Robert, his face an unrecognizable mass of bone and bloody tissue, waited to heal sufficiently and grow strong enough to endure surgery. Lord Inchmarnock knew what lay under the bandages. If it even looked a little better than it had done; even, please God, just a little better . . .

From which ancestor had the boy's beauty come? He looked like his mother, but stronger, and he looked like his father, but finer. He resembled the seventeenth-century portrait of a dilettante Inchmarnock, but there was nothing dissolute about Robert's finely carved features or about his character. What a lovely, happy little boy he had been. His father looked at the still figure in front of him, and his mind filled with pictures of an ethereal child in a sailor suit, running to him across the great lawns of Inchmarnock House, filling his life with love and joy.

There had been precious little joy during the last few months: there had been that first, almost unbearable joy when he had heard that his son, although wounded, was alive, but now the boy did not want to go on, had to be coaxed, cajoled and convinced that life could still be sweet. For me it's sweet, to have you here alive, my son.

'Beauty is only skin-deep, Robert.' To his abject horror, he heard himself mouthing platitudes and he tried to repair the damage. 'I mean, dear boy, the people who love you won't care ... It's you, laddie, the essential you that matters, and you're still there, Robert. And, in time, you'll feel better and ...'

Did the slit in the bandaged mask move? The voice was a snarl.

'Don't talk rot, Father. It may not matter to you ...' The bandaged hand reached towards his father and the voice grew gentler, no longer the horrible caricature of Robert's well-modulated tones. 'No, Pa, it doesn't matter to you.' The wounded boy-soldier sighed softly and stopped to gather his strength. 'But it sure as hell matters to me,' he said, and the anger and pain in his voice made his father wince.

'Robert, Mummy—'

'Can't even bear to look at me. What girl is going to look at me, Pa, if my own mother finds me so abhorrent?'

Lord Inchmarnock did not try to defend his wife. The boy had gone through too much already. Besides, try as he might, he could not forgive Julia for running away, for that was what she had done. It was not Robert she had been considering, but herself. Safely in London, she could pretend that all was well.

'There are nice girls . . .'

'Who won't mind being seen with a horror?'

'It's only the first operation, laddie. Each time it will get better.'

His whole body moved as Robert sighed deeply. 'It hurts,' he said simply. 'And I wonder how many operations I can take, Pa, and for what?' He stopped and there was silence for a time, while Sandy sat and tried to will his own strength into the broken body of his child. Then the voice came again. 'Is it the cricket season yet? If I'd stayed at Eton, I could have been captain. Winterton joined up – bought it, poor devil – and Nash and Thomson-Smythe. Not a decent batsman left in the side.' Again silence fell, and the father sat with his heart breaking. 'Has Victoria come back?' Robert asked after a time.

'She's a working girl.' Lord Inchmarnock tried to sound as calm and reasonable as possible. 'She'll come again as soon as she has a chance. Jolly decent girl. I've never met anyone who has worked in a factory before. Very educational experience. Good for the likes of us to meet real people, laddie. Puts a different perspective on life, don't you think? Flora Currie – you remember Auntie Flora?– She's like your Victoria. Brought up to believe that the sun rose and set on her head, and look at the work she does now.' 'Yes,' said Robert bitterly. 'She's a doctor. Horrid job for a decent woman, isn't it, dealing with all that ugliness and misery, and death.'

'And wonder, miracles and birth, laddie. She'll bring Victoria back just as soon as she can.'

'But I could feel her hands shaking, and she hadn't even seen my face. Her letters said I was like a knight in shining armour, Father. You must bring me a helmet from the staircase – to hide her hero's face.'

'She seemed like a nice girl, Robert,' said his father desperately. 'Flora thinks highly of her, and she always was a splendid judge of character: I mean, she adored me when we were youngsters.' He tried to laugh, but even to himself it sounded hollow.

'Victoria won't throw me over, Father. Were you there? *I won't leave you, Robert.* She is prepared to stick with me, but I have decided that I just couldn't bear to have any woman look at me with pity. And that's all it will be, you know. I don't want pity.' Robert stopped talking, exhausted by the effort, and Lord Inchmarnock hoped that he had fallen asleep. He stood up to fold the sheet more comfortably over his son's bandaged chest. And then the voice, despairing and hopeless, came again. 'Oh, dear God in heaven, Daddy, why won't they let me die?'

* * *

Arbuthnott Boatman enjoyed looking at fields of ripe grain. It was a comfortable feeling. For one thing, he admitted happily, it represented the back-breaking labour of other men, and all that grain meant food for the winter and, therefore, money in the bank. He patted his well-fed stomach happily.

'What do you see when you look at a grand field like that, Tam?'

'Ripe grain,' said the new tenant-farmer drily.

'Ah, you have no poetry in your soul, man. It should make you feel the warmth of coal fires for the winter; you should smell loaves baking in the oven.'

'Aye, and see money flowing into John Cameron's pocket. He's ages with my Davie, Mr Boatman, and there's one man running his health for the king and another living off the fat of the land.'

The lawyer sighed expansively. 'No more, Tam. There's a warrant out for his arrest . . .'

The farmer started up from the fence that had been supporting his thin frame. 'Land's sake, no: you can't do that. You can't drag the mistress through the courts. A decent woman couldnae hold up her head in the kirk after the talk that would flee about.'

'I have no idea what you are talking about, Tam,' Mr Boatman lied beautifully. 'A Dr Fiona Currie – you may well have met her, splendid woman – has complained to the police that a one-time lodger in the home of her respectable landlady has stolen a very valuable gold pocket-watch set with diamonds. He will be brought to justice.'

Tam looked at the lawyer measuringly. 'Jock Cameron was the finest man that ever walked behind a plough, Mr Boatman. His son, I cannae take it in, to be stealing from defenceless women, and not to be had up in court. Mind you, they'll need to find him. He'll no stay in the country waiting for the rap on the door. That lazy layabout is guy fond of foreign travel.'

'Even better – though you did not hear me say that, Tam. If the rightful owner of the farm is, as they say, of *unknown address*, then it is, of course, impossible to forward the rent to him. A fund would have to be established and in the course of time the rightful, or shall we say legal, owner, not returning to claim such funds in the time designated by the law, then they would naturally become the property of the next in line.'

'The lassie?'

'Aye, the lassie.'

The rock-hewn expression on Tam's face creased into a smile at last. 'Well, the lads will no mind working for Victoria. Got the best of her mam and her grandfaither in her, that lassie.' He removed his pipe from the side of his mouth and knocked the dead ash out on the sole of his hob-nailed boot. 'Now, I'd best get back to work, Mr Boatman. There's a wee more to farming than just leaning on a fence admiring the crops.'

'Ach, who knows, Tam. I always stand taller when somebody tells me I'm a grand figure of a man: maybe the crops grow better too, for a wee bit of praise.'

Tam looked at him sceptically. He was never sure how to deal with the lawyer's odd sense of humour. But if Mr Boatman had nothing better to do than lean over a fence and waste the best part of the day, Tam would not join him. He had promised to be back at the cottage in time to see that Davie had a decent dinner before he went off to Dundee to the doctors.

'You'll hae a cup of tea with us, Mr Boatman?'

'No, Tam, I thank you. I have another client to look in on, out this way.'

The two men shook hands and separated. Tam made his way back to the cottage, only to find that his son had eaten his dinner and gone off to catch the bus to the tram terminal. Miss that bus and there was a long walk before him.

* * *

Davie Menmuir did catch the bus and he did get to his appointment. Mind you, he was there far too early and had to sit in the waiting room twiddling his thumbs, while he waited for the doctor to see him. The alternative, however, was to be too late. It would never have occurred to him to point out the difficulties of arranging transport into Dundee. He was just grateful for the medical attention that was slowly, slowly making him feel almost whole again. He was so euphoric about the congratulations of the very pretty nurse at the hospital that, on leaving, he got on the wrong tram and ended up in Dock Street. The last time he had been near a harbour had been when the ship bringing him back from France had docked at Southampton, and then he had been in no fit state to appreciate his surroundings. Now he felt like a new man. That nice doctor at the infirmary had told Davie that, although he would never really be fit for labouring and was certainly unable to return to the army, the condition of his lungs was better than he or his doctors had any right to expect. With a little light work and plenty of fresh air, he could expect to live a productive life.

I'll have a wee walk along the river, thought Davie, who was wrestling with another problem. For Davie was in love, although he himself would never have used such a picturesque phrase. When his young wife had died within a day of their baby, Davie had believed that he would never love again. But over the years another woman's strength and kindness had caused him to be aware once again of the blood that flowed in his veins. He had never approached her – how could he? But now, now things had changed, and surely she needed him as much as he needed her.

Davie stopped for a rest and, with his back to the wall that paralleled Dock Street, looked up towards the Law, the ancient extinct volcano that now watched benignly over Dundee. A man came out of an alleyway and, with his hat pulled well down over his face, began to make his way up the street towards the Wellgate.

An expletive that he would not have wanted his mother to hear burst from Davie's lips and he began to run after the retreating figure.

John Cameron hardly knew what hit him. He heard a voice calling his name and began to run. He had no reason to suppose that the owner of the voice would be friendly towards him, and he was right. Davie forgot the doctor's warnings about *taking things easy*. Instead he remembered Victoria breaking down in his mother's arms when they had called with the surplus of the first strawberries. Anger lent speed to his legs and breath to his tortured lungs. He made a flying tackle, caught his arms around his quarry's legs and brought him down. There was no breath left for speech. The two men fought with every weapon at their disposal: Davie, a trained soldier, had the advantage of skill, while John had the advantage of good health. Back and forwards they rolled on the pavement, while passers-by berated them and sped on their way so as not to become involved. At last, when his strength had almost left him, Davie found himself on top, with his hands around the throat of his childhood friend. The terrified eyes looked up at him beseechingly, but Davie saw only Catriona and Victoria and, with the last ounce of his strength, squeezed. Sanity returned almost at once.

'Dear God in heaven, what am I doing?' He rolled off his opponent and lay for a moment with his eyes closed, while he desperately tried to suck in some refreshing and life-giving air. He felt sick, but whether his nausea was caused by the exertion or the awareness that he had come perilously close to taking the life of another man, Davie did not know. This was not Flanders. This was Dundee and he was a law-abiding man.

I must get a policeman, he thought. Maybe I've killed him. He struggled to his feet and, leaving John lying quiet on the pavement, he began to stumble towards the Wellgate, where he would be sure to find an officer of the law.

Ten minutes later, after he had haltingly and breathlessly convinced the constable on the beat that he had not only apprehended a wanted man but had probably strangled him, Davie returned to the spot where he had had his desperate fight.

There was no sign of John Cameron. Only a few spots of blood, probably his own, showed Davie that the fight had in fact taken place.

'He was here, constable, lying right here.'

'Oh, I'm sure he was, but you didn't hit him as hard as you thought you did.'

'I near strangled him,' said Davie simply. He looked around at the warren of small alleyways running up and down the street. 'What would he be doing down here?'

'There's several pawnshops in this area would no think twice about handling stolen goods, so your man was probably getting rid of his booty.' The policeman gestured to the busy harbour. 'A wheen o ships in the day as well, Mr Menmuir.'

'You don't think . . .'

'He's wanted for theft; he's probably avoided conscription. He knows you were away to find the polis. He'll no hang aboot Dundee waiting for us.'

'Can't you do something?'

'What? Go down to the docks and ask to search every vessel? They'd find me floating in the Tay as well, come the next high tide. Naw, I'll report this, Mr Menmuir, and I'll be glad to take your statement . . .' The bobby looked with compassion at the white, drawn face of the man beside him. 'And we'll get you a nice hot cup of tea afore ye fall down but, if you ask me, it's good riddance to bad rubbish.'

Davie looked at the teeming docks, at the closed doors and drawn curtains of the tenements around him. He would have liked to go to Catriona like a conquering hero, having fought for her honour and found the treasure that was lost, but, he thought wearily, he had achieved nothing. He had driven John Cameron farther into that underworld. Would Catriona thank him or hate him? Only time would tell.

9

VICTORIA LOVED EVERYTHING ABOUT Alistair Smart's office. She loved the dark-panelled walls, with here and there a watercolour bought on one of his trips to the mills in India. She loved the heavy leather armchairs and the worn carpet which he could easily afford to replace but never would. Each day, during all the months she had been working here, she found that she liked the funny bees-wax smell of his highly polished, mahogany rolltop desk, with its collection of pens and pipes and its meticulously arranged papers. The sole offering to modernity was the black telephone, which stood at the very edge of his desk, as though he did not really want it there but had been persuaded to endure its undoubted convenience. Victoria, standing in for the irreplaceable Miss Jessop, who was recuperating from a bout of flu, treated the instrument firmly and without fear.

She looked up now from her notebook and caught her employer's eye. Each was so surprised at being caught looking at the other that they smiled and went back to their work – one dictating and the other taking notes.

'You'll have those ready for me by lunchtime, Victoria?' said Mr Smart, unaware that it was already quarter to eleven.

'Of course, Mr Smart.' She smiled and went out to the outer office, where she had a desk beside that of Euan Gordon, the company bookkeeper.

Euan loved to watch Victoria at work. Everything had to be just so before she started and then, once she had her equipment arranged the way she wanted it, her fingers would fly over the carriage of the typewriter. He was right in assuming that she loved the process just as much as, or even more than, he did. Now he watched her arrange herself as if preparing for a long day.

'He's not wanting them done before dinner, is he, lass? You know, you can easily talk to him. He does listen. Miss Jessop takes no nonsense from him.'

'Oh, I'll send Peter down to Lamb's to get me a sandwich, Mr Gordon. I'd rather work through the dinner break than be late home.' She stopped delicately. One day soon she would have to tell everyone, or would she? Could they keep their horrible mess a secret for ever? 'My mother isn't too well at the moment, so I want to get the five o'clock tram.'

She went out to the main office to see the office boy, just as Mr Smart came in to ask her to add a rider to one of the documents.

'She's away to get the laddie to pick her up a sandwich, Mr Alistair. She's a good worker, that lassie, as hard working as she's pretty.' Mr Gordon had worked in Smart's office since he was fourteen years old and he was now almost fifty-nine. He could take his younger employer to task.

'Shame on you, Euan, a grandfather noting the charms of a female employee. You should be telling me about her typing speeds.' Alistair Smart smiled at his old friend and did not say that he needed no one to point out Miss Cameron's charms to him. Perhaps he was old enough to be her father, but he was neither blind nor uninterested.

'You know, Mr Alistair, I was that surprised when you hired a lassie.' Like most of the employees, Euan found Miss Jessop completely sexless – neither male nor female, just Miss Jessop. 'And I have to confess I thought you had gone too far with this "*Let's get ourselves firm\`y into the twentieth century*" business, but the girl has proved me wrong. She's bright and friendly without being forward. She works hard and she does her work well.' He stopped, remembering that Victoria had cheerfully decided to work through the firm's dinner break. 'She deserves to go far, Mr Alistair.'

Alistair Smart looked at his chief clerk. 'And so she will, Euan.' He put the paper down on Victoria's typewriter and turned to go back into his own office. 'We're well into this brave new century of ours. There's even talk of air travel. Can you imagine? One day, when Miss Jessop has retired, of course, Miss Cameron might fly to India on company business. I can't see it in my lifetime, mind you,' he added honestly. 'I can see her going to India, though. She'd be extremely useful to me, to the firm. But flying? What kind of fuel could they use to keep a machine in the air between Dundee and Calcutta? I have to think carefully about fuel when driving my motor between Dundee and Edinburgh. They'll never construct a flying machine that could go all that way without stopping.'

'What a dreadful idea, Mr Alistair. I hope never to see it. Can you imagine the confusion up there, although I suppose there is plenty of space. Anyway, that lassie will be married with a family long before the boffins have such an invention on their drawing boards.'

'Of course she will,' said Alistair Smart lightly, and he was surprised to find that he did not much like the idea of his efficient assistant being married.

Back in his office Alistair Smart pulled out the sheaf of letters from his mills in India. 'Blast this war.' In one way, it was good for business, which had never been better. But he had always liked a hands-on approach to business and had visited India once every three years since entering his father's firm at the age of sixteen, twenty-five years ago. His next visit was overdue and, although the managers in Calcutta were sound people, they too appreciated a visit from Head Office.

As well as the very necessary business discussions and appor-
tioning praise or blame, it meant more parties in an already
frenetic social round, new dresses for the wives and, more
importantly, new conversation.

If only this dratted war would just come to an end,
thought Alistair, *I could sail to India.* And then into his
head came a blissful picture – himself in white tropical
gear strolling along a moonlit deck with a girl ... *Any
girl? Certainly not Miss Jessop. How wonderful to take
Miss Cameron. She is so well organised and ...* He stopped
his wayward thoughts. Take a seventeen-year-old girl
to India? My God, if he was not arrested, he would certainly be laughed at by his colleagues. No, Miss Jessop –
the wonderful, sexless, but efficient Miss Jessop – should
go to India. If Miss Jessop will forget her fear of creepy-
crawlies, I will take her again, and the wonderful— No, he
would not describe Miss Cameron, even to himself. Miss
Cameron could easily run this office. They're all eating out
of her hand already. Pity she's so young (he refused to add
'and attractive') because it would be quite fun to show her
India. I bet she wouldn't ask for three-minute boiled eggs
at the hotel.'

He remembered his secretary's first visit to India and
the incredible patience with which the Indian staff had
dealt with her mounting paranoia. She would not eat any
curried dishes.

'Don't put that in your stomach, Mr Smart. I have ordered some poached chicken. Those spices merely cover up bad meat. Everybody knows that.'

She had almost been pleased when he had contracted dysentery. She, with her poached chicken and her three-minute eggs, had sailed through everything. In India she had eaten exactly what she ate in Dundee, prepared and cooked in exactly the same way as her elderly mother cooked it, and she had proved her theory. Maybe so, my dear Miss Jessop, but how narrow your life is, he thought.

No. Taking Victoria Cameron to visit the East could be a very enjoyable experience indeed.

Victoria was too busy thinking of her mother and Robert to daydream about the mysterious East. Dr Currie had taken another day off from her duties at the hospital and had gone to Edinburgh.

'I'll see Robert for you, my dear, and tell him that you will visit some weekend soon. Write him a note if you like, and his father will read it to him – or I will, if you'd rather.'

'I wish I could send something nice.'

'His father takes care of everything material, Victoria. It's a message from a friend that Robert needs.'

And so Victoria, mindful that other eyes would read her note, had written a stilted little message and given it to Dr Currie, before she lost her nerve and tore it up.

'I shall see Robert's father at the hospital,' said Dr Currie. 'He spends every moment he can there.'

But on the telephone Lord Inchmarnock had asked her to dine.

There was no harm, she decided, in meeting an old friend for dinner, even though the friend had been married for nearly twenty years to someone else. It was quite acceptable. After all, was she not a doctor and was the friend's son not very ill? To explain what the busy doctors in the hospital had no time to explain, in detail, to an anxious father was surely a kindness.

Flora took an early train to Edinburgh so that she could have a shampoo and wave, and she wore her soft blue woollen dress. It was a colour made world-famous by a young American socialite who gave it her name, Alice. And, like Alice Roosevelt, Flora knew what suited her.

They met in the dining room of the Overseas Club, and it pleased Flora that the comforting bulk of Edinburgh Castle filled the window where they sat. It had stood there for hundreds of years and had seen both comedy and tragedy enacted, often under its very roof, and still it stood there, calm, dignified, comforting.

Even the stress and worry over his son's condition had not detracted too much from Sandy Fotheringham's good looks and soldierly bearing, and his manners were as perfect as they had been all those years ago, when they had walked and hunted and danced their young lives away in an endless round of social engagements.

Why didn't I marry him when I had the chance? Flora thought to herself, as he held the chair out for her to sit down at the table. Or did I ever really have a chance? Did I even put up a fight after Julia appeared? Was I so used to being handed everything I wanted on a golden plate? Well, my dear Flora, those days are gone and, no doubt, that is a good thing.

She smiled up at Sandy as she sat down, and the smile revealed nothing of her inner turmoil. He returned the smile and there was one of those precious moments when time stands still and all worries disappear – little moments that are given to everyone, and which the wise snatch and keep safe. Victoria would have put the intimate smile in a walnut shell, but Flora knew nothing of walnut shells.

'They have some decent wine, Flora. I ordered this morning in order to save time – I hope you don't mind. I knew you would understand the lateness of our engagement, but I must spend as much time as possible at the hospital.' He tried to laugh. 'But don't worry. I remembered your sweet tooth and I've ordered a pudding.'

He was quiet as the waiter poured the wine and Flora felt that the interruption was giving him a chance to shape his next sentence. 'He's stopped asking for his mother, you know,' Sandy said when the waiter had gone.

Dr Currie's first impulse was to reassure him. 'Some people cannot take the sounds and smells of illness, Sandy, and to see a dearly beloved only child . . .' Dr Currie knew that they both knew she was lying, and she stopped.

'A less selfish woman would put the boy's needs first,' said Lord Inchmarnock angrily, then he remembered that he was discussing his wife. Bad form to discuss one's wife. Unforgivable to censure her behaviour. 'Forgive me, I didn't come here to air my own mistakes, especially to you. Delicious pâté.' He forced a smile. 'I wish you liked it. I always wanted to share everything with you, you know.'

'Friends,' said Flora, with perhaps a little undue stress on the word, 'don't need to share everything. They can appreciate their differences. Remember the hours and hours I spent watching you play cricket? Dear Lord,' – she laughed, a genuine laugh – 'what a soul-destroying game. Only thing that made it bearable was reading, when you couldn't see me. I went through several of the classics. Some might consider that to be two punishments in the same afternoon,' she finished lightly.

He reached across the table and touched her hand, and she let it lie there until he smiled and let go. And then he frowned. 'You're not wearing your watch. You used to wear it all the time, but, now that I think about it, you weren't wearing it that first time you came to see my laddie. Is that a message for me?'

She thought for a moment and almost lied, but he deserved the truth. 'It was stolen.' Her eyes filled with tears as she relived the moment when she had gone into her bedroom to check. 'My landlady's ex-husband. What an absolute cad he is, Sandy, and she is well rid of him. Unfortunately he seems to have disappeared. Perhaps he's gone abroad, I certainly hope so. He never was the slightest bit of good to them. You know the type of man, all charm and no substance.'

'Yes, my dear, I know the type, and this one took your watch?'

She nodded. 'I reported the theft to the police.'

Suddenly he was angry. Flora Currie in a boarding house in Dundee. She could afford better. 'I can't understand why you're living like that anyway, Flora. What would your father have had to say about it?'

'Catriona's house is clean and convenient. She does everything for me, even washes my clothes. I'm unbelievably undomesticated, Sandy, or just lazy. And it is difficult, especially since the war, to get decent help.'

'If only you had chosen me, instead of medicine, Flora . . .'

She could hardly breathe. *Chosen him, instead of medicine. Oh, you fool, Sandy Inchmarnock. What need would*

I have had for a career if your love had survived the test, but it hadn't. It had dissolved, just as the patterns Jack Frost leaves on the windows dissolve as soon as the first rays of the sun appear. That sun was Julia, and her rays had burned through everything. Flora tried to laugh, to be nonchalant and sophisticated.

'Oh, darling Sandy, you know you were knocked for six when Julia appeared like a comet, cutting a path through all you young men.'

They looked at one another, each surely seeing the other as they had been all those years ago. He looked away first, bowing his head in acknowledgement of the truth. He had been insane, with an insanity that had, unfortunately, lasted only a few years.

'Well, what was it my father's old coachman used to say? Ye mun drie yer ain wierd, and I have and I will. But my boy, Flora? What future is there for my boy?'

Instantly she was the consummate professional. 'He can live a full life, Sandy. They'll do wonders rebuilding his face, and the rest of his injuries will repair with time. Robert's main problem is what we call the will to live. His spirit will take longer to recover.'

'Will it ever recover? Will he laugh again? Will he enjoy life?'

'With you there to love him, and his mother ... She must be there to support him.'

'And the girl? She's a brave little thing. I see her refuse to flinch when she looks at him. Will she come back?'

'Oh, yes, Sandy. Victoria will come back. Some women are faithful, you know, against all the odds.'

She looked at him across the candlelit table and she could see the warmth, even the love, in his eyes. She prayed that he could see their reflection in her own. Was that all life held for them – reflections of what might have been?

'Julia's coming up at last,' he said, when he could bear the tension no longer. 'I'm taking the boy to Inchmarnock. He'll get better there, in his mind anyway.'

'That's nine-tenths of the battle.' Flora too was relieved that the spell was broken. 'I shall look forward to seeing Julia again. It will remind me to have a manicure. I can't remember when I last applied any polish.'

Julia Fotheringham, Lady Inchmarnock, unaware that her very presence could cause such a change in the lifestyle of her husband's old friend, did make the long journey from London to Edinburgh after Robert's operations: not immediately, so that Sandy might feel he had the upper hand, and not so long after the operation that her set might think her unfeeling. Robert's face, her husband told her, was decently hidden by bandages so, thought Julia, she could bear to see her beloved son again. Robert understood her feelings, even if her husband did not. But then, Julia thought, Robert had always been much more sympathetic and sensitive than his father, and she was coming for *him*, not because Sandy had almost ordered her to come.

She could also visit society's most controversial young poet, Siegfried Sassoon, who was, so a particularly dear friend had told her, recuperating in the very same hospital. This knowledge, naturally, had in no way influenced Julia's decision to steel herself to visit her son. She prayed that she would not break down and weep over Robert, and she prayed too that she would be able to lie convincingly and tell him that his hideously disfiguring injuries would make no difference at all to the feelings of those who loved him. It certainly had in no way changed hers. She would suggest that young Sassoon visited Robert with her. When she returned to London *everyone* would be thrilled to hear of her meeting with the poet.

Lady Inchmarnock was, therefore, not too happy to arrive at the George Hotel to find her husband in possession of the suite she had booked.

'Don't unpack, Julia,' he said. 'I've opened Inchmarnock. We're taking the boy home tomorrow.'

'Home?' The ready tears welled up in her eyes. 'Oh, Sandy, a mother's prayers have been answered. He's better. Our boy is better.'

Lord Inchmarnock looked at her beautiful face. What was it he had accidentally overheard an old friend say?

Julia Fotheringham's face has never been lived in. My God, how true it was.

'The lad is being sent home to recuperate from this operation, Julia, and to build up his strength for the next one. We're taking him to Inchmarnock, which he loves and where he may be happier. With both of us there to reassure him, he'll get well. He said a funny thing to me today: "*Inchmarnock's a walnut shell place.*" '

Lady Inchmarnock clutched at her husband's sleeve. 'Oh, Sandy, is his mind affected? There are no walnut trees at Inchmarnock.'

Patiently, but firmly, he removed the clutching hand from his well-tailored suit.

'I've hired a motor and a driver for tomorrow, Julia. The boy will be more comfortable and more at ease than on a train.'

'But the ferry . . .?'

'He likes the ferry. And the sea air will be good for him. I've ordered lunch to be sent up to you later on. I assume you are too exhausted from travelling to face the dining room.'

'I didn't sleep a wink on the train, Sandy, and had intended to take a little nap before dinner.' She stopped and looked around, but could see no real evidence of her husband's cohabitation.

He saw the frown of worry between her beautifully plucked eyebrows and smiled grimly. 'Rest easy, Julia. I'm bunking with old Charlie. Your sleep will not be violated. You have until three, and then I will fetch you in a cab and we'll go together to see Robert. Try to pretend that you are a loving mother.'

He was gone before she could throw something at him, or even think of anything devastating to say. It was grossly unfair. No one understood. How could she make Sandy appreciate the very real pain she felt when she saw their son – pain for the boy and for his ruined life, his destroyed hopes, not pain for herself. Oh, how dare he, how dare he? He could not understand her feelings. He had not carried the child as she had, in her very body for nine whole months. How could she have persuaded herself that he was a sensitive, loving man? He was a boor. She threw herself on the bed and enjoyed the indulgence of a good cry.

Three days later the Fotheringhams were comfortably resettled in their country home and Lady Inchmarnock found that it was not too painful to look at her son and to contemplate his future. She had had a wonderful idea that would make everything bearable. To this end she had sent Sandy's motor with its uniformed driver to fetch Miss Victoria Cameron. She felt that Miss Cameron could not possibly refuse to return with the driver. Who could reject an anguished mother's plea? What a lovely surprise it would be for Robert, who was now sitting happily in a shaded part of the terrace. Lady Inchmarnock rose as she heard the doorbell and walked quickly to her beautifully appointed rose drawing room. The private motor, then tea with a *real* lady in such surroundings. Oh, yes, her plan was so perfect.

'Victoria, my dear,' she said as the maid announced Miss Cameron. 'How very sweet of you to come at such short notice. I may call you Victoria? We're going to be such friends, I can feel it. I'm terribly sensitive, you know. It's such a handicap sometimes. India or China?' she asked so suddenly that Victoria was somewhat disconcerted, until she saw her hostess gesture to the ornate silver tray with its tea service.

'India, please, Lady Inchmarnock,' she said quietly.

Victoria had been surprised by the summons and had been in two minds over whether or not to jump when her ladyship called, but there was Robert to think of. If this afternoon tea had something to do with Robert, then she had no choice but to give up her one free afternoon and go. She wished that Dr Currie was at home so that she could discuss it with her, but since she was not, Victoria had made light of the summons when the chauffeur-driven Bentley stopped outside the modest house on Blackness Road. She was aware that the house and its occupants had been the subject of much speculation recently in the neighbourhood, and now here was more fuel for the flame of gossip. Still, she dressed in her new suit, worn only once since her first visit to Robert's bedside, and she sprayed a modest amount of eau de Cologne over her hair. The light perfume gave her courage.

'Should you not take a gift?' Catriona had asked. 'We always took eggs, or a nice boiling fowl, when we called on folk.'

'Don't worry. I won't let you down. You put your feet up and have a rest this afternoon.'

Now here she was with Robert's mother, who was offering her sandwiches no bigger than her thumb and a cup and saucer finer than anything she had seen outside the walls of a museum.

'And how is Robert, m' Lady?' she asked. Victoria was not going to be bullied by Lady Inchmarnock and she wanted to find out immediately the purpose of the visit.

Robert's mother looked at her measuringly for a moment. 'Do you know, Victoria, a pale-green Chinese silk blouse would be adorable with that suit,' she said. Then she added, 'He is so well, my dear. His father and I have every expectation that he will live a completely normal life.'

Victoria smiled at the words and visibly relaxed. She swallowed the tiny sandwich she had been holding in her hand and sipped from her cup. 'I'm so glad,' she replied. 'You said in your note that he was temporarily at home. That must be beneficial: you know how he loves Inchmarnock.'

Julia bristled. She did not need some upstart working-class office girl telling her whether or not her only son liked his home, but she forced herself to return Victoria's smile. 'Pearls are really the only suitable jewels for a young unmarried woman, but that suit does cry out for a discreet diamond brooch, don't you think? Sandy, Lord Inchmarnock, and I are so glad that you and Robert became friends, my dear,' she lied easily. 'In fact, that is why I asked you to come.'

Victoria rose. 'Do you want me to visit him, Lady Inchmarnock? Is he in his room? I'm sure my mother will have no objection, since you are here.'

Oh God, thought Julia, how distressingly working-class. What on earth did the mother think would happen if she were *not* there? Such dirty minds. 'Later, dear. Do sit down, Victoria. Robert is resting in the garden, on the terrace – it's such a lovely afternoon. More tea? No. Then I'll get to the point, shall I?'

Victoria sat down, her heart beating uncomfortably. She knew that she was not going to enjoy what she was about to hear. Surely Robert had not been discharged from the hospital in order to die at home. He had come through the operation well, Dr Currie had assured her.

'In some ways Robert will make a complete recovery. He can walk. His broken bones have healed. The damage to his internal organs will incapacitate him to a certain degree, but then, as I'm sure you know,' she added spitefully, 'he does not have to earn a living. It is his face, Victoria, and his spirit.' Julia stopped and tried hard to conjure up a picture of Robert's face. 'He's like me,' she said. 'He looks like me. Dark hair and eyes, beautiful eyes.' She laughed and blushed like a girl. 'I'm describing my boy, y'know – a sensitive mouth, but there's no femininity in his. A straight nose. The mouth so beautifully . . .' The picture just would not come. 'His face will never be rebuilt as it was. He will always be . . .' She stopped and pulled a handkerchief from her skirt pocket and dabbed delicately at her eyes, which were swimming with unshed tears. 'Oh, Victoria, can you understand a little of a mother's anguish?' she asked and began to weep softly.

Victoria sat, horrified. Had it been Catriona or even Dr Currie, she could have moved, done something, said something to offer comfort. What did one say? Anything would sound like a platitude, and she could not console this woman because she could not reach her in any way. 'I'm so sorry,' she said at last, 'but surely, surely we can make him see that his looks don't matter?'

Robert's mother blew her nose. It was the most incredibly refined and ladylike action and only succeeded in making Victoria feel worse than she had done before.

'I knew you would say that, Victoria, but all girls are not like you. Robert will feel like a pariah in society, my dear. Every time I see him, I am reminded of the obscenity of war, and I am his mother. I love him and I can't bear for him to suffer any more. What will be the attitude of some empty-headed débutante? I feel – I'm sure his father does too – that there is little real future for Robert in the world into which he was born.'

To Victoria's horror she leaned across the rosewood table and grasped her hand, and Victoria had to steel herself not to snatch it away.

'But you, Victoria. Even as he is, Robert can offer you more than you could ever imagine. Was it not pleasant to arrive exactly at your destination in a chauffeur-driven motor? Would it not be pleasant to throw that dreadful suit away, to wear pure silk against your skin, to put diamonds around your neck and in your ears, to live here, Victoria, as mistress of this house, to change this room and every other in this house as you see fit? I do not expect you to love him, my dear, and I'm sure that his health is such that he would not be a . . .' She stopped, while she searched her mind for the right adjective, and Victoria held her breath and prayed for the courage not to slap the beautiful, insensitive face. '. . . demanding husband. You would be rich, Victoria, secure for the rest of your life. There is even a cottage in the grounds where your mother would be quite comfortable. After all, it's not as if you and Robert will entertain.'

Victoria sprang to her feet and in one swift movement went to stand behind the chair on which she had been sitting. She clenched her hands on the rose silk and stared across the chair and the little table, with the remains of their elegant afternoon tea.

'How dare you?' she almost screamed. 'You are, without a doubt, the most insensitive and selfish person I have ever met in my life.' She stopped for a second as a picture of another selfish human being rose in her mind – that of her father – and that made her even angrier. 'You can't begin to understand, but I could never be bribed into marrying your son. I liked a boy I met twice, twice ... when we were children. To me he was St George or Sir Lancelot. I could have loved him, had I been given a chance, and perhaps he could have loved me – and wealth and power, and whether or not he is hideously disfigured would not have entered the equation. And nothing will ever get me to part with this *dreadful* suit – perhaps it's not *haute couture* and needs a little silk something here, and a teeny-weeny diamond something there, to make it bearable to a fine lady like you, but to me it's elegant and lovely, and a joy to wear, because someone who loves me and all my faults gave it to me, and you can't understand that either. I'm sorry for you, Julia Fotheringham, and my pity is another thing you can't understand. If Robert wants me to visit him in hospital I will go gladly, but I hope with all my heart that I never see you again.'

Victoria turned and fled from the room. Lady Inch-marnock stood, shaking, as she watched the flight of the only person in the world who had ever shouted at her. Neither of them saw the bowed figure of Robert turn from the window, where he had been standing for five of the most miserable minutes that he had ever lived through.

10

ROBERT WATCHED VICTORIA LEAVE THE room, then he made his way slowly along the terrace until he reached the windows of his father's study. How he had loved, as a small boy, to creep along here and then to jump in at the french windows. Each time his father had shrieked with fear. How old had he been before he had realized that Pa had expected the intrusion, had waited for it, lovingly. Dear Pa, thought Robert, dear old Pa.

He smiled a twisted smile at the memory and entered the study through those selfsame french windows. He went to the desk and sat down for a moment to rest. How he loved this room. How it spoke to him of his father. He ran his scarred hands along the top of the highly polished mahogany desk, along the oak case of his grandfather's favourite guns, and he breathed deeply, taking in that special smell of cigars and horses, books and Knight's Castile soap, which spoke so eloquently of Lord Inchmarnock.

How peaceful it was. He had always been safe here. As a small boy he had hidden – with Pa's connivance – from

Nanny and bedtime, under the knee-hole desk. Could I curl up there again, with Teddy under one arm and Pa sitting there, looking so patently honest? 'Gosh, nanny, has that scamp gone missing again? Try the kitchens. They absolutely ruin him there. I'll speak firmly to cook, I promise you I will.' And nanny had looked at him with a look that told him that she knew perfectly well that he knew that the much-maligned cook had nothing to do with little Robert's transgressions. Now Robert smiled at the panelled walls, as if they could see him and accept him – as he had been, and as he was now.

He opened a drawer in the desk and took out some of his father's heavy vellum crested notepaper. He fished in his pocket for his handkerchief and his trembling fingers encircled something. A walnut shell. He brought it out and struggled to open it. Even his fingers disobeyed him these days, trembling, trembling, like old Granny Inchmarnock's. But she was eighty, he thought, and I am just nineteen. How he had hated her trembling hands: they had frightened the boy Robert.

He had the shell open now and he smiled. She was right. Victoria was so very right. He could see the woods, first in their spring glories, then in their autumn dress, and always among the trees was a girl, a young girl, innocent, unaware. She smiled at him.

'These are private grounds,' she said primly, but with a dimple in her cheek, a dimple he had been able to see, almost to touch, in the bad days. 'It's against the law to pick flowers here.'

'They'll forgive a knight . . .'

He glanced up quickly from the walnut shell and his own face looked back at him. Photographs, photographs in silver frames, everywhere. Robert, a plump baby beside the Christmas tree with its breathtaking array of candles; Robert so solemn and unafraid on his first pony; Robert, even more aware of the weight on his young shoulders in his cricket whites, when he made the team; Robert, terrified, expectant, reluctant, in his first dinner jacket at his first dance.

He picked up a paperweight and smashed the shell, and the days of childhood and innocence disappeared and other days came flooding in. The Somme. The guns. The smell. The noise. The pain . . . The pain, and then Mother, Mother . . . buying him a wife.

'You're so right, Mamma,' he whispered, touching his scarred face with trembling fingers. 'No one could love this . . . except Pa. Oh, Pa, I'm sorry, I'm so very sorry.'

For a few moments he bent and wrote quickly on the expensive paper. He finished with a flourish, *Goodbye, Robert*, and then threw the pen from him, so that several of the pictures were splattered with ink.

In the hall the tweenies wondered whether or not they should try to *do* the study. They had finished everything else, but Jarvis, the butler, had said as how Master Robert had gone into the room, and he did so hate for the maids to see him.

'Poor lamb, he should get used to us being around,' said Milly solicitously to her friend Bess. 'Then he'd know we only see a hero what has suffered for our freedom.'

'It'll take—' began Bess but she never finished, for just then the silence of the great house was shattered by the blast of a shotgun. It was only too obvious that the soul-destroying sound had come from behind the closed door of Lord Inchmarnock's study.

The butler had met Victoria in her flight and calmly, as if every day of the week a guest rushed headlong from the house, he arranged to find madame's coat, madame's car.

'I prefer to take a bus,' said Victoria. 'Please, I would enjoy the walk down the driveway to the road.'

'As you wish, madame, but his lordship . . .'

'Can think what he likes,' wept Victoria. 'Please, I have to go, please.'

He opened the great door and she hurried down the steps. A path wandered off and hid itself among the rhododendrons and Victoria took it. She did not want the watching house to witness her flight. She ran and soon found herself at a pond, where a weeping willow bent over to admire its own reflection.

'Oh, dear God, this is the place. I've been here before.'

She stopped and looked around. Yes, it was the same spot where the boy Robert had met the girl Victoria. The great trees stood even taller now and once more their branches were visions of red and gold, yellow and brown. Under the trees, purple autumn crocuses were spreading themselves.

With eyes full of tears, she stood and looked at the archway created by the towering beeches. An autumn sun shone hazily through the leaves and she thought she saw a figure appear on the path – a boy, tall and slender. He shimmered and dissolved and she blinked against the tears and the sunlight, and there he was again. 'They'll forgive a knight going off to the Crusades,' he said and he held out his hand. It was autumn, but in his hand he held a posy of small yellow flowers.

'Robert, Robert, my dear, where did you get those primroses?' And then suddenly birds rose up in alarm from every tree, and the sky was dark with their wings and the air was full of their cries, and the boy was gone.

Her soul full of an unbearable knowledge, Victoria stood for a long time looking at the spot where the boy had stood, this moment and a lifetime ago. Then, chilled and unbearably anguished, she turned and, with head held high and tears streaming unchecked down her face, she walked down the path to the road.

She did not wait for a bus but walked along the river to the ferry. How calm, how peaceful, how beautiful it was. It was possible to believe that there was no evil in the world, no sadness, no madness, when one watched a great river. The sunlight rested on top of the still water and the underlying currents teased the rays and pulled them this way and that.

Victoria bent down and picked up a stone. She hurled it into the water to break that deceptive air of calm. There was too much evil in the world hiding just under the surface. Get it out, get it out and deal with it. The Tay was beautiful, smiling in the sunlight, but it was a treacherous river.

She felt slightly calmer after throwing the stone and continued to the ferry terminal, where she scrubbed her face dry with her handkerchief. She sat, until the ferry left, staring into space and, if she had but known it, her eyes were so full of unimaginable horror that two other passengers could not bear to sit near her.

She did not wait for a tram at the other side, but walked up to the Perth Road and out, farther and farther, until she came to Blackness Road. When she saw the dim light shining from the window of the room where Catriona waited, Victoria cried again and, heedless of the shock to her neighbours' sensibilities, ran until she was safe in her mother's arms.

Catriona rocked her and wisely asked nothing until Victoria was quiet.

'He's dead, Mother. I saw him in the wood, but he wasn't there. He was himself again, the way I want to remember him. Oh, his poor parents, his father.'

Soldiers are citizens of death's grey land,
Drawing no dividend from time's tomorrows . . .

Sandy Fotheringham, Lord Inchmarnock, held the slim little book that the other young soldier had given him at the hospital and he read the words from the last poem his son ever heard. The poet, Siegfried Sassoon, had himself read it to Robert. Now his father read it over the boy's open grave. The weather underscored his grief. It was a cold and raw day. The great trees in the churchyard held their bare arms up in supplication as he intoned his prayer. He had wept. Dear God, how he had wept. Not at first; not for some time after the remains of what had been the person he loved more than anything, or anyone, in the whole world had been tidied up and taken away. Only then had he raged like a wounded lion through the beautiful rooms of the house they had both loved, and which he never wanted to see again. Memories of Robert were everywhere in the great house, but too often the picture of what had been left of his son superimposed itself on the father's precious pictures: Robert in his baby clothes smiling up at his father; Robert, a plump toddler in his embroidered nightshirt running, squealing, up and down the corridors, evading capture and the inevitable bedtime, Robert, Robert, Robert . . .

Did anyone guess Sandy's agony as they saw his erect and proud bearing, his aristocratic head bent over the little book of poems as, in his well-modulated voice, he read the words of the soldier-poet who, better than anyone, exposed the futility of war.

> *. . . Soldiers are sworn to action; they must win*
> *Some flaming, fatal climax with their lives . . .*

Oh, sweet Lord, what was the flaming climax to my boy's life?

Julia Fotheringham too had read the sombre words. She would not talk of Sassoon when she returned to London's drawing rooms: he was for ever bound up with the horror that was Robert's final action.

> *Soldiers are dreamers; when the guns begin*
> *They think of firelit homes . . .*

An elegant, even beautiful figure in her black highnecked gown, she sat in her firelit home, winding the jet mourning beads round and round in her beringed fingers.

He's dead. My baby, my child, my son. So beautiful, so loving and kind, and he's dead. Dear God, what did I say to make him do this terrible thing? It wasn't me, it wasn't my fault. Oh, please, dear God in heaven, don't let it have been my fault. I couldn't bear that, and I have had so much to bear.

She crushed the letter yet again between trembling fingers, the letter that started *Dear Pa*, as if his last thoughts were only for Sandy: Robert didn't even want her to know what he was thinking. He had shut her out at the end. Why? Dear God in heaven, why? Didn't he understand that I couldn't bear for him to be unhappy, not like me ... He didn't know how empty our marriage has become. He was the priceless pearl, the only common unit that we loved, the precious chain that held us together – our son, our joy.

I see them in foul dug-outs, gnawed by rats,
And in the ruined trenches, lashed with rain,

The letter she had received from the boy-soldier slipped from Victoria's trembling fingers. She sat on her bed, looking out at the garden but seeing, through eyes swimming with tears, other trees.

What a waste! She wished from somewhere she could find stronger words, words that would express what Robert's loss – his terrible, dreadful way of ending his life – really meant. He had been so beautiful and so good. If he had grown up, he would have become a truly fine man, a good man. And his was not the only tragedy. In homes all over Europe girls were sitting on beds weeping for lost loves; mothers and fathers were asking: Why? For what has our child paid the ultimate sacrifice? Although Robert Fotheringham had taken his own life, he was as much a war casualty as any boy lost in battle. Would he have been a poet, a painter. . .? In spite of her numbing grief, Victoria laughed, a painful, croaking laugh. No, not a painter. He could paint no better than she. A teacher, perhaps. A man of vision. How many men of vision had died, together with the dreams they had not begun to realize? How many pieces of soul-soothing music would never be written? How many cures for diseases of the mind and body had died unborn, with their discoverers, in the Flanders mud? Why did they die? For Truth, Freedom, Justice, Right?

Oh, dear God, wept Victoria and she hugged herself for comfort against the almost unbearable pain. Don't let those words become trite platitudes. Let there be an end to war. Is there no great writer out there somewhere, no great statesman who can make the oppressors realize that their way is wrong, that every man has rights, that every man has a place in the great scheme of things? When will there be peace, so that we can mourn for the unachieved flowering of a generation's genius?

Victoria bowed her head again over Robert's last letter and sobbed. Could she have said something to change his mind from its dreadful course? Should she have visited him more often? Had he felt her first, involuntary withdrawal at the sight of his ravaged face? Oh, Robert, Robert, it did not matter, and I soon learned not to mind it. Did you hear me talk so cruelly to your mother? Did you misunderstand what I said? I did not say that I would not, could not marry you. I said I could not be bought.

She got up suddenly from the bed and went over to her bookcase. *Mansfield Park* still stood in its accustomed place and it immediately yielded up its secret: the petals of a flower so silver and fragile with age that she was afraid to touch them, for fear that they would disintegrate at the slightest touch. She bent her head and tried to breathe in their fragrance, but she smelled only a book that had lain too long unread on its shelf.

'I will keep them all my life, Robert, and I will remember you as you were. If I failed you, I am sorry. Rest in peace. Rest in peace.'

. . . Dreaming of things they did with balls and bats,
And mocked by hopeless longing to regain
Bank holidays, and picture shows, and spats,
And going to the office in the train.

Lord Inchmarnock finished and stood, with head bowed, as he prayed for his son and for all the other sons. And then his silent prayer was joined by that most poignant of sounds – the lone pipes. Where in the world, thought Sandy, had that eerie, mournful pibroch not sounded? The lament faded away and Sandy stooped and gathered a handful of good Fife soil. With his other hand he reached into his pocket and took out the walnut shell that Victoria had sent him by Flora.

'I'll try to remember only the walnut shell days, Robert, my heart,' he said as he threw, together into the open grave, the walnut shell and the handful of Inchmarnock soil.

He started to rub his hands together to wipe the clinging bits of dirt from them. Then he looked into the grave and saw the wooden box, and he stuffed his hands with their light traces of soil into his pockets. Would that I never had to wash them again, he thought. Would that I could keep this final, tentative connection with the boy-soldier who was the last in a proud line. He raised his head. He was almost alone. The many mourners were moving away towards their carriages and motor cars and, he was happy to note, their farm carts – his tenants, obviously.

'They're all to come to the house, Simon,' he said to his grieve, who was standing respectfully a little way off. He watched the man hurry after the tenants and sighed.

Thank God that is over, he thought. I lived for Robert. Perhaps Julia did too. Where will we find the strength to go on? Well, we'll start with the mourners. One duty after another. Perhaps that's all life is, a series of duties.

11

As winter approached, Catriona put her mind to the household tasks. If her mind was busy with the house and its welfare, there was less time to think of herself and her problems. She worked so hard every day that when she finally fell on to her bed at night, she slept like one dead, one who no longer had to think. In this way life became bearable. Victoria and Dr Currie watched her cope and each, in her own way, tried to help. If she would only speak about it. But since that night when, in her own mind, she had given way to weakness and had cried in her daughter's arms, she had shut herself away and brooked no argument.

'You can help me best by allowing me to go on with life as best I can,' she said.

Davie Menmuir was always there to help, too. He rarely spoke, but for some reason Catriona tolerated his presence and seemed to draw some comfort from his being there.

'I should hae a look at the gutters, mistress,' he said. 'There's already a few leaves come down and we'll not want the drains blocked.'

Catriona looked at him and sighed. If only she didn't always feel so tired these days, she could cope better. It was just tiredness that prevented her from climbing up that ladder herself and attending to the gutters.

'I'll hold the ladder for you, Davie,' she said, conscious as always of his emaciated figure. What a fine lad he had been, when she had first come to Priory Farm. But better not to think of those – what would Victoria call them? – walnut shell days.

Davie, for his part, hated to admit that he now needed a woman to help him do a simple chore. He began to reject her offer, but then thought better of it. That would give birth to the thought they were all avoiding. They might just have to mention why Catriona should not be holding heavy ladders.

They worked companionably and quietly together until Davie had been all the way around the house.

'Well, that's a grand job done, mistress. I'll wash up at the pump and be on my way home.'

So easy to let him go, to take his help for granted. But old habits of hospitality die hard.

'I've a rabbit stew in the oven, Davie. You'll take your tea with me afore you head out for the bus?'

He washed at the pump in the back garden, then went into the kitchen, where the table was now laid for two. How companionable it all looked: the coals glowing in the grate, the cat snoozing on the rag rug with old Flash curled up beside him, the dog's eyes wide open and following the path of his mistress as she moved slowly – not quickly and sharply as she usually did – from stove to table, from table to sink.

Davie sighed.

'You're tired, Davie,' said Catriona, misreading the sigh. 'Here, have some bread, I baked it this morning.'

'Bread dipped in rabbit gravy,' said Davie contentedly. 'I wouldn't call the king my brother with a meal like this in front of me.'

She smiled at him and cut another slice. 'Davie,' she began tentatively, 'I've been meaning to say thank you. You know, for that day in the town. Yon policeman told me how you hammered John.'

He blushed and stammered something incoherent.

'You're a good man, Davie Menmuir,' said Catriona. Then, afraid that she had said too much, and more than she had meant, she busied herself refilling his plate.

'I wonder where he's gone,' she said as she sat down. She neither knew nor cared where John had gone, but she had to make conversation, for Davie never would and they would just sit there, eating stew and avoiding what would one day have to be acknowledged. 'It was aye France he was off to before, but they'd no welcome him in the middle of this, would they?'

'There was two ships in the harbour that day, the policeman told me. One had come from India with a load of jute for the mills. The other was going to Mexico. Mexico,' Davie savoured the name. 'Have you ever heard of a place called Mexico?'

'Mexico?' Catriona thought for a moment. 'Is that one of thae places in Europe where they're aye having revolutions? I'm sure I've read the name in the *Courier*. Part of Spain, is it? I'll fetch Victoria's atlas. She was good at the geography.'

She got up from the table and went to the dresser, and eventually she unearthed a heavy green-bound book, which she carried back to the table and laid in front of Davie. 'Do you mind the geography lessons we had when we were at the school? Capitals and rivers.' Catriona laughed, the laugh of a carefree young girl, and he laughed with her.

'For a minute there you looked just like you looked the first day I saw you at the farm,' he said. And she saw admiration in his eyes and tensed.

'That was a lifetime ago,' she replied, 'and we're different people now.' She riffled quickly through the pages. 'K . . . L . . . M . . . Mexico. Goodness, it's half a world away. It's nowhere near Spain. That's the United States. Goodness, Davie, it's a place stuck on to the bottom of the United States of America. How could you ever get all the way to a place like that? And what language would they speak? They'd never speak English there, would they, Davie?' She held the atlas, and as he looked down at the huge green and brown mass that was Mexico, she saw his strong brown hands on her starched clean tablecloth. Those hands have never willingly hurt anything in their life, she thought. His wife should have lived. He should have had children. She felt a slight fluttering in her insides and sat down quickly. Davie jumped to his feet.

'Catriona, lass, you're unwell. What can I do?'

She ignored his use of her given name. She ignored the almost overwhelming impulse to break down and cry, and have him take care of everything as easily as he had rid her gutters of leaves.

'You can eat your stew, Davie Menmuir, and I will eat mine.' She closed the book and put it back in the drawer. 'Talking of jute ships minds me on Victoria. She loves her new job. I don't know how to thank Dr Currie for everything she has done for this family. Victoria would still be in that mill. Sometimes I have nightmares about it. Jock would have given heaven and earth to keep her out of the mills. Look at Nellie Bains. She took a way out of the mills, didn't she? Maybe more misery before her than behind her, though. An illigitimate child! Dear God, Davie. Can you imagine the shame of having an illegitimate child? And my Victoria took up with her again – even took her out to tea. I've nothing against Nellie, but I'm not Christian enough to want my Victoria associating with her.'

Completely unaware that she was causing Catriona Cameron such heartache, Nellie Bains was tackling her number one enemy – dirt. She was being helped or hindered by her son, Jimmy, who, perhaps because he was immersed totally in water only every Saturday evening, was fascinated by the lovely liquid slopping around in his mother's pail and kept getting in her way.

'If you put yer hands in that bucket again, I'll clout yer ear. You've dirty water up tae your elbows.' Nellie glared at her son, who grinned back at her with that engaging smile that turned her knees to water. 'I mean it this time, ye wee toe-rag.'

'That wean's got you wrapped round his pinkie, Nellie.' The voice came from up the stairs and Nellie lifted her head and looked up through the wrought-iron banisters.

She sighed. 'The dirtier that water, the happier the wee rogue is, Mrs Dow.'

'Ach, I'll come down and mind him for ye.' Mrs Dow removed her ample bosom from where it had been resting on the banister and followed it down to the landing that Nellie was scrubbing. 'Tell ye what, Nellie. It's a braw day. I'll tak the wean doon to the drying green and give him a wee push on the swing.'

Nellie looked at the girth of her neighbour and at the swiftly moving lightning bolt that was her son. 'Are ye sure? He's a right wee handful,' she said, pushing her damp hair back from her forehead, but Mrs Dow gathered the baby up in her arms and he buried his dirty face in her neck quite cheerfully.

Nellie smiled. 'Thanks, Mrs Dow. You're a grand neighbour.'

'Lassie, lassie, it would be a poor world if we couldnae help one another.'

Mrs Dow set Jimmy back on his feet again. It was safer to walk hand-in-hand with him down the stairs. She held on to the banister with one hand, Jimmy with the other, and Nellie watched their progress, Jimmy's feet touching, at the most, every third stair.

Ach, he'll be safe enough wi Mrs Dow, thought Nellie, She's never drapped a bairn yet. And she knelt down to get on with her once-every-five-weeks job of washing the stairs, the landings and the stairwell.

It had been a rainy month and there was an amazing amount of mud on the stairs, hence the dirty water. Still, without wee Jimmy's help, she got on more quickly.

Two urchins took delight in running up part of the stairs that she had just scrubbed and then, with an almost believable 'Sorry, missus', ran back down again. At the third attempt Nellie collared one of them. 'Run doon my clean stair again and I'll skite ye both off that wall,' she said. After that they contented themselves with making occasional rude noises at her from the mouth of the close.

Wee toe-rags, thought the good-natured Nellie. *My Jimmy'll no behave like that when he's big. Mind you, if I get what I'm wantin, there'll be nae stairhead for him to play in.*

That thought cheered her up and she bent to her scrubbing with renewed energy. The stairs would be dirty again before nightfall, but for a few perfect hours they would be as clean as Nellie Bains could make them. She fought the dirt as fiercely as her man was fighting his enemy, *somewhere on the Front.* Eventually she finished and stood, with aching back, watching her son squealing in delight as he soared through the air on the makeshift swing. It was good to rest after her hard work and Nellie took satisfaction from the sight of her child and the knowledge of the clean stairs behind her. She should take him upstairs and feed him his tea. There was some broth left and, if she soaked a slice of stale bread in it, the baby would be perfectly content.

Seems a shame to dirty my clean stairs right away, though, she thought and went over to the green to play with Jimmy. Mrs Dow cheerfully surrendered her charge and Nellie gave herself up to one of the real pleasures of motherhood.

'Wheee,' she yelled, as she pushed the wooden swing into the air.

'Wheee,' answered Jimmy, as well as he could while the wind tried to blow the breath from his little body.

Nellie stood pushing until she was exhausted and, finally refusing the repeated entreaties of 'More', she climbed happily back up her already dirty stairs.

Five hours later she was back downstairs with the three-legged milking stool that had been one of her legacies from her family's tied cottage at Birky. It had been too rickety for the dairy maid and so it had been deemed good enough *fer a wee bit lass like Nellie*. Nellie had been savouring the last of her plate of deep-fried chipped potatoes, liberally sprinkled with salt and vinegar, when Mr Flett from across the stairs had knocked on the door to remind her that she was also supposed to renew the gas mantle. It had got broken in what he had called a *stramash* when the next-door pub closed its doors the previous Saturday night.

'And here's me, on my own without a man, going out to a dark closie at this time of the night. Do you not think that self-righteous bugger could hae done it himself and told me how wonderful he was the morn's morning?' She checked that Jimmy was asleep, left the door unlocked so that she could get back in and hurried down the dark stairs. She eyed the broken mantle and she eyed the stool. Since Jimmy's birth she had not been quite the slip of a girl that she had been when she had inherited the stool. She sighed, but decided that life would be easier for everyone if there was light in the close. She positioned the stool and balanced tentatively on it.

'Tak care noo,' a male voice boomed out of the darkness and Nellie dropped the shade with fright. How often had her mother told her not to get herself into such situations?

Nellie took a deep breath and peered into the poorly illuminated close, where the figure of a man loomed. And then her generous heart began to beat, but not with fear – with anticipation. It was a soldier: from her precarious perch on the stool she could smell the dirt and sweat that no doubt he himself no longer noticed. She placed her hands on her hips and swayed provocatively towards him.

'They've nae baths at the Front?' she asked pertly.

'Naw, Nellie lass. There's an awful lot Dundee could teach the French. I'll no be too dirty for a wee kiss?'

Too dirty! Too dirty! Nellie threw herself off the stool and into his arms and for a few blessed moments the ill-lit stairwell was the most beautiful place in the world. At last the soldier pulled himself away.

'I'm lousy to, Nellie. The wee buggers are in my hair and under my arms and places I'll no mention, but gin I'm scrubbed you're going tae see them for yourself.'

'I cannae wait, Tam Sinclair,' said Nellie boldly and almost pulled him to the stairs.

He laughed. 'Away, ye bold lass. Ye'll need to boil everything, including me.'

'Pity I wore my brush out on the stairs,' she laughed, close to tears. 'For it'll take more than water to get the dirt off you. And the smell of you. Can you no smell yourself?'

'Ach, I'm past smelling, or feeling, or even hearing, Nellie. We've had that much of everything, we notice nothing now.'

'Is the war over then, lad?'

'Naw. I finally got some leave, and if God is as good as you're always telling me He is, then it'll be over afore the end of my furlow.'

'Furlow. Now there's a word for the wean.'

'How is he, Nellie? Is he well? Does he remember me?'

Their arms around one another, they had reached the door of their tiny home. Nellie opened it and Tam saw a welcoming fire, polished linoleum and the crib. He tiptoed, in his great mud-caked boots, over to where his son lay. They looked down at the child, who lay like a reluctant angel on the pillow. His thumb was in his mouth and his dark eyelashes fanned his plump cheeks.

Tam stretched a filthy finger down to his son and gently touched the small head. 'This is real, Nellie. I never knew it till now, but this,' he gestured at the child, 'was what we've all been fighting for these last years. I've seen dead bairns, Nellie, and I suppose I prayed to hold mine in my arms.'

'Well, we'll get ye clean first,' said the practical Nellie, who could scarcely contain herself at hearing words like that from her Tam. She wanted to cry, she was so happy, so she took refuge in making herself busy. 'I'll boil some water and you get out of those clothes. Pit them in the sink at the stairhead. I'm no having any of your lodgers crawling along my settee.'

'Nellie. How can I get to the stairhead without my clothes?' demanded the modest Tam.

Nellie put her hands on her ample waist and laughed with joy into her man's dirty bearded face. 'This close has seen worse, Tam my lad, a lot worse,' she said and turned away, so that he could not see the tears of joy in her eyes. 'Wrap yoursel in a blanket off the bed, ye daft gowk, and I'll meet you at the door and take it back along to the sink.'

Tam tiptoed out on to the landing and quickly began to undress. The top half was easy, but once he had wrapped the thin, clean blanket around his shoulders, getting his lower half undone without dropping his covering was difficult. He was reminded of the days of childhood, modestly trying to preserve his dignity behind a threadbare towel at family picnics.

'Cover yourself, our Tam,' his mother's voice came back to him. Not a voice with which to argue. He had become so used to taking orders that it had never occurred to him to argue with Nellie.

'Yes, sir. No, sir.' How many more times would he say those words? And later there would be a job in this brave new land for which they were fighting and dying, and he would be back to saying, 'Yes, sir. No, sir.' But at least he'd be living. Sometimes the dying was the cleanest part of it. 'Dear God, don't let me tell Nellie any of the real truth of the glory. Glory!' He stood at the sink and the tears for his lost innocence made tracks in the dirt on his tired face. Oh, he was fell tired. Oh, to hold Nellie's warm, clean body, to lose himself and his memories in her, to be reborn, the old Tam, who had never stolen, never lied, never killed.

'Tam Sinclair, if you don't come back in this house, I'll be forced to dae something I tellt my mother I'd never dae up a closie in Dundee.'

He laughed. 'Nellie, Nellie. I'll no lay a finger on you till I'm clean.'

'Well, stop standing there like a tumshie in a field, Tam. Come on.' Her arms were round him and her breath was warm on his neck. He could feel her warmth through his towel. Her voice was no longer bold, but the real voice of the real Nellie. 'I want to make the most of every moment we've got together. First we'll get you clean and then I've some soup, Tam. Then, well, you know what we'll do, and then we'll sleep, stuck thegither like two spoons in a drawer. But ye'd better get a move on, for that son of yours is up with the birds and he's oot of the cot and in my bed.'

Tam saw the picture in his mind and it was a lovely picture. 'Ach, Nellie,' he said as he thrust the blanket into the sink and began to sprint, as naked as the day he was born, for the haven of his home, 'that would never never do.'

Her laughter and then her lovely self followed him, and he heard the bolt shoot home in the door.

12

Las Estrellas, Mexico

CONSIDERING THAT SOME OF THE battles of the bloody civil war had raged very close to them, the tiny village of Las Estrellas looked quite lovely in the sunlight. The bunting, hung everywhere to celebrate the end of the civil war, added to the air of festival. Ragged, barefoot children ran shrieking around in the dirt, sending clouds of red dust scurrying into the air. The dust immediately draped itself on the nearest object – dog, or peasant, or sidewalk table. For the children it was good to run for the sheer joy of being alive. For years they had run – from bullets, from machetes, from plunging horses – and they had run quietly, their eyes staring in horror, soundless mouths wide open, too terrified to scream. Now they ran and yelled in the hot sunshine and their elders sat at the rickety wooden tables and washed the dust down into their stomachs with warm beer or fiery tequila, distilled from the Mezquite that grew everywhere in this otherwise almost barren land. A hairless dog chased its own tail until it was exhausted and then it too lay down in the dust.

John Cameron, brown as a nut from his months with the guerrillas, sat at a table on the verandah where there was some shade and sipped the raw red wine that was produced in the area. Now that this blasted war was at last over, maybe the peons could get back to tending their grape vines, most of which had withered and died in the past few years. He laughed at himself for his bad luck in running away from one war, only to be caught up in another one, and for his good luck in managing to make money – even though he was unsure as to the value of pesetas in real terms – out of that war. Gun-running was extremely profitable, and here in Mexico there was money to be made if one had a brain and no conscience.

'Madre de Dios,' he said and sat straight up in his chair. One of the sons of the local *padrón*, Don Alejandro Alcantarilla Medina, was riding past on a magnificent stallion. But it was not the horseflesh – superb though that was – or even the dignified, aristocratic bearing, the almost insolent arrogance and self-confidence of young Don José Luis, the *padrón's* eldest son, that drew his eye. The young *hidalgo* had his sister with him. She was riding, as aristocratic Spanish girls often did, behind her brother, her arms around his slim waist: she had no fear of the strength of the dancing horse, for was not José Luis in complete control? *La dama* Lucia, sixteen years old, and home from her convent school for the first time in months, was wearing riding dress: a wide, blue skirt exquisitely embroidered around the wide hem, which fanned over the rump of the horse: a matching short blue jacket that was also embroidered with – could it be? – gold thread, over a man's-style ruffled shirt, of a whiteness that almost blinded John's eyes. Her black curls were trapped against their will under a severe gaucho hat, and her dark eyes twinkled with excitement, even more brightly than the diamonds screwed into her perfect little earlobes.

Don Alejandro had locked his precious only daughter away for her own safety as the war had raged around his ancestral acres. So today, at last, she was happy to be free, to be with José Luis, to be . . . admired. She knew that the gringo at the table admired her. Had she not seen his eyes almost start from his head as she and her brother made their stately way along the dusty main street? It would be fun to tease him, especially since José Luis could not see her naughtiness. She forgot everything that dear Mother Mercedes had taught her about the wicked, lustful ways of men and she devastated John Cameron with her smile.

'Ay, *caray*,' breathed John Cameron in his newly learned Mexican Spanish, 'did you ever see a plum so ripe and ready to fall from the tree?'

Pedro Robles looked around, fearful that the very dust might listen and report the insolence of this foreigner to the *padrón*.

'Sh! How you are stupid, Señor, even to look on the face of Don Alejandro's daughter. He would whip the skin from your back. And *la dama*? She would spit in your face.'

John laughed. No woman – not even Catriona when he had bid her farewell – had done that. 'Yours, I'll grant you, Pedro, and who could blame her. But, believe me, *amigo mio*, the lady who can resist the charms of John Cameron hasn't yet been born.'

'You have learned much of our language, Señor Juan,' said his companion, a shifty-eyed *paysan* in dust-caked jeans, 'but not enough of our culture. You might as well touch the moon as the daughter of *el padrón*. Just to look at her with bold eyes could cause her father or her brothers to cut out your heart. Men disappear in Mexico and no one who is wise asks questions. And who will ask for you? Be on your guard: you are not safe here. You have no nation: you could just disappear. And who would mourn?'

John upturned the wine bottle to find that it was indeed empty and reached for his other drink. He threw flaked salt onto the back of his left hand, picked up the roughly cut lime in his right, licked the salt from his hand and squirted the lime juice into his mouth, as he had seen Pedro and the others do, before draining his glass of tequila. He winced; not a drink for a gentleman. He gestured for a second bottle of wine, his gaze still on the straight little back of Lucia Alcantarilla Medina. It was doubtful that he had even heard his friend's warning. Perhaps it was the masculine, but yet so feminine, riding habit. Or perhaps it was six lonely months under cold Mexican stars. But he longed to see the girl's face again, to hear her speak. Her voice, he knew without hearing it, would be as beautiful as her smile.

He would go to what passed for a hotel and pay for a hot bath and a shave. 'Learn from a master, my friend. All I need in order to have that rich young beauty eating out of my hand is time: time and a little Scottish cunning.'

He stood up, picked up the rather dirty bottle of wine and threw some thin coins on the tabletop. He looked down at Pedro and smiled inwardly. 'And I have plenty of both.'

For days he waited, starting from his chair at the sound of any horse's hooves, but no bloodstock pranced down the dusty streets of Las Estrellas. John rented a horse and rode out to the Alcantarilla ranch but he was turned away by well-armed, well-fed, well-clothed guards.

'Private land,' they said. 'No road this way.'

Or this way or that way. God in heaven, did the don own the whole of Mexico? If Mexico had suffered during the civil war, the Alcantarillas had not. Herds of fat cattle grazed on the land guarded by a veritable army of well-mounted men.

'You can ride for three days, Señor Juan, and not get to the end of *el padrón's* land. Give up this foolish idea,' advised Pedro. And John, unused to horses or leather saddles, rode back to town and soaked his sore bones in tepid, dirty water and dreamed of black curls and flashing Spanish eyes.

And then there was the *corrida*, the bullfight. And the best bullfighters in Mexico came at the invitation of *el padrón* to fight his best bulls in the ring: a celebration of peace. Afterwards there would be dancing in the streets to the music of a *mariachi* group, who were coming all the way from Cuernavaca to play for the *fiesta*.

'*Mariachi*?' asked John, without too much interest.

'It is from the French, Señor, *le mariage*. We were ruled by the French, you know, and they left us much of their food and their customs. The *mariachi* was music for the marriage, and now it is just music for pleasure, for joy. Now it is Mexico.'

'And what is happening?'

'In two days there will be the bullfight. Then everyone will eat too much, and drink too much and love too much.' He laughed, the laugh of an experienced man. 'And it will be *la Navidad* before we find relief from the headache, and maybe some of us will never find relief, for there will be more mouths to feed next spring, and there will be angry fathers and brothers.'

John went into the hotel and he washed his one good shirt and polished the silver points on the end of his string tie. If everyone was coming to the *corrida*, he would see *la dama*.

She came in state, like a queen, her father silver-haired and ramrod-straight beside her, her brothers riding beside the carriage, they and their magnificent horses looking as if they had been carved from the selfsame pieces of fluid metal. Lucia threw roses in the dirt at the feet of the Mexican women, who cheered her and wondered at her milky-white skin, her dress of silk and lace, her jewels.

It was the first time John Cameron had seen a heavy cream-coloured lace mantilla arranged on shining curls of the bluest black.

'Every woman should dress like that, Pedro,' he said. 'She's beautiful, innocent and yet provocative.'

'She's danger, señor.' But John did not know enough Spanish to realize that Pedro had used the noun, danger, instead of the adjective, and perhaps he was not clever (or wise) enough to understand the subtle difference.

He made his way through the crowds to a spot where he could run in the street beside the rose-filled carriage like the peasants. He picked up one of Lucia's discarded roses and, when he saw that she saw him, he kissed the rose and threw it back into the carriage. She looked at the dusty rose on the immaculate cream lace of her skirt and she picked it up.

She's hooked, he thought. She'll keep it.

But Lucia Pilar Francesca Alcantarilla Medina knew who and what she was, and she looked saucily into John's eyes as he ran beside her carriage, and she dropped the rose into the dust and turned a haughty cream shoulder to the man who had almost fallen under the hooves of her brothers' horses to throw it to her.

'Bitch,' he snarled. Then he laughed, for it was a game, and the game was no good unless both could play. And in the flower of the Alcantarillas he had met a worthy adversary.

He made a point of walking near the flower-filled box with its green and red bunting. Then, when he saw that the girl had spotted him, John stared at her indifferently and turned away, and when he turned again she was talking animatedly with her brothers and fanning herself furiously with her exquisite ivory fan.

For weeks he teased her. She did not know that he watched the dusty road out of Las Estrellas to see the clouds of dust that told him she might be condescending to visit the town. When he saw her, he looked at her coolly, although the blood was leaping through his veins. He turned away as her carriage passed through the streets and went into the nearest shop, as if his business was so much more important than the sight of a young girl. At last, one day, she avoided her *duenna* and tricked the youngest of her brothers into riding with her into town.

'Go, Alvaro,' she ordered imperiously. 'See if there are messages for Papa at the telegraph office. I will wait here and drink a glass of water.' And the owner of the bar scrubbed a tabletop with his best towel and washed and cleaned a glass until it shone, then, reverently, he filled it with water and handed it to the *padrón's* daughter.

'Lucia,' began Don Alvaro.

'Who will hurt the daughter of *el padrón*, Alvaro? Go.'

The young man shrugged his shoulders and went. Don Alejandro could forbid his daughter nothing. He would scold her for sitting in a café, but it would be her brother who would feel the real weight of his anger.

And who will hurt her? thought the young man, who had not seen the gringo gun-runner sitting in the shade.

John did not understand every word Lucia had spoken. He was lost in the musical notes of her voice. He watched her sip the water, and then he noticed her scarf slip from the shoulders of her shirt and fall to the floor. Such an old ploy. He laughed and she pouted, and after he had made her wait just long enough, he moved forward and picked it up.

'*Gracias*, señor,' she said, her voice and her eyes kept low. Her little hand was held out for the scarf, but John bowed low and then pushed the scarf into the pocket of his tough denim trousers.

She did not know what to do. She was so young, he thought. Then, unbidden, came the picture of another girl of about the same age. His daughter, Victoria.

Angus

Rain was beating down on the streets of Dundee.

'It's the stotting kind,' old Euan Gordon told Victoria, and he traced the rain's passage with his hand. 'It comes down and then it goes back up.'

'We need it,' said the daughter of the farm. 'If it just lasts the right time and gets everything well watered. But, have you noticed, Mr Gordon, that rain either lasts far too long and floods everything or it doesn't last nearly long enough. Very perverse thing, rain.'

Mr Gordon was quite taken aback. The climate was his favourite subject of conversation, but he was not used to having the discussion taken seriously. Miss Jessop would merely have said, as she always did, 'so it does, Mr Gordon, so it does.'

He was so disturbed that he almost forgot to tell Victoria that she was required in Mr Smart's office.

When he did remember, she grabbed her notebook and her pencil, smoothed her hair – how like a woman, thought Mr Gordon – and hurried into the office.

Alistair Smart was standing at the window watching the rain, the stotting kind. 'Ah, Victoria, thank you for coming in.' He gestured to the rain. 'You should see it in India – so heavy sometimes that it could knock a wee thing like you clean off your feet.' He pulled out a chair. 'I have a proposal to put to you. Sit down, my dear.'

Alistair Smart had been standing behind his massive desk when she had entered, clutching her notebook. Today's departure from the norm made Victoria nervous. Usually, because he was a very courteous man, he stood up when she entered the room, but he never came out from behind his desk. What on earth could he be going to say? She hoped she was not to be dismissed. With so many men coming back from the war looking for work, it would be inevitable that some women lost their jobs.

She was so caught up in her own feelings that she did not notice that her employer was as nervous as she herself was.

'I'll get right to the point, Victoria,' he said and she braced herself for disappointment. 'I would like you to come out to the Calcutta office with me.'

He said it as if he was saying nothing more significant than 'I would like you to run out and pick up a *Courier*.'

She said nothing. Calcutta ... India ... The mystical East. He had actually said he wanted her to accompany him to Calcutta.

'I can see you are somewhat taken aback, Victoria. Let me explain. It's obvious that the war will be over in a few months. I must see what has been going on at the mills out there. Usually we have someone on home leave every year, and although we have had several written reports there is nothing quite like seeing for one's self. Don't you agree? And the admirable Miss Jessop says that her one trip to India has cured her for ever of wishing to travel. She says that if she sails as far as the Isle of Arran on her summer holidays she will have spent as much time in a boat as she wishes. I cannot do without a secretary, Victoria, and Miss Jessop herself has suggested that you should accompany me. I have given the matter a great deal of thought. You are very young, but we have worked together for some time now. Dr Currie encouraged me to ask you and, since she is, as it were, your reference, I have decided to ask you. You would be perfectly safe and all the conventions would be followed. I am sure you need have no worries on that score. If, however, you feel that you are too young, that your mother would worry about you on such a long voyage, I will understand, but I will have to find someone else.'

He stopped and Victoria nodded vigorously. Her mouth had gone dry and she could not speak. Calcutta ... to go to Calcutta . . . the Straits of Gibraltar, Suez, Port Said . . . Bombay, overland to Calcutta. Oh, yes, oh, yes. She could almost feel the heat between her shoulder blades; she could smell the spices, the exotic flowers. She could hear the temple bells, the call to prayer. She came back to earth with a bump.

She could see her mother struggling bravely against the tragedy that had overwhelmed her, trying desperately to pretend that it was not happening. She could hear a young girl's voice promising, 'I will never leave you, Mamma, never.' But she had never believed that promise would mean that she would lose an opportunity like this. What an incredible chance. To work in this lovely office had been the answer to her prayers. But now this, to travel under her employer's protection, to be paid a wage, for she would be working, and yet, at the same time, to see sights that most men never saw. She had to go; she *had* to go. It was too cruel.

The colour drained from her face so rapidly that Alistair Smart thought she was about to fall.

'I can't, Mr Smart,' she blurted out. 'I would love to go, and I can't tell you what it means to me that you asked me, but . . . I can't leave my mother.'

She turned, groping at the same time for her handkerchief, and hurried from the room.

Alistair Smart stood for some time just looking at the closed door. She had said no. He could hardly believe it.

He had thought that she would jump at the opportunity of safe, escorted travel. He had seen the initial joy and excitement in her face and he had been sure that she would accept. In fact, it had never occurred to him that she would refuse. He sat down wearily in his chair. He was . . . disappointed. No, it was more than that. He was hurt. She had said no. She did not want to travel across the world with him. Was she afraid? No. She knew that she was safe. Good heavens, he was her employer, and old enough to be her father.

Why, in the name of heaven, you old fool, does it matter to you? he asked himself. Why do you suddenly feel bereft, as if all the lights have gone out? It can't be, no, it can't be that . . .

He thrust the thought away and, drawing a ledger towards him, began to work.

Victoria took refuge in the lady's room – a facility added by old Mr Smart upon the hiring of Miss Jessop, and which should now, more properly, be called the ladies' room. Mr Smart, Senior, had had very Victorian notions of the sensibilities of females and, besides the usual offices, there was an enormous *chaise longue* – possibly for combating fainting fits or the attacks of hysteria from which all decent women, he was sure, suffered. In its thirty-year occupation of the little room at the end of the executive corridor, nothing more weighty than Christmas parcels had rested upon it. Now Victoria threw herself down on it and christened it with her tears.

I have to get over this disappointment before I go home, she thought. *I could not bear poor Mother to know how very much I want to go and oh, please God, don't let me resent my promise to her. I can't leave her now. I want to be with her. Her dreadful situation is partly my fault. Oh, John Cameron, what a cruel charmer you are. I hope there is nothing of you in me, and I pray that you never ever hurt anyone else.*

She sat up, feeling melodramatic and slightly silly. *Where are you, John Cameron? Oh, dear God, forgive me, but I wish he were dead.*

Then, since that was an appalling thing to say about anyone, and doubly wicked about one's own father, Victoria Cameron knelt down, rested her head on the *chaise longue* and prayed for forgiveness.

13

DAVIE MENMUIR WRESTLED BOTH WITH the root and with his inclinations. The root was causing serious plumbing problems in the Blackness Road house and was proving the very devil to haul out. Four years ago, before this bloody war had started, he would have had that root out and the garden tidied long since, but he wasn't the man he had been: there wasn't the strength in the injured body that there once was. Despite his efforts to control it, Davie began to cough and wheeze and, fearful that Catriona would look out of her window and see him, he stumbled behind the resurrected gooseberry bushes and lay there until the spasm had passed. What he thought best for Catriona had ruled his life for years now, and he had spent so much time battling with his own feelings and desires that trying to do what he thought Catriona wanted came second nature to him. But, at the same time, sense and practicality told Davie that something had to be done – and soon. How long could Catriona pretend, or perhaps deny her condition?

'The hale street knows, lassie,' he told the root, when he went back to the fight, 'and I'll no have them lace-curtained wifies condemning you. The god Respectability hides some fell queer goings-on.'

As if as a sign to him, the root finally yielded up the battle and capitulated, sending both victor and vanquished backwards into the bushes. Davie swore, picked himself up, and hauled the rest of the monster out of the pipe. Then he carried it, waving over his shoulder like a giant serpent, down to the bottom of the garden, where he put it on the bonfire with all the other garden rubbish he had been accumulating all afternoon. He watched the roots writhing in the flames and then, when all danger from the fire had gone, he washed his hands at the stand-pipe and went in to do battle with Catriona.

She looked surprised to see Davie enter without knocking, but there was a faint smile of pleasure in her tired eyes.

Ach, lassie, lassie, he thought, can you not give someone else a share in your burden? What joy it would be to help you. But he had had too many years of not expressing himself and stood tongue-tied looking at her.

Catriona looked back at him and, as if she sensed his feelings, she put her hands protectively over the voluminous apron she had taken to wearing.

'You know then, Davie?'

'Aye.'

'And yet you don't condemn.'

At this Davie forgot his habits of taciturnity and grabbed her hands. 'Lassie, lassie, could I have killed him for you, I would have.'

Abruptly Catriona sat down and he pulled out one of the wooden chairs from the table and sat near her, almost close enough to touch her, if he could summon up the courage to do so.

For some time they sat without speaking, Catriona with her head bowed, apparently looking at the work-worn hands in her aproned lap, and Davie looking tenderly at her red-gold head with its streaks of silver. At last Catriona began to speak, haltingly.

'I was so ashamed, Davie, and afraid that you . . . that everyone would think I had . . .' She could not continue.

He leaned forward but he did not touch her. 'Nobody that knows you could think you would encourage him, Catriona.' There, he had said her name, but if she noticed she gave no sign.

'I did not fight at first, Davie.' She looked up at him unflinchingly, straightforwardly. 'You have to know that. It was like a dream, and then I realized what was going to happen, what was happening, and I fought but . . . it was soon over. And I prayed, really for Victoria, that nothing would come of it, that I could just forget it, put it away like a horrible nightmare. Dr Currie forced me to accept what had happened to me, what was happening. I was terrified, so ashamed, and I thought of the shame to Victoria, her embarrassment when people found out. After . . . after that night, perhaps I worked too hard to try to let nature take a natural course, but then I thought: poor wee soul, it's not your fault that you are coming so unwelcomed into the world. I'm having John's baby, Davie, and although in the beginning I would have done almost anything to get rid of it, later sometimes I was almost glad. When he moved, Davie, when he told me he was alive and growing . . . my heart melted.

'When John left – well, when his father wouldn't allow him back – and he never tried, not once, to contact me or even to see Victoria, I still thought of myself as his wife. Even after the divorce went through, I never thought of remarriage. I loved John so much; it took a long time to tear him out of my heart. And when he came here, well, he was Victoria's father, and then I've always been a very practical woman, and I talked myself into thinking that he really would pay his way, that maybe we could come to some sort of civilized relationship.'

She looked down at her lap again. 'Divorced, with a daughter; how I have prayed and thanked God that my mother never lived to see me divorced. The shame of it, Davie, but I was brought up to endure what must be endured. To many, maybe myself included, I was beyond the pale of respectability. I decided to devote myself to Victoria, to do my best to give her a decent home. And when John came and I saw him work his charm on her ... But I thought he might truly come to love his own child. That would be natural, wouldn't it? So I felt that I had no right to stop them loving one another. And now this ...'

She smiled at him tentatively. 'Am I making any sense? The neighbours, some of them, began to avoid me and I lost my nerve. I haven't been outside the door in weeks, not even to the kirk. The shame of divorce is nothing to the shame of this. Victoria is my comfort, and then there's Dr Currie. I thought she would find new lodgings – and who would blame her? – but there's two of them prepared to fight for me.'

'There's three, lass, if you'll let me.' Davie laughed aloud with joy. For weeks he had been trying to find the words and now, when he had not even been thinking, the right ones had popped out by themselves.

Catriona looked at him. She did not understand his laughter. 'What are you saying, Davie Menmuir?'

'I'm saying that I've admired you half my life, Catriona Cameron. I'm saying that I've learned to respect you even more these last few years. I'm saying that when I was a lad, I fell in love with a lass and we had a good marriage, and I wouldn't want a moment of that changed, but I'm saying that it's no an untried lad, but a man, that loves and wants you, Catriona Cameron, as he has never wanted any other woman.'

As if surprised by his words, Davie fell quiet.

'But, Davie, I'm soiled and you . . .'

Soiled? Soiled? How could she think that of herself? Anger swelled inside him until he thought he might start to cough again. He fought his illness more strenuously than he had fought the root in her plumbing and interrupted her.

'I have little to offer you, lass, but my name and my heart. I can't bring you riches, or even a regular wage, but when I'm well I'll work all the hours God gives me, and I could do a lot round here for you. Did you know I've become a grand cook? Isn't it my mother herself who says nobody makes better pastry.'

Catriona smiled. 'But the baby, Davie?'

'Is more mine than his. Was he not here only for the begetting? I'll love him, Catriona. Och, lassie, the birth of an innocent baby is a reason for joy in this sorry world! That young laird that was buried – did wee Victoria love him? Will a marriage and a new wee brother or sister not help to heal her wounds and all?'

Catriona stood up and went to the range. She lifted the lid from the pot that stood there and mouth-watering smells filled the small kitchen. Davie felt his tastebuds quiver in anticipation.

'I don't know what she felt about the poor laddie,' said Catriona as she stirred. 'I'm not sure that she knows herself. And lately she's been so busy helping me and sustaining me. You should see her walk to the tram with her head held high. I'm so proud of her, Davie.'

'And so you should be. She's Jock Cameron through and through, is she not? And she's her mother's daughter too, Catriona Cameron. You never give yourself credit for that girl. When she did well at the school it was because she was her grampa's girl. You, and only you, should get the credit that she's turned out such a nice lass. And another thing you don't seem to want to admit is that she's no a wee lassie any mair: she's a grown woman. Victoria deserves her own life, Catriona. For her sake, if not for yours or mine, marry me.'

There, he had said it. Marry me. That was it. He wanted to marry her. She thought she was shop-soiled goods, and he thought that he was only half a man, but his loving heart was intact. He could love her and work for her and protect her, if only she would give him that right.

Catriona moved away from the range and put her hands on the strong back of one of the kitchen chairs. She gripped it hard. He could see her knuckles standing out.

'Oh, Davie, it's not right to marry just to give the baby a name, to save what little reputation I have left, to release Victoria – although Victoria mustn't be made to feel that she has to stay. I want her to go out, to meet young people, both boys and girls. This great love of hers – how could it be love, Davie? They were bairns, and she must get over his death and open her heart again.' She stopped and they looked at one another. Was Victoria the only one who was to open her heart to a new love? Catriona took refuge in stirring her soup again and then she turned back to him, standing there so anxious, so caring. 'And I never suspected . . . I couldn't bear to be married out of pity. You do pity me, Davie. No, let me finish. You're a kind and loving man, a decent man and maybe you're mistaking pity for something else. Maybe you're just giving it another name.' She looked up and met his gaze squarely, unflinchingly. 'Besides, don't misunderstand me – and, oh, God knows, Davie Menmuir, that I don't want to hurt you or throw your gift back in your face – but I don't know what I feel about you. I know I've come to rely on you. I know it makes me happy when you are here. But is that enough?'

'It's enough for me.'

Catriona looked at him, at his honest, fine-boned face with the lines of both pain and laughter etched deeply into the skin. He had been a soldier for a long time, but he still had a farmer's eyes, keen and clear. He saw birth and death as equal partners in the game, each with its rightful place. He was a good man. A woman would be proud and lucky to have such a husband. But was it fair to him?

What have I to give him at my time of life? I'm forty-one years old. I have a daughter a step away from her eighteenth birthday, and . . .'

Whatever else she thought she had was lost in an unbelievable pain that ripped through her. It was so sudden and so intense that nature controlled her intellect and Catriona moaned and clutched her middle. Sweat broke out on her forehead and she stumbled forward and gripped the table for support. Cloth, dishes and cutlery fell unheeded to the floor.

'Oh, God, Davie, the baby,' she said and this time she screamed as another searing pain struck her.

Davie had his arms around her. They were strong. 'There, there, my lass,' he said, automatically using the words and the tone that he had adopted naturally with his master's animals in like circumstances. 'There, there.'

'Use the telephone, Davie,' gasped Catriona. 'It's easy. Lift the receiver and ask for Dr Currie's office.'

The telephone. He couldn't deal with that new-fangled machine. He would run down the road and get a cab, and perhaps a policeman.

The telephone, Davie. Please,' groaned Catriona. 'You'll see, Davie lad, it's easy.'

He looked at her, lying moaning in the chair. The telephone. If a lassie like Victoria could handle it, so too could Sergeant Davie Menmuir, late of the Black Watch. Davie gritted his teeth, straightened his shoulders and hurried out into the hall.

Nearly five hours later, Davie sought comfort in his mother's kitchen. He sat in the big chair before the fire, stretched his stockinged feet out to the brass fender, lay back on her cross-stitched cushions and let the heat soak into his cold bones. 'I had to leave her,' he said in a voice harrowed by pain. 'It's no human.'

'Ach, Davie lad, there's nae place for a man at a birthing. The hospital doctors know fine what they're doing. Catriona's in good hands.'

Davie looked up at his mother and took the mug of hot soup from her. He needed both its warmth and its sustenance.

'It was just, they knew I had nae business there, nae right.' His tone was so despondent that his parents looked at one another over his bowed head. Was he thinking of his young wife, so cruelly dead before her baby was even big enough to be born?

'Catriona's a strong woman,' said Bessie Menmuir firmly. 'It'll be different this time.'

'Aye,' said Davie sadly, 'and me as much use as I was the last time I was near a birthing.'

If their widowed son's obvious interest in their former mistress was not one they would welcome, the older

Menmuirs gave no sign. They were country people, accepting birth and death as one accepts the changing seasons – perhaps not always to be welcomed but, in their words, to be *tholed*, or accepted.

'The land's looking grand, Father,' said Davie, trying to cheer up his parents and himself. There was nothing they could do for Catriona and it would be better to think of something – anything – to keep his mind off the swift pace of events after his first, quavering use of the telephone. 'That trust fund must be growing like the winter wheat,' he went on, as if he had nothing else on his mind.

'Aye, lad,' agreed old Tam, as he bent towards the fire to light a taper for his nightly indulgence of a good pipe. 'Mr Boatman is a very astute fellow, and as honest as the day is long, and him a lawyer,' he added, as if the two were not naturally compatible. 'To let your English school teacher rent the house, and have me and my own men do the work the way we always did it for old Jock, was inspired thinking. Do you not think so, Bessie?'

Bessie Menmuir was not in the habit of handing out praise. She avoided the opportunity again. She ignored the talk of lawyers and trust funds, neither of which she knew a thing about, and went straight to the real issue.

'Well, what *was* inspired thinking was for our Davie to take the tram hame. A good meal and a good sleep in your own bed, Davie.'

'Aye,' agreed his father. 'Mistress Cameron will need her friends more than ever when this is over, and you'll be little use to her if you're sick.'

Davie looked up. Had his father stressed the word 'friends'? There was no time to question him though, for from the yard came the sound of a hooting car horn. Who would come calling at Priory Farm who also owned a motor car?

All three Menmuirs rushed to the door and threw it open.

Outside, a fraction of an inch from the heavy iron gate of the steading, stood a car, and climbing out of it were Dr Currie and Victoria. Victoria ran to Mrs Menmuir.

'It's a boy, a bonnie wee boy, and my mother is fine.'

'Over already?' breathed Davie. 'And she's fine – and a wee laddie.' He looked up at Dr Currie and took over from his father, who was obviously too overcome to act the host. 'You'll come in, Dr Currie, and wet the bairn's head?'

Dr Currie bent to enter the little cottage and its warmth reached out to her. 'I'd be delighted, Davie, and Victoria assured me of a good tea, Mistress Menmuir, if we can impose.'

'Impose, impose, what a word for a cup of tea and a bit scone.' Davie's mother bustled around, thought Victoria, like one of her own hens. Bessie had never entertained a lady doctor before, but she was serenely at ease. Everyone who came to the Menmuir door would receive the same welcome: what we have we share.

The whisky was passed around and Victoria took a cautious sip. Then she put the glass aside and gave herself up to enjoying being back in this cottage, which she had visited a thousand times as a child. Dr Currie was giving the Menmuirs an abridged account of Catriona's labour and delivery and, Victoria saw with delight, was appreciating her whisky as much as Davie and Tam.

'I'll have her moved to a private room, Mrs Menmuir,' the doctor was saying. 'That way there is a little more freedom for visitors. And if you can convince matron that you know what you are doing, who knows, she just might let you hold . . . Victoria's wee brother.'

'Oh, how wonderful,' said Victoria. 'You know, I never really thought until you said those words, Dr Currie, but I have a brother – and one day this farm will be his. Don't you think Grampa would have loved to have had a grandson?'

The four older people looked at one another and then looked away again.

'It's a grand, clear night, Victoria. Wrap yourself up against the cold and see that nowt has changed,' said Davie. 'We'll have our drink and then it's me that will help with the tea.'

Victoria smiled at the gentle man who was coming to mean so much to them. And, after wrapping her shawl warmly around her shoulders, she went out into the crisp night air.

She laughed again as she saw how nearly Dr Currie had missed the gate and then she stood and looked up at the sky. The stars were so bright she felt that she could almost touch them. And as she stood holding her breath, as she had done all those years ago in this selfsame spot, a streak of silver flashed across the sky and disappeared into nothingness.

A shooting star. A baby is born and a star has died: nature's balance. Will I be the first to tell you of shooting stars, little brother, and of walnut shells? I'll fill one tonight and I'll put your birth in it, and Dr Currie and the Menmuirs, and the shooting star and the lovely sound the cattle make there in the steading as they stand together to keep warm.

She walked across to the gate and looked over the top at the milling beef stirks. One stayed near the fence and did not flinch from her hand as she touched his soft, warm nose. 'And I'll put your courage in, little stirk, and this starry sky, and the joy of seeing lighted windows and knowing that people you love are in there, waiting.' She breathed in the smells of the farm, the wood smoke from the cottage fire, the warm breath of the animals. 'This is me and this is mine. It will always be home – no matter where life takes me.'

The door of the farmhouse opened and a river of light spilled out into the darkness. Then the light was broken by the dark figure of a man.

'Tea's on, lass,' came Davie's voice. 'Come in afore the cold gets you.'

And Victoria had a feeling that she would often stand there in the years to come, and that Davie's voice would call to her across the darkness, as would another voice, that she had not yet heard but for which she was prepared to wait.

'I'm coming, Davie,' she said and he heard the smile in her voice.

14

DAVIE MENMUIR'S STARCHED COLLAR THREATENED to rub a line on his neck. He stuck his calloused fingers inside it to try to ease the stiffness. That was better. It was the Sunday tie; how he wished he could take it off. He had his Sunday suit on, too, and he was carrying a parcel and, quite frankly, he felt a bit of a fool.

There was a surprising number of men visiting the Dundee Hospital for Women, but only a few were there to see new babies, as most babies were born at home. Davie moved across the antiseptic waiting room to position himself beside another man. That way, he thought, he could blend in better. He hated the antiseptic smell. It made him remember the trenches and the military hospital. It made him remember pain and, more importantly, fear, and he did not want to be reminded of the fear. It was strange to think that the selfsame smell could be associated with birth.

The other man held up his parcel to Davie. 'Wallace's pie for the missus,' he said. 'She hates the food here. She's dying for a beer too, but I was scared to risk it.'

The door opened before Davie had an opportunity to explain the contents of his own brown-paper parcel, and the nurse appeared. She was as starched from head to toe as Davie was around his neck and he stood awkwardly, his bonnet in his hand. How clean she looked, how efficient. Perhaps she wouldn't let him in.

The nurse did not smile. She looked them over one by one, and each expectant visitor was left feeling inadequate in some way.

'Dae ye think she's starched underneath as well?' whispered the man next to Davie. 'If this is the nurse, God helps us all when the matron sees us dirtying up her nice clean hospital.'

'This is a hospital,' said the nurse, glaring at them both, 'not a variety hall.' Suddenly she stopped as a loud 'atchoo' split the frozen air. 'Who sneezed? No one with a cold may come in. How old are you, miss?' She swooped on a girl who stood with her mother.

'Thirteen, miss.'

'Too young. Come, the rest of you. No more than two to a bed and do not, I repeat, do *not* touch the beds at all. When the bell rings, do not dawdle. Leave at once.'

'Righto, sergeant,' said the happy-go-lucky man beside Davie. Davie admired his bravery. The nurse did not.

'Mr Menmuir?'

Davie clutched his parcel. She was looking out for him. Why?

'Yes, nurse,' he said.

She smiled graciously. 'Mrs Cameron has been moved out of the general ward to the room that Dr Currie reserves for her private and special patients. If you will follow me.'

Thankful that he had asked his mother to put a crease in his trousers, Davie followed the starched back down a long corridor, through some swinging doors and into yet another corridor.

'Mrs Cameron is in room B. She may have her young man with her . . .'

Davie held out his hands for inspection, as he had done all those years ago at school, and the nurse smiled gently. 'It never occurred to me that your hands would be dirty, Mr Menmuir. I was just going to ask you if you were the one who sneezed. We don't want our young man catching a bad cold, do we? No? Then in you go. I think Miss Cameron is there too.'

Victoria was indeed in the room but Davie had eyes for no one but Catriona. She was lying back against the pillows and, to him, she looked like the young girl who had come to Priory Farm twenty years before. He felt awkward. He had never seen her with her hair down, and he had certainly never seen her in a nightgown. He blushed and she smiled at him and held out her hand.

'Well, Davie, have you come to see the bairn?'

'Aye, and your good self.' Somewhat nervously he handed her the parcel. 'The lady at Draffens said it was quite respectable and fitting to buy this.'

Catriona had undone the string and opened the parcel. In her hands she held a fine knitted shawl. It had cost Davie a princely 14s 11d and he had swithered between the shawl and a lovely bedjacket at the same price, but had decided, in the end, that the jacket was too intimate a gift.

Catriona held the soft wool between her fingers and did not look up.

He panicked. 'It's to put round yer shoulders, but if ye don't like it . . .'

She looked up and he saw that her eyes were filled with tears. 'It's the finest shawl I've ever had, Davie, and I'm proud to put it round my shoulders.'

Victoria smiled as she thought of the drawer full of Catriona's own exquisite hand-knitted creations.

'And what about this young man?' she asked Davie, who was still gazing in a tongue-tied way at Catriona. 'Have you no time for him?'

For the first time Davie noticed the little crib near the window.

'Isn't Dr Currie wonderful?' Victoria went on. 'Mother gets to have Baby . . .' She stopped and laughed with delight. 'We can't keep calling him Baby. We will have to choose a name for him. Think, Mother. Will you call him after one of the royal princes?'

Catriona shook her head. She had had plenty of time to think of a name for her baby. 'Andrew, I thought,' she said. 'A good, strong Scottish name and all his own, no one else's.'

Victoria leaned over the crib. 'Hello, Andrew,' she said softly and picked up the tiny shawl-wrapped bundle. 'Here, Davie, do you want a shot? He won't break, you know,' she added, as she saw the look of mingled hope and dismay on Davie's face.

'Pretend he's a lamb, Davie,' said Catriona.

'What, and throw the pair wee soul over my shoulder? No, I'm no frightened tae touch him, just amazed at the wholeness if him. Would ye look at the fingernails.'

'Mrs Cameron. I'm sorry to disturb at visiting hours but there are forms to be filled in.' It was the nurse again. She read off Catriona's name, address and date of birth. 'The father's details aren't down here, Mrs Cameron. I take it our gallant soldier is still at the Front.'

Catriona and Victoria looked at one another.

'No, he's not at the Front, nurse, he's . . .'

'My wee brother and I have no father, nurse,' said Victoria firmly. 'You may just leave that bit blank.'

Catriona looked at Davie, and she saw the love and tenderness in his eyes as he held the infant in his arms and gently soothed him. He looked up and smiled at her, and Victoria saw the look that passed between them.

'Mother?' she questioned.

'Maybe you're wrong, Victoria,' said Catriona, although she still gazed at Davie. 'Maybe wee Andrew is going to have a daddy, after all.'

The nurse was becoming impatient. She could sense the atmosphere in the room, but she had too much work to do to wait while these people ironed out their lives.

'That's all very nice,' she said, 'but there's still a space on my form.'

'Menmuir,' said Davie, but the beaming smile on his face was directed at Catriona. 'David Menmuir, Esquire.'

15

Las Estrellas, Mexico

JOHN CAMERON HAD NOT FULLY appreciated the difficulties he would encounter in trying to form a relationship with the daughter of Don Alejandro. The girl was escorted everywhere by one or other of her brothers. There was always a stout Mexican matron in heavy black silk with her in the coach, or in the motor car when the *Padrón* wanted to show the villagers that their sleepy part of Mexico had moved firmly into the twentieth century. And there were always servants running behind and beside her to pick up anything she might drop, or to anticipate her slightest wish – to pick that flower, to hold and soothe that baby, to visit that church.

La dama Lucia became very devout in the weeks after the *corrida*. 'I have not done all the things my dear Mother Mercedes asked me to do, Papa,' she said demurely. 'I have not prayed novenas or visited the sick and so, from now on, I will visit the mission regularly and light a candle at the statue of the Virgin.'

Don Alejandro could deny her nothing. Besides, he knew that none of the men in the village would dare to raise their eyes to stare at his daughter. If he knew of the *gringo* gun-runner – and he must have known, for he was informed of every single thing that happened in his village – it never occurred to him that his gently reared and cosseted Lucia would find the bold stare of those blue-grey eyes a challenge.

John contrived that they should meet in the garden at the mission, and there he fell in love with her halting English as much as with her beautiful dark eyes. She, for her part, loved to hear about that wild, beautiful country far across the world, where there was grass all year round, and rain, and soft, delicate flowers so unlike their own strident, exotic reds and oranges.

'Stay here and pray enough for both of us, Inez,' she ordered her *duenna*. 'I was allowed to walk alone in the gardens at the convent. What harm can come to me here? Besides, I must be a little free sometimes, to walk, to pray, to dream.'

And John Cameron watched her enter the garden and set out deliberately to seduce her. For him it was a game. He had never known anyone like her.

He did not listen to Pedro's warnings. He laughed at them. He thought Pedro's fears and grim forebodings of swift and frightening restitution were the result of too much tequila, too much raw red wine.

'This is not the Middle Ages, Pedro. Good heavens, I'm only talking to the girl. I'm helping her improve her English. She's quite good – learned it from some old nun in a convent – but it's stilted, book English. Her father should be paying me.'

'He will, Señor Juan,' said Pedro seriously. 'I beg you to be careful.'

And since neither Lucia nor John liked to be told what to do, they enjoyed their rebellion, and what had begun as a game became much more serious.

Lucia told John how to get on to Alcantarilla property without being seen by the guards, who were really there to look for stray cows and did not expect stray adventurers. One night, after she had been sent to bed while her father and her brothers remained smoking their cigars and drinking their imported brandy, she let herself out of a side door and made her way to a dried-up creek some distance from the great house and hidden from it by some sage brush and stunted bushes.

And there Lucia Alcantarilla was kissed for the first time by a man who was not related to her, and she liked the experience very much indeed.

My God, she's so ready, thought John as the soft, white hands caressed his sunburned neck and the soft, red lips parted under his.

He thrust her away. 'Lucy, no,' he said and wondered at the words he heard being spoken in his own voice.

'Don't you like kissing me, Juan?' she asked. 'Me, I like it very much.'

John looked down into the dark eyes, where the tears sparkled as brightly as the jewels in her ears, and he was almost lost.

'Lucy, you don't know what you're doing, but I do. I'd best go now – before it's too late.'

She wanted to cling to him, but she remembered her noble birth. An Alcantarilla would never beg: they did not have to do so. 'You will come again, Juan,' was all she said, 'to tell me of this Scotland and your estate.'

'We'll meet at the mission,' he replied, and that was what he meant. It was foolish to trespass on her family's land and yet more foolish to dally with an innocent young girl, who did not really understand the forces at her command, even if she pretended to. But John was lonely and Lucia Alcantarilla was very beautiful, very desirable and very rich, qualities that he had always admired in a woman. He found that he could not keep away from her. And several times he rode out to the ranch, where he waited alone and cold by the creek, and Lucia did not come.

Then one night he heard a soft footfall and there she stood in the moonlight and he thought he had never seen anything so lovely. He kissed her and the blood leapt in her veins, to pulse with the blood that was leaping in his. Much later she struggled only a little when he began to undo the buttons of her gown.

Lucia had been told little of the real ways of men and nothing at all of the desires of women. She did not know what was happening, but the sensations clamouring in her body made her breathless. She could not bear it, but she did not know what it was that she could not bear. She clung to John as tightly as he clung to her, and she went where he guided her, and she screamed at him for ease of this torment. Then at last there was a wonderful explosion of release and Lucia lay back, exhausted, exhilarated.

John lay against her for a few minutes and then came terrifyingly to his senses.

God in heaven, what had he done? He pulled himself away and began to tidy his clothes. He did not look at her. He did not want to see her again. Would there be a look in her face, in those great eyes, that would tell the world – and especially her father – what they had done? He shivered.

'Is that what men and women do together, my Juan?' she asked wonderingly. 'Well, I like it very much, and Inez was wrong. It did not hurt at all.'

'You must go back to the house, Lucia.'

She twined her soft arms around his neck. 'When will you come again, my Juan?'

He pulled the arms away, but gently. 'Lucia, I must go, and you must go back quietly to the house and . . . and have a good hot bath. The ground is dirty. Look at your dress.'

She shrugged. When had Lucia Alcantarilla Medina needed to consider her dress? 'It is nothing. I will give it to one of the maids. Tomorrow, you will come tomorrow.' And he promised that he would, so that she would turn and run back to her house.

He had to get away, to get out of the state and then out of the country. He would like to run tonight, but he was waiting for a bank draft from . . . a client. Too much money to lose. Oh, but the girl had been sweet. Wonderful . . . He would like to go back, again and again, but that way spelled madness. He was not as fearful of *el padrón* as the peasant, Pedro, but he knew that no man would like his daughter's virtue taken before her wedding. John smiled to himself. 'Some Mexican aristocrat is in for a surprise. He'll thank me for waking her so gently.' He hoped Lucia's husband would see her initiation in that light. But now he had to make his arrangements, he had to get away.

My John, my Jean, my Juan. He was tired of them all, these clinging women. Why could they not love lightly, as he loved, and not seek to own him? Much against his will, he stayed in the village of Las Estrellas and went every day to the telegraph office and he waited, and while he waited he sat in the *cantina* and drank young red wine, and the wine warmed his blood and he thought of Lucia. He had to see her again.

Did the wine cloud his judgement? He was not quite so careful this time as he rode to the Alcantarilla ranch. Lucia was sitting on a tree stump by the creek and for perhaps the first time in his life, John Cameron felt some regret when he saw her. She was beautiful – even more beautiful than she had been just a few weeks ago – but she was pale and the great, dark Spanish eyes were sad.

'Lucia,' he said softly.

She looked up and saw him, and what man could have resisted the joy that he saw springing into her eyes?

'Juan, oh Juan. I thought you didn't love me any more.'

'Love you?' He rushed to her and knelt at her feet and put his head against her legs. 'Love you? Oh, Madonna, I adore you, as I have never loved any other woman. But, Lucia, I'm not worthy of you.' For once John Cameron spoke the truth, but the girl was too young, too innocent to realize this.

She was not so young that she did not understand the danger in which they stood.

'You are a crazy man to come here in the day, my Juan. My brothers have such feudal ideas, especially José Luis.

He is a medieval man, my brother, and thinks to marry me to one like him. You must go away . . .'. She saw the disappointment in his face and smiled. 'Only a little distance into the hills, *mi corazon*,' she said coaxingly. 'There is a hut. See, I will draw it for you in the sand. The *vaqueros* use it, but not at this season. I will come when I can.'

He held her close. 'Come now,' he begged.

'Oh, Juan, you will never understand. Trust me: we have to go so slowly. To my brothers and Papa you are as nothing. We have to think, to talk . . . Go.'

He got up from the ground at her feet and thought that he would ride back to town. But then he looked down into her eyes and decided that it would be as well to wait in a hut as to wait in the dusty, dilapidated heap of clapboard structures that was Las Estrellas.

She came that night, bringing bread and wine, but they did not talk and they did not think. And for two weeks John hid in the hut and waited for Lucia Alcantarilla Medina. And he was as drunk with her young freshness as he was with the raw Mexican wine.

'I must go into town soon, Lucia,' he whispered one night as he kissed her goodbye. 'My money will be here and I can't risk losing it, especially if I am going to prove to Don Alejandro that I can support his daughter.'

'Soon, Juan. Maybe next week. It's not easy for me to get away. That's why I was so late tonight. Alvaro insisted that

I play cards and I could not say no, or my father would have been suspicious. Alvaro is my favourite and I love to play cards with him. Or at least I did, before I met you.'

'We should take a break, *querida*. I will go into town to wait for my money and you can be a loving daughter, just for a few days. Now, don't be careless.'

But Lucia had been careless. She had not seen her brother as he stood by the creek and wondered who had drawn a map in the sand to a *vaqueros'* hut, and why. She did not see the trembling and the ready tears in the eyes of her maids, as they prepared her for bed each night, for she was too anxious for them to be gone so that she could throw on some riding clothes and steal from her father's house. She was in love with love, and with the power she had over this foreigner. She was half-frightened and half-exhilarated by the efforts she had to make to outwit her *duenna* and her brothers and father, and by all the restrictions that had pinned her, like a butterfly to a collector's board, since the day she was born.

John left the hut reluctantly, but the money was too important to lose. He took up his place at the table in the little *cantina* and it was there that Don José Luis Alcantarilla found him.

John Cameron had never been so near the aristocratic figure of José Luis and he found himself wishing that he was not quite so close now. The young man's powerful figure in his beautifully cut clothes, his very air of supreme assurance and arrogance thrust the near-squalor of the room into stark relief. José Luis Alcantarilla Medina was sublimely indifferent to the effect he had on other people, but he was not unaware of it. He smiled now at John Cameron, but it was a smile that did not reach those beautiful, dark Spanish eyes, eyes so like those of his enchanting sister.

John returned the smile. He had seen the young don several times from a safe distance, had seen the respect and, yes, the fear in the eyes of the Mexican peasants when the don and his younger brothers passed. Now Don José Luis was standing there in front of the rickety table at which John and Pedro sat, and the power emanating from him was almost palpable. Pedro, who had managed to combine grovelling with jumping to his feet, was already sweating with fear, but John would not sweat. He would bluff his way through this encounter as he had done through many others. It was obvious that his relationship with the girl had been discovered – or was it? Why the wait of several days? Surely, if the don knew, then he, John Cameron, would now be lying bleeding in the dirt.

Everything depended on Lucia. How much had she said? To what had she confessed? God, that Mexican moon had driven him mad. Otherwise he would not have, not have . . . He looked into the young man's cold eyes. Did he know what John had done with his sister? A shiver of fear passed down his spine, but he would not abase himself here.

'Don José Luis,' he said, rising to his feet. 'This is an honour, sir. May I offer you a drink? Though I regret to say that this *cantina* does not serve the vintages that men like you and I usually enjoy.'

'It is a *cantina* for peasants, Mr Cameron,' said the young man, 'and the wine is good enough. It comes, after all, from my father's vineyards.' Don José Luis watched the flush of embarrassment travel up from the gringo's neck, and again he smiled. It was not a pleasant smile. 'It is of my father that I wish to speak. His excellency wishes you to join him for dinner. You will come too.' He gestured to the cowering Pedro and, without waiting for a reply, turned and left the room.

'When does he mean?' began John.

'Now.' Pedro was almost in tears. 'He expects us to follow them. I do not like this, Señor Juan. No way would the don and his family eat with me. He has found out that you are a nuisance to *la dama*.'

'Stop grovelling,' snapped John. 'If the don has heard of a little dalliance, he has sensibly decided to become acquainted with the one his daughter favours. This is the twentieth century, man, not the middle ages.'

'No, Señor Juan. This is Mexico, and *el padrón* is king. He will never accept you into his blood, and he will banish *la señorita* Lucia to a convent before he allows her to sully her bloodline.'

In spite of his bravado, John was more than a little concerned by his henchman's obvious fear. 'It will be different when he finds out that I too am a landlord, Pedro, that I too have acres of fertile farmland.' Mentally he thanked the ill-luck that had made him unable to sell the Priory. It would perhaps be necessary to *exaggerate* a little, but since he had no intention of returning to Scotland, it was highly unlikely that any of the Alcantarillas would compare the actual acreage with his description. For the rest of the long ride to the *hacienda* he sharpened up his descriptive skills.

The house came as a surprise. He had been some distance from it on his visits to the creek and had not expected anything quite so grand. It was long and low, all on one level, and lights spilled from every one of the many windows. They had ridden for miles into the desert, but before the house there was a green lawn, a fountain surrounded by blooming flowerbeds and some strange but lovely bushes with bright red leaves.

His host, looking like a portrait from an old schoolbook, was on the verandah to meet John. Like his sons, *el padrón* was tall and slender, with the incredibly straight carriage of the lifelong horseman. He was dressed in black, but they were the evening clothes of a Spanish grandee, not the riding dress usually favoured by his sons. There was no smile on his cold face as he greeted his guests.

He dismissed Pedro to the servants' quarters with a gesture and preceeded John into the house. His two younger sons stood before a fireplace of Moorish tiles imported from Spain. Of *la dama* Lucia and Don José Luis there was no sign.

'You would like to wash the dust away, Mr Cameron. My son is doing the same in his room, and Soledad will show you where you can ready yourself.'

An elderly woman in stiff black silk smiled graciously at John and showed him into a well-furnished bedroom. The air was full of the scent of the white lilylike flowers that stood in a bowl on the table, and John saw a basin, a pitcher of water and a soft, clean towel arranged beside the flowers. Soledad gestured to the silver-backed brushes on the dressing table and then withdrew slowly, closing the door behind her.

John almost rubbed his hands together. 'God, what class,' he said, 'what style, and in a God-forsaken place like Mexico.'

Quickly he washed his face and hands in the scented water, brushed his hair and tried to remove at least the top layer of dust from his clothes. Satisfied with his appearance, he took the towel and wiped it across the toes of his boots, reflecting, when he saw the dirt transferred to the towel, that only a servant would see it and the servant's opinion of her master's honoured guest did not matter. He dropped the towel on the floor and returned to the large hall, to find the tableau hardly changed since he had left it. A peasant woman in a richly embroidered blouse and skirt brought him a glass of sherry. The glass was of fine crystal, and the sherry was subtler and smoother than anything he had ever drunk.

'My daughter will join us when her brother is ready, Mr Cameron,' said the don in his perfect English. 'She is a very silly little girl and I should beat her – so say her brothers. Well, except for Alvaro, who takes her side always.'

John met the measuring glance of the youngest of the brothers, but his smile was not returned. Don Alvaro's softness was reserved for his sister.

'Your daughter is enchanting, *padrón*.'

'And very foolish. My first thought when Jaime' – he gestured to his second son – 'told me of her indiscretions was to send her back to her convent. I kept her here because I am an old man, and I had sorely missed her laughter for three long years.'

'You were right, Don Alejandro,' said John.

'I was wrong, Mr Cameron,' said the old man and his voice bit with the accuracy of a rattlesnake, 'but I do not make the same mistake twice. My daughter is spoiled and headstrong.' John almost winced at the contempt in the voice as he continued. 'She says she will marry you, Señor Cameron. I have brought you here to renounce her within her hearing, and before me and my sons.'

Before John could answer, there was a flutter of skirts and a sound of running footsteps, like castanets, on the cold tiles of the floor. Lucia freed herself from her brother's arm and threw herself at John.

'No, Papa, I will not give him up. You may do as you wish.'

'Foolish child,' said the don coldly. 'But come, Mr Cameron, we are civilized people, and José Luis tells me you are a connoisseur of fine wines. We will dine. Remember your breeding, Lucia, or Jaime will be forced to take you upstairs to your nurse.'

Lucia flounced over to her brother Alvaro and pouted at Jaime and José Luis. Her father smiled.

'She is a child pretending to be an adult, Mr Cameron, and not yet worth the regard of any real man. And no real man, of course, would dally with a young girl in the grounds of a mission, and assuredly not on her father's land – and never against her father's wishes.'

John coloured furiously. Damn these aristocrats. What made his daughter so special? All women were the same, everywhere. How much did the don know? I could tell you a thing or two about your precious, innocent little daughter, my oh-so-patronizing señor. Wisely, however,

John decided to say nothing, but to follow his host into a large dining room where a huge, carved wooden table stood flanked by twenty superbly carved chairs. There was fine plate on the table and the glasses at each place were of the finest crystal.

'We have selected a French meal in your honour, Mr Cameron. I am told that you have spent some time in France and, as you no doubt know, France and Mexico share a cultural heritage.'

John smiled, man to man – naturally he, as a man of the world, was familiar with Mexico's history. No need for the don to know that it was a chance conversation with Pedro that had taught him all he knew. What did trouble John was the fact that his past seemed to be an open book to his host. What else had this haughty man learned?

The meal was superb and the wines that accompanied each course better than any John had ever tasted. As one glass followed another, John relaxed. What a set-up. Thank God that his late lamented father had insisted on a divorce. If the old fool could see me now, thought John, a grandee among grandees. I hope you're looking on with envy, he said to the memory of Jock Cameron.

Don Alejandro's cold voice cut through John's warm thoughts. 'It is time to banish Lucia to her *duenna*, Señor, so that we may enjoy our cigars, like the men of the world we are.' He stood up and walked to his daughter's chair.

'I ask you now, in her hearing, to say that you have realized that the gulf between you – of culture, education and breeding – is too large to be bridged.'

John choked on his wine. What had gone wrong? A few seconds ago everything had been going swimmingly. He recovered and looked up. Lucia was staring at him, her eyes wide in terror. How beautiful she was. He remembered her boldness tempered by her innocence and shyness, her sweetness, her passionate response. A few weeks ago he had been praying that he would soon be out of her life for ever. Now he felt that he could not give her up. Perhaps it was time to settle down again.

'I cannot, Don Alejandro. Your daughter has entered my blood like a drug.'

Don José Luis sprang to his feet, a knife in his hand. 'Easy to let her out, gringo.'

'No, no!' It was Lucia. She jumped to her feet, her yellow skirts flying around her ankles like a host of exotic butterflies. She threw herself at her brother's chest and he held her easily and gently, as he would have trapped the butterflies.

'Little vixen,' he said. 'This foreigner is not worth your little finger. I will cut his fingers off, one by one, and give them to you to play with.'

'Silence.' The cold voice cut through the excited cries. 'Such melodrama, José Luis. We do not wish to frighten

Mr Cameron. Listen to me, señor. Never will I give permission for my daughter to marry you. I would rather return her to her convent and have her take the veil.'

'No, Papa, no,' cried Lucia. 'I must marry him. I have ... we have ...' She stopped, confused, unable to meet her father's eyes.

'I know what you have done, Lucia,' said the don and his voice was like ice.

Lucia looked at him and at John, then she put both of her beautiful little hands on her stomach.

'No, Papa. It's too late.'

Don Alejandro stood up and for just one fatal moment he looked like a very old man. Then the colour returned to his face. He took his daughter from her brother's arms and looked at her very gently.

'Is this true, Lucia, or a story?' But he could not doubt what the girl was too terrified to tell him. 'So,' he said sadly and he turned away. Lucia relaxed against her brother, who held her again. The *padrón* walked to his high, carved chair and sat down and for some time no one spoke.

Then at last Don Alejandro looked up and a wordless communication passed between him and his eldest son. 'So,' he said, 'I thought we were to have a funeral tonight, but instead we are to have a wedding. Jaime, go to the mission for a priest. Alvaro, take your sister to her *duenna* and have her dressed in her prettiest gown. And,

José Luis, take Mr Cameron upstairs and find him something decent to wear . . . for his wedding clothes. I will stay here and make the arrangements.'

John smiled. He had not expected the don to capitulate quite so quickly. He was to marry Lucia. He had never really believed in his wildest dreams that he would be allowed to marry her. He was not quite sure, however, that he did in fact want to marry her; she was so young. Another young girl's face came into his head and he dismissed it. So what if Lucia was even younger than his own daughter? He banished the thought. She was beautiful and very, very wealthy. He would be a faithful husband, at least until she became fat like the peasant women who had waited at table. He smiled and followed the silent figure of Don José Luis.

He did not see the look of hatred and calculating cruelty on the face of the man who had just ordered his wedding.

This time José Luis led John up one flight of stairs to another bedroom, even more ornately furnished than the first one. It felt as if someone lived there and since the wardrobe, when opened, revealed rows of hanging clothes, John decided that it was probably José Luis's own room. The young don rifled through the suits and eventually selected one, which he threw on the bed. He went to the dresser and found shirt, tie and cufflinks, and then from another wardrobe he withdrew a pair of hand-made leather shoes.

'Try these,' he said coldly. 'I will wait outside, unless you would like me to play valet.'

John decided correctly that the last remark was facetious, and he laughed and began to peel off his clothes.

The shirt and suit fitted surprisingly well, but the shoes, although beautifully soft, were perhaps a little too narrow for perfect comfort.

'Their cobbler will soon get my size right,' he said to himself, as he took one last, admiring look at himself in the mirror.

Then he went out and joined the young man who was about to become his brother-in-law and together they walked down the wide staircase.

John Cameron had never seen anyone more beautiful than Lucia Alcantarilla in her wedding gown. It was a high-necked white lace gown that contoured her young figure so perfectly that it could have been sewn upon her form. A necklace of pearls the size of pheasant's eggs hung around her neck, and there were more pearls in her ears and entwined in her glossy black curls. In her hand she held a crucifix formed of yet more pearls and tiny, perfect diamonds. Through the exquisite matching lace mantilla that covered her head John could see her eyes shining like the diamonds in her hands.

'I have no ring,' he had gasped to his prospective brother-in-law, who had wordlessly handed him a thick gold band set with dark-green emeralds.

'Her mother's,' said Don José Luis and his eyes had glitered, not like the diamonds, but like the eyes of a snake.

I am not young Joseph's favourite relative, thought John, trying to shake off the cold feeling at the nape of his neck.

It was not the happiest of weddings. Only the bride was smiling. The priest from the mission conducted the service as if he could not wait to get back to his cell to fall upon his knees in prayer. Don Alejandro was grim-faced as he gave his daughter in holy matrimony, and his sons knelt with bowed heads and made automatic responses to the prayers.

'You will wish to change, Lucia,' said Don Alejandro at the end of the service. 'The cooks are preparing a feast: you have plenty of time. José Luis will take Juan to his room to rest until you are ready. José. You have the room arranged, with everything as I ordered?'

'*Si*, Papa. Everything is perfect for him.'

Don Alejandro took his daughter's hands in his and looked down at the winking emeralds on her finger. 'Go with your nurse and take off your mama's dress. You look very beautiful, Ninita, almost as pretty as Mama.'

Lucia pouted, threw her brand-new husband a kiss, lifted her lace skirts and hurried up the staircase, the lace mantilla floating around her shoulders.

'Juan,' said Don José Luis and pointed to the staircase.

John went with the young don and the two men walked side by side to the first turn of the stairs. They stopped and looked back. The *padrón* was standing, his other sons beside him, motionless, silent.

John shrugged. It would take time, but he would win them round.

Don José Luis led him down another corridor to a room with magnificently carved double doors.

'My father keeps this room for very special guests, Juan,' said José Luis. 'I trust you will be comfortable.'

'Is this the bridal suite? Will my wife join me here?' John refused to be intimidated.

'Dona Lucia's rooms are on the other side of the house. Please, allow me to open the door for you. See, it is a beautiful room, no?'

John stepped inside the door, and immediately José Luis closed it behind him and John was alone. The room was sombrely furnished with heavy Spanish furniture, but there was an embroidered red satin cover on the huge bed and coiled in the middle of the bedspread . . .

John gasped and turned desperately, his hands clawing at the door handle but although it turned, the door did not open. He had been locked in.

'José, Don José Luis, for God's sake,' he whimpered as he turned again to look at the bed. 'For Lucia's sake. Help me.'

'It is for *la dama*'s sake, swine,' came the cold voice from the other side of the door. 'You think to despoil the jewel of the Alcantarillas. May you rot in hell.'

There was the sound of scuffling, a strange rattling, then silence followed by a scream that soared around the wooden rafters and died away, as Don José Luis unlocked the door and, without even looking in, turned and walked away.

16

AT ELEVEN O'CLOCK ON 11TH November 1918 Tam Sinclair was still with his regiment in France. His heart was, however, in a wee flat up a close in one of the less salubrious areas of Dundee.

It's over, Nellie, it's over, his heart sang across the miles, *and gin somebody tells the laddies over there who are still shooting at yours truly to stop, I'll be coming back to you, to you and wee Jimmy.*

There was a defiant hail of bullets over his head and he ducked automatically to avoid them.

'Haven't you got a home to go to, Fritz?' he yelled, as soon as he could stand up again, across the mud. 'I've a girl and a bairn waitin' for me.'

Dear God, I'm no the laddie you met at the mill, Nellie, I'm a man sure, and I'm coming home to marry you and to be a father to wee Jimmy.

'You should see my lassie, Fritz,' he yelled again. 'That clean and wholesome I can smell her from here, so sweet the breath stops in my throat with the longing for her. Have you got a lassie?'

'Sure, Jock.' To his surprise a voice came back. 'Is Helga und two babies, girls.'

'Mine's a boy,' shouted Tam. Then he realized that he was having a conversation with a German, the enemy, and in English. The wonder of it amazed him for a moment. 'Where did you learn to speak the King's English?'

'In the school, Jock. You learn German?'

'I never learned nothing. All my learning I did here,' he yelled and then he added softly, 'or in Nellie's arms.' He shouted across the mud, 'Are you married?'

'Of course,' came the reply.

This German was that good at his English that he did not even think before replying. Wait till Nellie hears about this.

'In the church,' the soldier went on. 'You too, Jock?'

'No, but it's the first thing I'll dae, Fritz. I'll marry my Nellie in the kirk and I'll take them out on the town and into the country, where Nellie wants to be. I'm going to learn farmin.'

'Farming? Such hard life, Jock. Me, I like the city. I work in a bank, nice and clean. You come one day to Germany. Is so beautiful a country and the people are good, Jock.'

The people are good, Jock. Tam looked around at the desolation. Three-quarters of a million dead on the British side. One and a half million injured. Who knew how many the Germans had lost. But the people were good.

'You're right, Fritz. The people are good. Anytime you're in Scotland . . .'

'The people there are good?'

'Och, aye, Fritz. The people there are good.'

And then 'Jock' and 'Fritz' realized together that there was silence around them. No guns pounded, nothing crashed or erupted in flames, no one screamed. They had not shouted their last sentences at one another.

'Hey, Fritz, do you think your officers have finally got the message?'

'I think so, Jock. Excuse, please, I am crying like a baby. Are we at peace?'

'Well, I've been at peace for a few minutes, Fritz. It's your lot what's been doing the shooting.'

'Funny, Jock, but I am more frightened now than I was before. Four years, Jock, four wasted years.'

'Ach, it wasnae wasted, Fritz. We've learned our lessons. No more wars. Your lassies and my wee laddie will grow up in peace.'

'Please God, Jock.'

'I doubt He's got much to dae with it, Fritz.' Tam had never learned much about the deity. There had been a bit of hellfire and brimstone on the one or two occasions he'd been forced to go to Sunday School, but he could not say or think God and war in the same breath, as it were. War certainly existed, but did God? 'Kiss your Helga for me.'

'And you too, Jock. Kiss Nellie for me.'

Tam laughed. He could just imagine Nellie's response if he was to tell her that he was kissing her for a German soldier he hadn't even met, but whom he would remember for ever. He found himself praying, though, that the war was really over, that there had not been some terrible mistake and that the first moment he lifted his head it would not be shot off by his friend Fritz. But, his head still whole and entire on his shoulders, he duly sailed for home, and Nellie.

'Wash your mouth out wi' soap, Tam Sinclair,' was what Nellie said, when Tam finally arrived home and told her *This kiss is from my good friend Fritz.* 'Thae Germans started this hale thing.'

'Nellie, Nellie,' laughed Tam, as he held both her and Jimmy in his arms, planting kisses on each of them wherever he could. 'The people dinnae start wars. It's the high heid yins, and Fritz was just like me, wearying to get hame to his wife and his wee lassies.'

'His *wife*, you say,' said Nellie archly.

'Aye, lass. Nellie Bains, will you – and wee Jimmy – marry me?'

'We will, Tam,' replied Nellie softly.

'And we'll ask your friend Victoria to help me get a job on a farm. I haven't a notion what tae dae, but I'll give it a shot. I've it all worked out, Nellie. First, get ourselves married, then a job on a farm and a nice, wee tied cottage where we can raise Jimmy in good, clean, fresh air.'

'If that's what you want, our Tam,' said Nellie, who had dreamed of nothing but a cottage in the country since the day she had started work in the Dundee mills, 'that's what we'll do.'

Catriona and Davie were to be married on Saturday, 21st December 1918. Victoria was at work, making lists of all the things that had to be done, for the wedding and for the holiday celebrations. She should have been typing letters for Mr Smart, but her mind was firmly on the exciting events to take place on Blackness Road and on the heart-to-heart conversation that she had had with her mother.

Now that the house was in good shape, with a new tenant joining Dr Currie in January and Davie there to help, Catriona had tried to persuade Victoria to think again about further education.

'You're eighteen, Victoria, and you've been the best daughter any woman could ever have wanted, but maybe it's time for you to move on, to think about your own future. I'm that happy I can scarce believe it, but I don't want to hold you back any longer.'

'I made a promise, Mother, to stay with you for ever.' Victoria had smiled teasingly at her mother, who was blushing like a young bride. 'Am I supposed to believe that I will be in the way and will be cast aside now that you have found Davie?'

Catriona had looked as if she did not know whether to laugh or to cry, and Victoria had put her out of her misery. She'd placed the little box containing two hand-embroidered pillow slips – a wedding present from an elderly neighbour – down on the pile of similiar boxes all waiting to be acknowledged and had sat down on the floor at her mother's feet, in the way she had often sat as a little girl.

'I'm so happy for you, Mother, you know that. I've always liked Davie and you love him, and that's wonderful. I have been doing a lot of thinking, and part of that thinking says that a newlywed couple shouldn't have to have a great girl underfoot all the time.'

Catriona had stroked the shining, dark hair. 'You're my daughter, Victoria, you'll always belong here. Your grampa always wanted you to go to the university—'

'It's too late, Mother,' Victoria had interrupted. 'I've thought about it, but I don't have entrance qualifications and I don't want to go back to some cramming school to get them. I really love working at Smart's. It's interesting. I'm learning a lot and I'm skilled, Mother, and getting better all the time. I can't think what I'd want to study now if I went to a university. I don't think I ever really thought too much about it.'

'But you'll live here at home with me and Davie, and wee Andrew?'

'For a while, Mother. Who knows? Maybe one of these days I'll get a chance to travel the world.' She would never tell her mother that she had been offered the chance to travel in luxury to India, but had rejected the opportunity in order to stay with her. 'And somebody who's never been farther from Dundee than Edinburgh would surely jump at the chance to do that.'

Now Victoria dragged her thoughts back from the happy little family in Blackness Road to concentrate her mind on invoices, bills of lading and various letters to type for Mr Smart. She worked steadily for almost an hour until the quiet hum of activity in the office was shattered by Euan Gordon.

'How on earth am I supposed to do that?'

At the interruption Victoria looked up from the work she was trying desperately to finish. 'What's the problem, Mr Gordon? Can I help you?'

'It's Mr Alistair's trip to India, Victoria. It's on again, now that the war is definitely over, but everything has to be done so quickly. He's taking presents – Keillor's Marmalade, if I can get any. Does he not remember there was a war on, no sugar and even fewer oranges?'

'You'll manage something,' began Victoria, but she bent her head over her typewriter again as Mr Smart himself came in from his office.

'And could you make sure that the shipping company has the tickets sent here, rather than to the house, Euan?'

'Yes, Mr Alistair.'

Victoria's heart was beating in a strange way. India . . . India. She was aware that her employer had stopped at her desk, but she refused to look up. If she had, she might have seen the wistful expression in the man's sad brown eyes. 'What a pity you can't accompany me, Victoria. What an opportunity, what a chance for advancement and, of course, speaking quite selfishly, I can't imagine how I am to manage.'

Victoria's heart began to sing. She could hardly believe it, but it looked as if she was going to be given a second chance. Oh yes, oh yes, she would grasp the opportunity. She looked up and Alistair Smart saw the flush on her cheeks and the brightness in her eyes. 'Well, actually, Mr Smart, now that Mother is to be married again, she has actually encouraged me to think of my career.'

'Do you mean that you will be able to accompany me after all, Victoria? I won't have to try to break in some stranger to my ways? Splendid, simply splendid. Arrange it, Euan.' And having dropped his bombshell so casually, he turned and went quickly into his office, leaving his two employees gazing after him.

He closed the door and leaned back against it, his heart racing. Why this euphoria, you stupid old fool? So you are to have a secretary after all. It's relief you should feel, not this . . . this . . . Oh, what is this joy that makes me want to caper like a child on Christmas morning? Yes, yes, to have a competent secretary will make life so much easier. That's all it is.

Behind him, in the general office, Victoria wondered how she could ever handle the events of the next few months competently. She was going to India, to India. But first, first, there was the wedding.

It was as perfect as they could make it. Catriona and Davie were married in the register office. Victoria and Tam Menmuir were the witnesses.

Did either Catriona or Davie think back all those years to when, at different times in the same wee Angus kirk, they had stood happily making the same promises? They had vowed then to be faithful and to do their best and each had kept faith. Now they stood and promised to love, honour and cherish one another.

Victoria cried. This time it would work out. These two lovely people, who meant so much to her, deserved to be happy. She prayed for their future.

She turned and saw Davie's mother, tears of joy running down her cheeks, her lips moving in silent, impassioned prayer. Victoria tried to send her a message. It will be all right: this time, for both of them it will be all right.

It would not be the fault of their friends if anything went wrong. After the simple wedding they all went back to the house on Blackness Road and Victoria was amazed by the number of well-wishers who crowded into the little house. Arbuthnott Boatman was there with champagne that he must have bought before the war. Bessie Menmuir and Catriona had, from austerity rations and generous gifts of produce from the farms, created a meal that many a guest would talk about for years.

Tam Sinclair and his wee Jimmy, each scrubbed and polished as clean as only Nellie could get them, stood gaping at the sight of a spread that surpassed their wildest dreams.

'Well I tell you, oor Nellie,' said Tam, as he held his family close against his side, 'if these are farming folk and this is the way they eat, I'm glad I've got my name doon for a job out at Birkie.'

'They're no all farming folk, Tam. That thin, kinda elegant woman is a real lady doctor. She's taking wee Andra while Mrs Cameron's away ... No, wait, it's Mistress Menmuir noo.' Nellie sneezed as the bubbles of the first champagne she had ever drunk in her life went up her nose. Then she laughed and drank Tam's, because she had drunk hers too fast and had barely tasted it.

Poor Tam was quite happy to hand it over. 'Don't tell them I didn't fancy it, Nellie,' he said and smiled with real pleasure as the new man of the house handed him 'a dram, Tam? A real drink?'

'See that toff with the doctor,' giggled Nellie. 'I hear he's a real live lord. Victoria says he's been twice tae the house tae see the doctor, and the net curtains the length of the street have been twitchin' like nobody's business. He's a married man, but the rich are no like you and me.'

Tam watched the expression on the face of the real live lord as he talked to the lady doctor.

'Oh, aye they are, lassie,' he said. 'They just wear better clothes.'

'There's Victoria's boss,' said Nellie and she waved enthusiastically at Alistair Smart who, with great good humour, waved back. 'He lives in Broughty Ferry. Did ye ken everybody that bides there's a millionaire. He's lending Catriona and Davie his gate-house for the weekend. Can ye believe that? A house for a man that does nowt but open the gate.' She was silent for a moment. Even the champagne had no strength here. 'He's dead, that man, in the war.' The champagne was playing havoc with Nellie's train of thought. 'You're about the only one here that came back in the one piece, Tam. Some of them never came back . . . Davie's brother, the auld minister's laddie, half the farm laddies . . .'

'Here, Nellie, hold our Jimmy while I get you a nice cup of tea. That fancy wine's gone to yer head.'

Tam went off and was nearest the front door when there was a knock. He opened the door to Catriona's former minister.

'How could I not come, Catriona, and you too, Davie, to wish you well in your new life together and to say a blessing on this marriage of yours.'

For the second time that day Victoria watched Bessie Menmuir weeping tears of joy. The old woman held the baby, who had wakened up to join in the party, and her tears mingled with his as he cried for his supper.

'I'll give him his bottle,' said Victoria and she whisked him off to the kitchen.

Alistair Smart followed her there and jiggled wee Andrew up and down while Victoria warmed his milk. Then he stood and watched her as she held the child.

'There is something so powerful in the image of a woman feeding a baby,' he told her. 'Men look . . .' He stopped, because he could find no words.

'Sweet,' Victoria finished for him. 'Men look sweet. Except men like Davie, who are used to looking after small things. He looks just right.'

Alistair looked down on her bent head as she attended to her small brother. *You look so right too, Victoria*, he said to himself, *so very, very right.*

'I'd best go back to the party, my dear,' he said, suddenly conscious of the intimacy of the moment. He was disappointed that Victoria did not even look up from her all-important task as he left the room.

Sandy, the fiddler from Priory Farm, had driven the minister to Dundee, and wee Andrew stopped sucking on his bottle when the new sound danced into the kitchen.

'So you're a music lover, are you, my wee man?' Victoria asked her brother as she burped him. 'Well, let's change your nappy and then I'll take you back and dance a reel with you.'

In the corridor she met Dr Currie and Lord Inchmamock. Their set faces showed Victoria that these two were the only unhappy guests at the party. Victoria smiled shyly at Sandy Inchmamock: she could never really be at ease with him. He was Robert's father and Robert was dead, and Victoria had never been able to find the right words of consolation for him. Are there any words to help deal with things that are unbearable? Is it enough to say, 'I'm sorry. I wished I had known what to do, to say. I wish I could help.'

She turned sideways now, with the baby in her arms, to let them pass her in the narrow passageway.

'There's no one in the kitchen, Dr Flora,' she said. 'If you were to start making the tea, you could have the place to yourselves for a wee while.'

'Bless you, Victoria. Try to get us ten minutes of peace and quiet,' said Dr Currie and she led Sandy into the kitchen. 'Have you any idea how to make tea, Sandy?' she asked lightly as she saw him look round in amazement. The entire house was smaller than his kitchens at Inch-mamock. 'Sit down, my dear. Perhaps it will be easier for you to explain if you don't have to look at me.'

'I want to look at you, Flora. I want to spend the rest of my life looking at you.'

Flora Currie wanted desperately to hear those words. They were sweet, as soothing as any medicine she had ever been able to prescribe for a patient, and as healing. But she could not listen: she had no right to hear them.

'Well, you can't, Sandy,' she said almost jovially, 'so do stop being silly.'

'We talked about divorce,' he said baldly. 'I'm going to divorce Julia or, at least, I'll see to it that she can divorce me.'

The words thundered out against the sounds of merri-ment from the front room.

Flora almost fell down on the three-legged stool by the stove. 'Oh, my very dear,' she began, her hands held out in supplication. You can't. Julia would be a pariah. She would no longer fit in the nice little mould she has made for herself. You can't do that to her. You're a man – all the chaps at your club will laugh heartily and say, "Heard about Inchmamock, the old dog", and they'll continue to ask you to dine and shoot. But Julia will be ostracized. She won't be allowed at court. Sandy, you can't do that. She'll shrivel and die. Hasn't this year been hard enough?'

'It was Robert's letter, Flora. Have you any idea how the boy's words haunted me in the middle of the night – night after night? We talked. Julia and I have talked more since . . . since Robert died than in our entire married life. She as good as told a shocked, traumatized child that he was incapable of inspiring real and lasting love. She tried to buy your Victoria for him.'

'Oh, God, he heard that?' Victoria had told Dr Currie of the events leading up to Robert's suicide, of her horror and her own feelings of guilt that, at the one time it counted, she had not said die right dung.

'She said she couldn't be bought—'

'She meant only that money wasn't necessary, Sandy. Victoria liked Robert. If she had—'

It was his turn to interrupt. 'I know, Flora. The children might have made a go of at least friendship, if they had been left to get on with it. But Julia pushed before either of them was ready.'

'She meant well, Sandy. Oh, dear God, you have lost your only child. Don't lose your wife too.'

'The boy I have in my heart and soul,' he said sadly. 'My wife I lost a long time ago. How like you to think of her, Flora, but she wants a divorce too. She has a . . . friend. I'll give her the grounds; it's quite easy to do, you know. Some people make a nice little living out of, shall we say, indelicate photographs. At least Julia won't have the trauma of being the one divorced. She can divorce me and, as for money, even after this damn war that's not a problem. I'll sell the estates up here, the stuff that's not entailed – I couldn't bear to be in Scotland without my laddie – and Julia can take the proceeds and live abroad. She's actually talking about the United States. Titles still count there, even with some of their top society people. It's too soon, of course – maybe in a year or two – but I wanted to ask you . . . Will you wait for me, Flora?'

Flora leaned forward on her three-legged stool. She put her arms around his neck, as she had done twenty years before, and she kissed him lightly on the lips.

'I'd wait for you for ever,' she replied softly.

It was unfortunate that Agnes Johnstone, Catriona's next-door neighbour, should choose just that moment to come into the kitchen to see what on earth was happening to the long-promised pots of tea.

17

VICTORIA THOUGHT SHE MIGHT BE sick with excitement. She was not; but she was very sick with the motion of the great liner as it sailed across a stormy Bay of Biscay.

Her first thought, when she could stand up again without wanting to die, was that she should have been working. This was not a pleasure cruise; she was a working woman. The stirrings of joy began to defeat the qualms of nausea. She was going to India. She staggered up on deck to look for her employer.

Alistair was standing by the rail, wrapped in a long fur coat, deep in conversation with another traveller, but he hurried across the deck as soon as he saw her. 'My dear Victoria,' he said with evident relief. 'How nice to see you above decks. Come, stand by the rail and enjoy the sea breeze. Or would you prefer a chair out of the wind? There will be quite a change in the heat in a day or two. Would you believe you shall soon have to guard your complexion?'

Victoria, who had heard from the medical officer that her employer had asked for her constantly and had ordered several delicacies to tempt her palate, smiled at him warmly. 'I have wasted enough time already, Mr Smart. I am quite ready to take dictation.'

'My dear girl, get yourself well. Enjoy the voyage. There's dancing every night, and as soon as the sun comes out we shall have deck games. I hope I have not lost my skill at quoits. There is to be a treasure hunt too, and although you have missed your first opportunity to dine with the captain, we have been asked to cocktails. I have no idea what a cocktail is – some new craze from America, I suppose – but I am assured we will enjoy the experience.'

'Sounds fun.'

Fun. That was not a word that had figured too much in Alistair Smart's vocabulary. He usually preferred a good book. The ship's library possessed the latest John Buchan and he had put his name down for it. He took a deep breath and told his secretary of the fancy-dress party that was to take place. It was only right that she should enjoy such frivolity.

By the time they were approaching Egypt, Victoria had forgotten her appalling sea-sickness. The ship was full of young army officers and their wives, young men who were going out to work in the jute industry, civil servants. Victoria soon found herself an accepted part of a lifestyle she had previously only seen from the outside. The army, however, preferred to keep to its haughty self.

'Their loss,' laughed Victoria, who quite forgot her employer for long hours of every day, as she walked and talked, and ate delicious food and danced away the glorious starlit nights. She met Mr Smart at mealtimes and, after dinner, he would ask her for one dance. Then he would retire to his cabin.

'We haven't done any work, Mr Smart,' Victoria would remind him every few days.

'Plenty of time for work, my dear. Enjoy yourself.'

And Victoria did.

And then there was the treasure hunt. The clues did not seem, to Victoria, too difficult. She worked them out, one after the other, and ranged over the ship in search of the next clue. So did Captain Edward Welborn. They met behind the second lifeboat from the right.

Eddie Welborn was quite happy to find himself behind the lifeboats with Miss Cameron. He had wanted to speak to her since she had first appeared on deck, but too many constraints had got in the way. First, as an officer raised from the ranks, he felt insecure as a member of this august ruling class of officers and gentlemen. He had been told that Victoria was 'trade, m'boy, and you don't mix with shopkeepers, not if you want to wear a gong one day'.

Eddie was not sure that he wanted to become a general. He wasn't even sure that he wanted to stay in the army. He had gone in because there was a war on, and his father's little Lake District farm could not support three sons. He had become an officer because, he said, 'everyone else bought it'. The general who had recommended his promotion remarked, 'best foot soldier I've seen since the Boer War.' Eddie was going out to India to see if he might like to leave the army and take a good job in jute. But he knew he would hate the sun: it had already blistered his skin. How he could bear three years of it, in or out of uniform, he simply could not imagine. He had sat in the shade with a book for two weeks and listened to Victoria's laughter, wishing that he had enough courage to defy the rules, as he had once defied the German army.

'So she's a shopkeeper,' he had argued with himself, 'and you, Edward Welborn, are a sheep farmer in funny clothes.' But until he had found himself behind the lifeboats he had not plucked up the courage required to defy convention.

The two young people looked at one another and at the hiding place contained in the clue. Who would reach for it first?

'You go,' said Eddie.

Victoria looked at his honest, freckled face and the clear blue eyes and she smiled. 'No, you go,' she replied. 'If I'm totally honest, I have to say you were here first.'

Eddie looked at her and thought that she was even prettier than he had believed and that her simple flower-patterned evening frock was much more becoming than all the expensive creations that the officers' wives were wearing. 'Shall we work together on it?' he asked now. 'After all, either you will follow me around or I will most certainly follow you.'

'Sounds good,' said Victoria and blushed. 'I mean, the working together bit.'

'Come along then. Twice I heard giggling. There are others looking for our clue.' Boldly he took her hand and Victoria shyly allowed it to rest in his. His skin was not so soft as she had thought it would be. After all, he was an army officer. She wasn't sure what they did, but she was sure it involved delegating, rather than doing.

'Your skin's quite hard for a gentleman,' she said and blushed again furiously at her boldness.

Eddie looked down at his hand. 'It's masquerading,' he laughed. 'It's a farmer's skin and it's taken four years of war to soften it.'

A farmer. In seconds their shyness was gone, like snow in summer, and Victoria heard all about the difficulties of sheep farming in the Lake District. In return Eddie was told a little about the Priory, about Grampa and old Tam Menmuir, but nothing about John Cameron.

Hand in hand they continued the hunt and, two hours later, to their great surprise but even greater joy, found themselves the winners.

'The prize is a bottle of bubbly,' said the ship's captain, 'and you shall receive it at the ball on the last night. I take it you'll be partners.'

They looked at one another. Victoria knew perfectly well what the military said about the others on board. Civil servants might be tolerated. Trade was anathema, unless they were owners of the firms – and even then they were suspect. She also had to think of her employer.

'We shall certainly be there, captain,' said Eddie boldly, 'and I shall ask the young lady to have the last waltz with me.'

'Yes, please,' said Victoria and blushed again, for surely sophisticated world travellers did not say such naïve things to young men.

Eddie seemed to see nothing amiss. 'Would you care for some tea before . . . retiring, Miss Cameron?'

Miss Cameron would care. They sat in one of the ship's lounges and drank tea and ate delicious little butter biscuits. And they talked and talked until Victoria felt that there was nothing she did not know about the Welborn family. She in turn told Eddie almost everything about her own family. But she could not bring herself to speak about her father, so she skirted over Andrew's birth.

Eddie, for his part, had heard about the baby's birth and the marriage some weeks later of Victoria's mother and stepfather, and he had reached his own wrong conclusions. But he had never before judged anyone without seeing for himself and he did not start now.

It was after two in the morning when Eddie, with a soldierly salute, left Victoria at the door of her cabin, but it was some time before she fell into a deep, untroubled sleep. She sat watching the moon on the water from her porthole and thinking that really life aboard ship was romantic and Eddie Welborn was the nicest young man. Catriona would like him. But how would she meet him? Catriona lived in Dundee and Eddie Welborn was going to India and might well stay there. Victoria smiled at the moon.

'What's for me will no go by me,' she told it and, happier than she had been for some time, Victoria Cameron slipped into bed and was soon sound asleep.

'I won the treasure hunt,' Victoria told Alistair the next morning at breakfast.

'I know, my dear, with a Captain Edward Welborn.' He held up the daily newspaper that was printed on board. 'Well done you. I hope you have saved your prettiest frock for the ball. I shall certainly come to see you receive your prize.'

'You won't mind if I give it to Eddie? I slowed him down a bit.'

'Not at all. Now, perhaps we could make a few notes about letters to send back upon arrival in India.'

He watched Victoria as she bent conscientiously over her notebook. Eddie, she had called him Eddie, and they had only just met.

But that's as it should be, he told himself. You are her employer, Alistair, and she is young enough to be your daughter.

Unbidden, the ghost of another young girl came into his mind. It was an old memory and had been locked firmly away, so it was rather hazy. No, Victoria is nothing like Mabel. Mabel was fair and frail and . . . But there is something in the tilt of the head, in the clear, untroubled look in the eyes. Almost enjoying the pain, Alistair remembered.

Where's your pride, Alistair? She's an office girl. She'll never command respect.

He should never have listened to his father. He should have married his Mabel. They could have had a year before the dreaded tuberculosis took her. No point in wondering whether money could have helped keep the killer at bay.

The remainder of the voyage was not enjoyed by Alistair Smart. Victoria and young Welborn were soon inseparable and, as if to rub salt into a wound that he could not know was gaping, Eddie came every day to ask punctiliously for

Alistair's permission to take Victoria away – to dance, to play deck tennis, to swim, to walk in the moonlight, hand in hand, around the deck. Alistair watched them and he tried to be happy for Victoria. And, because he was a thoroughly decent man, he made no excuses about pressure of work to keep the girl by his side.

'This is as it should be,' he said. 'Every young girl should have a shipboard romance. Good heavens, what would it be like to go back to Dundee and not to have flirted madly with a gay young blade?' And he almost convinced himself that it was he who had begun the whole thing and that he was quite proud of himself.

Victoria, for her part, was experiencing thoughts and sensations that she had never before encountered. Robert had been a dream, a fairytale and, like too many other fairytales, it had ended in horror. She had not been in that lovely library with the boy when he pulled the trigger, but too often in the night she had awakened with a cry, sure that her sleep had been disturbed by the blast of a shotgun. She had been able to tell Eddie about Robert and he, who had seen more horror than Victoria could ever imagine, had held her hand tightly and prayed for the courage to hold her in his arms and to kiss away the nightmares.

And all too soon they were approaching Bombay.

The noise, the smell, the heat, the crowd – it was all overwhelming.

Victoria and Alistair disembarked at Bombay, the gateway to India since Charles II had been given it as a wedding present from the father of his Portuguese wife. They were to stay in a hotel suggested by the firm for a few days, before setting off on the long, dusty train journey across the subcontinent to Calcutta. Victoria's earliest childhood memories were awakened by the sight of the overworked horses that pulled the Indian taxis. Oh, Grampa would have laid about him with a whip, had he seen his own animals so badly abused. Her anger helped her tolerate the amazing smells of India as they trotted towards the hotel.

Alistair Smart was not so lucky, and the smell of urine and dung, and dirt and incense, and ... and ... stuck in his throat and tortured his eyes. He was made even more unhappy when he saw that the unattached soldiers from the ship were also unloading their baggage at the hotel. He had watched Victoria floating around the deck in the arms of Edward Welborn and had forced himself to smile with everyone else at the attractiveness of the young couple. And he had consoled himself that the army was off to Delhi, while he and Victoria were bound for Calcutta.

Two nights after their arrival he sat in his white dinner jacket among the palms of the hotel foyer and watched Victoria and Edward dance with each other again.

He's holding her too close for decency, he raged, and then he scolded himself for being an old fuddy-duddy.

'Tomorrow we're off. By the spring that boy will be nothing but a memory.'

The music stopped, but Victoria and Edward did not. They continued to waltz out of the ballroom and into the fan-cooled foyer.

Alistair could do nothing but sit quietly and pretend to be engrossed in the week-old *Times*, while Victoria and Edward stopped and gazed at one another.

It was like one of those dreadful Hollywood films, except that the piano player was no longer playing. Edward was not much taller than Victoria. Alistair watched him bend his head and kiss her. He watched as her arms stole up around his sunburned neck.

I hope that hurts, Alistair thought to himself. Then, because he was a good man, he tried again to find the answer to the crossword clues. *I should have said . . . But I couldn't . . . She is in my employ. She is young enough to be my daughter. We are going to Calcutta tomorrow. She will forget him. Please God, let her forget him. But why? Why should she forget him? Because he is an army officer, Smart, and you think he will go away and forget her, and she will be hurt.*

Once again he buried his head in the newspaper and, oblivious to everyone and everything, Victoria and Eddie wandered out on to the verandah.

'I love you, you know, Victoria.'

'I know.'

Eddie looked at her. He was not experienced at telling young women that he loved them, but he had a suspicion that 'I know' was not exactly the answer he had expected.

'And?'

'Oh, Eddie, I'm confused. I don't know what love is. I love my mother and my wee brother. I loved my grandfather. I don't know what I felt for Robert, but it's not the same as I feel for you. I always saw him as a knight in shining silver armour . . .' She fell silent, ready almost to burst into tears. She knew that this conversation was probably the most momentous of her whole life and she did not want to spoil it.

'I'd look stupid in armour, Victoria, and I hate horses. Well, they hate me. They always want to stand on my feet. I'm no god. I'm a normal man and I want to see you every day for the rest of my life. Now that, to me, is love.'

'It would be nice to see you every day too, Eddie,' said Victoria simply. And she smiled shyly at him and he held her hand again.

'Now, you're going to be in Calcutta for three months and then back to Scotland.' He was once again the experienced army officer – capable, in charge. 'I must go to Delhi with the regiment, but I can be demobbed almost at any time, Victoria. And I want to go back to the Lake District and try to find a tenancy somewhere. I know a lot about sheep. We could write to one another. There's a bus or a train from Scotland that passes quite near us, so it must go back the other way as well. We could see one another. My mother would be happy to meet you.'

'Yes, Eddie, and my mother would like to meet you. My stepfather's father still lives on my grampa's farm. It would be interesting for you, wouldn't it, to see a Scottish farm?'

'Yes, it would. Victoria, I'm rather tired of talking. I'd quite like to kiss you again, if you don't mind.'

Victoria did not mind, and by the time she went to bed that night she had quite decided that life would be insupportable if she was not to see Eddie Welborn every day of her life. How she would live through the next few months she could hardly imagine.

18

WHILE VICTORIA PLAYED DECK TENNIS and quoits in the sun, Priory Farm trembled under the weight of a deluge.

Tam Sinclair stood in a ditch up to his knees in muddy water. He stretched his aching back, whacked his freezing hands against himself to try to restore the circulation, and laughed.

Better than crying, Tam me lad, he told himself. *Only difference between this and Flanders is that no one is shooting at you.*

He bent again to his task. He had to clear the ditch or the water would pile up in the fields, and then the topsoil and the seed would run on to the roads. Up down, up down. He shovelled and threw the piles of rotting vegetation over his shoulder. Then he came across the small heap of bones and the bile rose in his throat, so that he retched. For a horrible moment he could smell death again and he could hear the whining of the shells, the dull thud of the guns, the screaming of the horses and men.

For a long moment he leaned all his weight on his shovel. 'Hold it, Tam lad. It's nout but a wee rabbit eaten by a stoat: a wee Scottish rabbit eaten by a wee Scottish weasel.'

Almost tenderly he laid the bones on the side of the ditch and put his raw hands into the mud to pull out more.

'Well, that was stuck in one overflow pipe,' he congratulated himself, as the water began to run more fiercely and the level went down. If only the wind would stop, or the stinging rain that lashed his cheeks. It was impossible to see what he was doing. He worked on blindly, and where the tears of cold stopped and the raindrops began he did not know.

'They can stuff this bit of farming,' he told himself, as he wiped his wet nose with an ever wetter hand.

The one constant joy of farming was that the sun dictated the hours. Tam worked on until he was in danger of cutting off his legs in the dark, then he pulled himself out of the ditch, shouldered his spade and his axe, and set off for the cottage where he and Nellie had set up home after their ne'erday wedding in the wee kirk. One family's tragedy was another wee family's good luck. There were tied cottages available, and work for man and wife to go with them. Nellie cleaned twice a week for the school teacher, who did not mind Jimmy as long as he neither heard nor saw him; and Tam struggled along at Tam Menmuir's side and tried to learn and love an alien way of life.

The curtains were open so that the firelight danced out to meet him. Nellie would draw the curtains only once her man had found his way home. Tam shivered as the icy water ran down his neck and his frozen feet squelched in the pools lying in the soles of his boots, but he kept his eyes on the glow from his home.

He opened the door and there was Nellie.

'Och, Tam love, ye're frozen. Come on to the fire. Jings, man, look at yer hands: they're bleedin' with the cold.'

Tam closed the door to shut out the rain and leaned against it, as he eased off his sodden boots. The warmth from the fire hurt his hands and the wood smoke caught in his throat and eyes. Jimmy appeared from the kitchen, his nightgown trailing the ground and his fat little arms holding some protesting kittens, who were mostly upside-down.

'Put the kitties down, laddie, afore they scratch you. No, don't come to Daddy till I'm dry. And what have you and Mammy done the day?'

'Ach, we've had a lovely day at home just the two of us, Tam, while you were out there in that. Can ye smell that stew? There's rabbit in that, and a pigeon.'

Tam sat and watched the steam rise from his socks and he laughed at Nellie as she laboured over his poor, calloused hands.

'Them's a working man's hands, Nellie Bains Sinclair, no a fancy school teacher's lily-whites. They're perfect for dandling wee laddies and cuddling big lassies.'

'You be sure it's only the one lassie, Tam Sinclair,' said Nellie, putting away the ointment. 'Noo, is that no better? How are you feelin, love?'

Tam smelled the stew and the fire, and he looked round the front room with its box bed and its dresser containing Nellie's granny's best plates. He saw his son rolling among the kittens on the rag rug and he saw the love in Nellie's eyes.

'Will I tell you what I feel, Mistress Sinclair? I feel something I thought I had lost for ever in the hell-holes of France. I found it in the hell-holes of Angus: wasnae there more than enough water to float it back to me? I feel happy, Nellie, just plain happy.'

Nellie lifted Jimmy, who had twice rolled against the fireguard, and he protested loudly.

'Jimmy Sinclair, you'll bring this hoos aboot oor ears. Time he had a brother, Tam Sinclair,' she suggested archly. 'He's spoiled. Mrs Menmuir's got him as fat as a Christmas pig with her baking, and here's you thinkin the sun rises and sets on his heid.'

'Brawest sight in the world, Nellie lass, a healthy, happy bairn. Mind you, two healthy, happy bairns would tak a lot of beatin'. We'll just have to grin and bear it, lassie, until we're sure his brother is well started.'

'Let's get you warm and dry and fed, Tam Sinclair, afore ye start your grinnin' or ocht else.'

In the West End of Dundee Mrs Murray Gow, née Emily Simpson, was feeling very happy too. Her star was in the ascendant. Murray, her husband of eleven months, two weeks and three days, who had shone at the Harris Academy, had been promoted to manager of the bank and had also become an elder of the kirk. Only this morning he had told her that he thought they might move in a year or two to Barnhill. Barnhill! A detached house would need at least two maids and a gardener – Murray could not dig potatoes after a day spent sorting Dundee's finances. She would ask Pa – discreetly – to get them the latest in sanitary conveniences. If Murray continued to do well, Pa might even be able to move his own plumbing business from the Hilltown. Not that there was anything wrong with the Hilltown – fine people, all of them.

She sat in the waiting room to see dear Dr Braithwaite. She was not quite ready to announce that she and Murray were to be blessed . . . So difficult – everyone would know that she and Murray, well . . . It was an act sanctioned by the church, but better that no one knew just yet. Better that the neighbours dwelt on the sterling work that she and Murray had done during the war and on the wonderful fund-raising she was doing for those poor soldiers who had given their all, or nearly their all – they were coming back, after all. And she was there twice a week with solid half-crowns, clean boots and changes of clothes. That nasty man who had yelled that he didn't need charity, he needed a job, had been so misguided. But she had forgiven him, and had smiled understandingly as she had picked up the half-crown from the corner where it had rolled. She returned it to the pile, waiting for the next unemployed veteran – and the next, and the next.

'Mrs Gow, doctor will see you now.'

The starched nurse knew who she was. Emily bowed at her slightly and rose to follow her into Dr Braithwaite's consulting room.

'Wait a minute. This isn't the way to the doctor's rooms.'

The nurse turned. 'Dr Braithwaite has an emergency at the Royal, Mrs Gow. He asked Dr Currie to see you.'

Emily stood quite still where all the waiting patients could see and hear her.

'Currie? Not Dr Flora Currie?'

'Yes, Mrs Gow, but Dr Currie is even more qualified in obstetrics than Dr Braithwaite. That was one of the many reasons why he hired her.'

Emily could not believe her ears. Obstetrics – the nurse had given her business away. How mortifying! Not only that, but she was to be seen by a woman doctor, *and* one whose name featured in the less salubrious papers. Should she make a stand now? Was it time to show Dundee that Emily Gow was not like other women? Yes, it was. It would be painful to make a scene, but one had one's principles. 'Make me another appointment,' she said rather too loudly and a teeny bit squeakily, because she was not, at heart, a fighter. 'I have, after all, another six months to go. Quite frankly, nurse, I'm surprised that dear Dr Braithwaite hasn't fired that . . . that scarlet woman.'

The nurse was angry. 'Mrs Gow, please!'

'I did not want the dear doctor to hire a woman doctor. How unfeminine to wish to be a medical person – so unladylike. But that he continues to sponsor someone who figures so luridly in the less professional press shocks me.'

The other patients were beginning to look embarrassed, worried or angry, and Flora had come out of her office to see what was causing the delay.

Emily saw her and, although she would have preferred to have attacked without her victim's knowledge, did not draw back.

'I'm sorry, Dr Currie, but everyone is talking about it. I know the papers say that dear Lord and Lady Inchmarnock are not to divorce, but I have heard it from a friend of mine who saw you last Christmas at a very – well, quite frankly – a very working-class party.' She stopped for a second in embarrassment. What was her friend doing at such a party? 'It was a function that my friend attended mainly to keep on pleasant terms with all her neighbours, and you were seen, deny it if you dare, kissing Lord Inchmarnock.'

Flora stared at her in horror. Should she deny it? Should she say that she and Sandy were childhood friends? Should she ignore it? The papers speculated constantly about the Inchmarnocks. *Grief-stricken peer seeks solace* had been one rather kind headline. What would they be like when the divorce actually came through . . .? Even in the twentieth century divorce was looked upon as almost more abhorrent than murder. Sometimes excuses were found for murderers.

'I shall find another physician,' finished Emily grandly and she swept out.

Flora watched as two, then three other patients rose. 'I'm sorry, doctor,' said one as she passed. 'I just can't afford to be associated with anything not quite nice.'

Me neither, thought Flora as, with her heart plummeting into her expensive leather shoes, she ushered in her last remaining patient. No man and no career either, if things continue like this.

'Come on, Dr Currie,' whispered her patient. 'I think you're the best doctor in Dundee and I need you to help me birth a live baby this time.'

Flora smiled down at the girl who had suffered three miscarriages in as many years.

'That's what's important, Sarah, my dear. And we'll do it this time, together.'

After she had examined young Mrs Black and sent her happily on her way home, Flora had time to sit down and write to Sandy Fotheringham, but she did not mention the problems with her patients. Poor old Sandy, she felt, had more than enough problems of his own. He was determined to be a free man and had gone off promising to let her know the outcome of his attempts to give his wife due cause for divorce. It all seemed so sordid and hopeless, and sometimes Flora wondered if it was worthwhile. She loved Sandy, she always had, but she had lived without him for a long time. She was no longer a giddy young thing. She had her work and the ache in her heart no longer bothered her. At least, she was very little aware of it.

She posted her letter on the way back to Blackness Road and then waited patiently for a reply. Sandy did not write or telephone. He arrived himself and they went out to a hotel for dinner.

'It was so sordid, Flora. The woman reeked of cheap perfume and the room ... peeling wallpaper, damp patches, cigarette burns and such tawdry finery.'

He looked at Flora, so clean, so elegant somehow, even though he could see she never really made an effort. It was just Flora, just the way her bones allowed the clothes to drape themselves over her as if they had been made there, her hair going grey and being allowed to show its dignity. He thought of his wife and of how much time she spent adorning her face and her person. The results were beautiful, but contrived. Here was a real woman. Not like that ghastly woman in the hotel. She had had the audacity to laugh at him – not out loud, but he had known she was laughing.

'This is all dreadfully embarrassing.' How stupid he had felt saying that, but the words had burst out before he could control them.

Sandy Fotheringham, Lord Inchmarnock, had looked around the hotel bedroom and had barely repressed a grimace of distaste. It was a hotel that had never before known his patronage and certainly never would again. He could hardly believe the seediness of the décor or the rank atmosphere.

'What do you want me to do?' God, what a fool he felt. He had absolutely no idea of what steps one took.

The lady in the scarlet and black négligé pouted at him. 'Come on, darlin', you've surely been to bed with a woman before.'

That was not the kind of flippant remark that was calculated to endear her to her unwilling customer. 'Please, let's not make this any more distasteful than it has to be.'

'Sorry, love,' said the woman. What was her name? Miss Lulu-Belle de Chastelaine. In other circumstances he might have laughed. 'Look, it's a job. You want a divorce, or your lady wife wants one. I need the money. Slip off your dressing gown and get into bed. For pity's sake, I won't bite. I get in beside you, snuggle up, make it look a bit compromising. Bob takes the pic, gives it to your wife, who weeps over it and shows it to your nice expensive lawyers – and that's it. D.I.V.O.R.C.E. and you free to marry. Couldn't be easier.'

Sandy did as he was bid. It was all so sordid. Why could they not end the marriage in a dignified and civilized manner? Hadn't he come across an anthropological record somewhere that said divorce was achieved by saying three times, 'I divorce thee, I divorce thee, I divorce thee'? That seemed eminently civilized to him.

Miss de Chastelaine slipped into the bed beside him and manoeuvred her not inconsiderable weight closer to Sandy. She looked at him adoringly, the door burst open and there was a loud flash, the smell of powder and the door closed again.

Sandy threw off the girl. 'That wasn't how it was supposed to be. That wasn't the photographer I met earlier.'

Lulu-Belle lay back on the pillows and reached for her cigarettes. She lit one, inhaled heavily and blew smoke at him through her mascara-laden eyelashes. 'Sorry, darlin', but a girl's got to think of herself. You're the answer to a prayer, you are. That picture, which will appear in all the papers tomorrow, is my passport to at least six months on the West End – well, just off, near as makes no difference. You'll still get your divorce, of course – or at least her lady-ship will. We looked you up, *Mr Fotheringham*. You know what they say about need, ours being greater than yours and all. No hard feelings?'

In the elegant Dundee hotel dining room Flora looked at him and smiled. Poor Sandy. She saw seediness and taw-driness every day. He had got off lightly, but still, he had been fooled and cheated. He had not known that Miss de Chastelaine was a third-rate actress: but he should have known, with a name like that.

She removed one of the pile of newspapers from the table in front of her. 'Some of my patients have been bringing these tabloids in. This one says, "The beautiful Bella" – and she is lovely, Sandy—'

'Good heavens, Flora, how can you say that? So, so . . .' He was lost for words.

Flora ignored the interruption. '. . . has a contract at the Variety, but has vowed never to open her heart about your affair. How noble of her!'

He had had enough of jokes at his expense, even from Flora. 'Dash it, Flora, I never set eyes on her before that day.'

'I know,' she said simply and she smiled at him. Then her face changed and became sad and Sandy did not like what he saw.

'But you have to face that this changes things, Sandy my dear, for both of us. You've become a dashing blade and I've become a notorious woman. Everyone knows it's a set-up, but they think it was done because we are . . . involved.'

'But that's nonsense.'

'I know it. You know it. But please try to think rationally. Forget your wounded pride and the humiliation, and think clearly. My reputation has to be whiter than white, Sandy. My authority depends on it. My patients don't want to be treated by a scarlet woman.'

He stood up angrily and walked over to the window. Outside, the garden was full of Michaelmas daisies and chrysanthemums, serviceable flowers but no less lovely for that. For a moment a picture of the scarlet, brown and yellow colours that the house at Inchmarnock wore in the autumn blotted out the Dundee streets and the pain gripped him, as it always did.

He turned again to look at her and held out his hands. Flora went to him and they leaned close together, each taking comfort from the presence of the other. The small private dining room was empty but for themselves, but their need for each other was so great that, had it been full of other diners, it is doubtful they would even have noticed.

'I've thought and thought, my darling, and it seems to me that Fate, in the person of the delectable Miss Lulu-Belle, has stepped in. There is no reason to wait now. Julia can divorce me as quickly as she likes. She will have everyone's sympathy. "Heartless bounder, not enough that she has to lose her child, but old Sandy gets himself involved in a scandal." We can move away, Flora. Even with the proceeds of the house sale going to Julia, I have far too much money.' He held her away from him and looked into her compassionate, understanding eyes. 'Some would say the war was good to me; there's irony for you. You don't need your patients, Flora. Marry me and you'll never have to work again. You can snap your fingers at all the narrow little minds that revel in the misery of others.'

'That doesn't describe my patients, Sandy. Oh, some of them have been quick to judge, but I'm never surprised by human nature. I want to marry you. This . . . unpleasantness won't make me change my mind, but . . . Oh, darling Sandy, I never really thought about the commitment I am making to you. I'm a doctor, and there are people who depend on me. Please, dear, don't interrupt. I know there are other doctors, but patients don't see things that way when they are frightened. There are people I have to help through things – birth, death . . . I can't just abandon them, not without warning. Give me some time. Give us both some time – for you to be divorced, to finish the sale, for this appalling nonsense to die a natural death. I'm asking you to go away, Sandy . . .'

He could hardly believe what he was hearing. To go away. She wanted him to go away. Where could he go without Robert, without her, that would not plunge him into everlasting misery? His son, his bright little boy, was horribly dead, and Sandy had climbed out of his grief, taking comfort in the knowledge of Flora's friendship and then her love. And now . . .'

'Flora, please. I've lost Robert, must you . . . No, no, forget I said that. I make you sound like the prize I get if I'm good, like Nanny in the nursery. "Eat all your toast soldiers and you shall have a chocolate biscuit." Forgive me, I'm not myself. It's all so . . . galling, mortifying. Of course I understand. You need time, space. We both do. I'll go to town and help Julia. There are things she must want from Inchmarnock, Robert's things. We must go through the treasures together. Some of Inchmarnock is entailed, you know, the house itself. My cousin or his son will inherit.' He stopped as the memory of the boy who would not inherit intruded on his present grief. 'I shall write you often and, when you are ready to see me, even just for dinner . . . I'll stay at my club, I think. That would be best, it's so impersonal.'

Oh God, oh God, he thought, *please help me to get through this added misery without breaking down. Quick and sure is the best way. Like putting down a beloved old dog. Have to do it oneself. Less pain that way.* He reached into his breast-pocket and took out a little gold-wrapped packet. 'Not an engagement gift. You see, dearest, I will never presume. Just a . . .' He handed her the packet. 'I won't even kiss you, Flora. I do, in my heart and soul, every minute of every day. Goodbye, best beloved.' And he was gone, and Flora saw the door swing shut behind him, and she heard him running down the great stone stairs. She knew that she could have called him back and he would have come, and he would never have left her and she wanted that so badly, so desperately. And she bit her lips to stop herself calling out his name.

She held the packet against her cheek for a moment, feeling the warmth of his fingers, and then she opened it slowly. A watch, almost the image of the one that John Cameron had stolen, lay on a bed of velvet. She took it out and, through her tears, read the inscription picked out in diamonds on the back. Twice she rubbed her eyes. No, it was not exactly the same.

Sandy loves Flora – always.

19

Victoria spent most of the voyage back to Britain writing letters to Eddie. When she worked with Alistair Smart, or sat with him in the ship's dining room, she did not notice that he had changed subtly from the kind, thoughtful man who had sailed to India just a few months before. He was still kind and still thoughtful, and therefore seemed to Victoria to be just the same nice, old Mr Smart. But he no longer waited after dinner for one dance and, since Victoria spent the evenings walking around the deck looking at the moon, and wondering if Eddie was seeing the same moon, she failed to notice.

They arrived back in Dundee in a downpour and Victoria laughed with joy.

'Yes, my dear,' smiled Alistair Smart rather sadly, 'some things never change.'

Catriona, Davie and wee Andrew were at the station to meet them, and after Mr Smart had greeted the family, he was taken off in his chauffeur-driven motor car while Davie loaded Victoria's bags into a hired taxicab. She had acquired so many souvenirs that another bag had had to be bought – 'They are so cheap. Mother, you won't believe the prices. Wait till you see the brass plate I've brought you for the front hall, from Tibet.'

'This seems like money for jam, Catriona,' said Davie, as they squashed together in the back of the cab, 'money for taking folk home from the station.'

Normally Catriona would have agreed, saying that when the good Lord gave folk legs, He expected them to use them. But today she could think of nothing but the elegant woman who sat beside her, hugging wee Andrew, who in turn looked up wonderingly at the almost brown face above him, from his big blue eyes.

'You're that brown, Victoria, and you're taller and thinner. You're not a wee girl any more,' said Catriona, when they arrived at Blackness Road.

'She's been round the world and back, Catriona, and here's me thought I was a big man, with my free trips to France.'

Victoria laughed. 'India's not around the world, but it's a long way away. Mr Smart bought me a camera, Mother, and I've got some lovely snaps. I'll show you an elephant, Andrew, a great big elephant with a big, long trunk and funny teeth that stick out of his jaw.'

For a few minutes she was the young, silly Victoria as she pretended for her brother that she had a trunk and big ears. Andrew, however, who had never even seen a picture of the strange animal that his sister was trying to portray, was singularly unimpressed.

When they looked at the photographs Catriona noticed, but did not mention, that there were more than a few snapshots with the same young man in them. In one, a rather indistinct picture of a young woman standing under a huge arch that appeared to be formed of carved elephants, the same young man was standing with his arm casually around the girl's waist. Victoria looked at it for a long time, rather dewy-eyed, but apart from a dismissive 'Well, that's Eddie Welborn. I told you about him in my letters', she said no more.

Before she went back to work, Victoria had three days at home to rest and tell her family all about her experiences. They sat up night after night, exclaiming over the picture postcards, the Chinese porcelain, the embroidered blouses, the sandalwood boxes and, for Andrew, the carved wooden dolls that Catriona showed him and then put away on a shelf above his head, before they ended their short lives in his mouth. Victoria seemed to have remembered every meal consumed, not only on both voyages, but in the luxurious hotels in which she had stayed. And so well did she recount her experiences that Davie felt he could almost smell the curries and taste the fruits with their wonderful names. How much more exciting 'papaya' sounded than 'apple'.

'I shall try to prepare a curried meal, Mother,' said the new, sophisticated Victoria. 'I have brought packets of spices with me.' And Catriona and Davie looked at one another and wondered anxiously if their Scottish digestions were a match for the exotic East.

Victoria saw the looks and laughed. 'Don't worry. Here's me that can barely boil an egg properly talking about oriental cookery. It'll just be a wee sauce on your mince, Davie, just to give you an idea. Some of it I just couldn't eat, but Eddie has a digestion that a horse would envy.'

Had she any idea how many times the word 'Eddie' came into her conversation, or how her voice dropped and her eyes softened at his very name?

*

After three days Victoria went back to work and it was amazing how quickly the little house got back to normal, except that every morning Victoria was the first to rush to the front door to see if the postman had left any letters, especially thin blue ones. It was some weeks, of course, before he did and every day that he did not, Victoria retreated angrily upstairs to get ready for work. And, as she worked, she blamed the blameless postman for not delivering her letters.

'It cannae be that you are expecting a letter, lassie?' laughed Davie, and at the twinkle in his eye Victoria laughed herself out of her ill-humour.

'Waiting's so hard, Davie,' she said.

Davie smiled and there was a lifetime of experience written in his smile for those who could read. 'There's me could write a book about waiting, lassie.' He leaned forward and gently touched her hand, so softly and quickly that she felt she could almost have imagined the intimate gesture. 'It's aye worth it, though, lass, aye worth it.'

Victoria smiled at him fondly and tried to be patient. And the days went on, and eventually two or three blue letters came all at once, and then again there was a wait.

Victoria went on working for Mr Smart, and she continued to write her own letters after tea in the room that looked out on to the garden so carefully tended by her stepfather. She set herself to helping her mother, and she loved and appreciated the time that she had been given to get to know her little brother.

Most days she stayed at the office at lunchtime and ate a sandwich, but on the days when it was just possible that a letter might arrive, she hurried home at noon, and Catriona treasured those days.

One warm day Catriona greeted Victoria at the door. 'You will never guess who I met in Muirhead this morning?'

Victoria took Andrew in her arms and was rewarded with a very wet kiss on the cheek. 'Tora,' he said rapturously and then immediately struggled to be put down.

'Who, Mother?'

'You are so brown, Victoria,' said Catriona, ignoring the question for a moment. She had still not got used to having her daughter home after almost a year away in India, and she never tired of her daughter's stories. 'It's actually becoming. Oh, what was I saying? Elsie, Elsie Morrison. You remember Elsie?'

How could Victoria not remember Elsie, her first real friend. But had she been a real friend, for she had never been a recipient of the secret of Victoria's first love? Only *Mansfield Park* knew that whole story.

Unaware that her daughter's attention had wandered, Catriona went on. 'She was fascinated to hear about your travelling. She's left Glasgow and is back at home. She is, would you believe, one of these dreadful "votes for women" feminists. She is actually, behind the scenes, I should add, going to work for one of these ardent reformers. What's the expression, dear, the Power behind the Throne? Locally, of course, in the first instance and then, who knows?'

Victoria obligingly set up some skittles for her small brother and watched his pleasure as he immediately knocked them down. She pictured Elsie, her one-time best friend, who had accompanied her on so many rambles, who had been there every time she had met Robert, who had dumped her when the Camerons had fallen on hard times.

'Perhaps with a view to becoming a councillor, Mother, or even, one day, Member of Parliament?' asked Victoria drily.

Catriona, an ardent believer in the natural order of things (man first, woman a long way behind), laughed at her daughter's nonsense. 'Away with you. What will you say next? Anyway, she is quite anxious to hear your views on votes for women, suffragettes and suffragists. According to Madame Elsie, she absorbed these notions practically at the breast. Her own mother went to all those dreadful meetings which the suffragettes held in Dundee before the war and, since Elsie was one girl among all those boys, her mother took her along too. Goodness, my poor mind was spinning with all the stories and the new ideas. She's sure that now you are travelled, you will agree with her. She's a great fan of Neddy Scrymgeour and thinks that his bad luck has run out . . .'

Even in India, Victoria had kept abreast of local Dundee politics and she knew the name Edwin Scrymgeour, the prohibitionist candidate and vociferous critic of what he saw as a corrupt city corporation, who had fought and lost every election since 1908.

'What bad luck?' she asked. 'I never heard of anything unpleasant happening to that family.'

'Well, it's surely bad luck to lose so many elections, dear – embarrassing too, I should think. Anyway, Elsie says his share of the vote in Dundee has crept up to twenty-eight percent and she thinks that he'll defeat that dreadful Churchill at the next election. You know, that man isn't really interested in Dundee. He just sees us as a safe seat. I think Elsie wants you to help her to help Neddy Scrymgeour kick him out. I did hint, delicately, that perhaps you might be rather too busy next year, but she asked if she might drop in. I was delighted to tell her that we have a telephone and that she should try ringing you first.'

'She's teaching, I suppose?'

'Oh, aye, at a primary school along the Perth Road. Primary Four she has, forty-three eight-year-olds. You could forgive anybody anything who has to suffer that day in, day out.'

Victoria was not so sure. 'If she rings while I'm at work, you could ask her to the harvest dance.' She looked up at her mother. 'I've not thought about it for a long time, but she was at that awful dance when Grampa died. All her brothers were in the Forces – no, one was still at home. I still miss Grampa, Mother, There are so many things I want him to share.' Victoria heard her favourite sound and stood up. 'Quick, Mother, watch Andrew, that's the dinner-time postie.'

'Well, I was sure you weren't coming home these dinner hours for my cooking,' said Catriona fondly as she carried Andrew into the kitchen and tied him into his chair.

Victoria hurried out into the hall and saw a thin blue letter on the rug at the front door. She carefully teased it open and read it three times, before following her mother into the kitchen. She was blushing as she saw her mother's happy, knowing look.

'He's coming home, Mother. He's had enough of the army and hates the thought of an office job. He's coming back to Britain. He'll go first to see his family and then, oh, Mother, he's coming here. There's a question he has to ask me.'

'And what will you say, love?'

Victoria smiled, but did not answer the question directly. 'It'll mean that I'll go away again, Mother. You know that, don't you? He hopes to have saved enough at least to get a tenancy somewhere. The Lake District, perhaps.'

Catriona removed too big a piece of bread from her son's mouth. 'I wouldn't have it any other way, Victoria. I left my mother. She left hers. Besides, if we all learn to drive one of these dreadful machines like Dr Flora, we can see one another often. The twentieth century is a grand time to live in, don't you think?'

'It is indeed,' agreed Victoria, but she was thinking of Eddie Welborn and of the very exciting developments in her personal and public life, certainly not of politics, or of the real place of women in their new society. 'Now I'll need to eat this up quickly and get back to work. Mr Smart's up in the air a bit just now. We've been asked to join a conglomerate of all the big jute industries. It's all very exciting, but nerve-wracking. Cox's, Gilroy's, Kyd's, oh, all the big companies want to form a textile conglomerate. This was a good year for jute, but things are looking a wee bit shaky now. Calcutta's beginning to undercut Dundee. Luckily Mr Smart has his own family mills in Calcutta, but it's still . . .' She stopped and laughed as she saw the look on Catriona's face. 'Marriage and motherhood have changed you, Mother. You were always so interested in business.'

'Oh, I still am, dear, but you'll find that marriage changes your perspective on things. Right now, Davie's lungs, Andrew's teeth and your happiness are the most important things in my life and so whether your boss – nice and generous as he is – makes two million pounds' profit this year or twenty million isn't really top of my list.'

'Marriage, if I get married,' Victoria said as archly as only a girl who has had a written proposal of marriage can, 'won't change my interests, Mother. I think I'll phone Elsie when I get home and go along to one of her suffrage meetings. Eddie wouldn't want a wife who knew nothing but the price of potatoes.'

'Sixpence halfpenny a stone,' said Catriona immediately and they both laughed, well pleased with one another and the shape their lives were taking.

Dr Currie drove them all out to Priory Farm for the harvest dance. She had the night off, but refused to participate in the festivities. Some brightness seemed to have gone out of her since Lord Inchmarnock had sold as much of his Scottish estates as was not entailed and had gone away. She was still as hard-working as ever, if not even more so, but her laughter was not heard so often and her car was driven more sedately and rarely came screaming to a halt just inches from disaster.

'I have letters to write and case notes to make, Catriona. I'll come back for you all later.'

She drove off and the family was soon caught up in greeting old friends, who admired Victoria's sophistication and Andrew's new tooth with equal enthusiasm.

Because of several nights of working late before the formation of Jute Industries Ltd, Victoria had been unable to attend one of Elsie's meetings, so they met for the first time in many years at the harvest dance.

Victoria wondered if she would even recognize her old friend. Had she herself changed beyond recognition? Victoria stood at the door, where she had stood with Grampa, and waited for Elsie – Elsie who had taught her to dance, Elsie who had suggested that they go sketching in those enchanted woods, Elsie who had not wanted to dirty her expensive shoes in the unrestored Blackness Road house. Forgive and forget. Elsie had lost five brothers in the Great War. Maybe such an experience would have turned Victoria too into a fighter.

She saw Elsie arrive and it was as if it was all those years ago, although this time Elsie arrived without her usual fraternal escort. The two surviving brothers obviously preferred to be with their own families. The women looked at one another's burst into tears and, with their arms around one another's waists, went and sat in a corner, as it seemed for hours, talking about their lives since they had last seen one another. For Elsie those years had been mainly at university, where she had first become interested in politics. Now she was back in Dundee in her first year of teaching.

'But you've done so much, Victoria. It's hard to believe you won't be twenty till next year.'

'I've never really thought about it, Elsie. I was usually far too busy to think about what I was doing, what with school and Grampa's death and the mills. I'm glad that's over, but I don't regret working there.'

Elsie gave a delicate shudder of distaste. 'You can't mean it, Victoria. When I think of how you were raised. Your grampa worshipped you. We were sure he'd leave you the farm. My mother thinks there was maybe some funny business with lawyers there.'

Victoria thought of their dealings over the years with Arbuthnott Boatman. 'Nonsense, Elsie,' she said sharply. 'Grampa just never got round to changing his will. Perhaps he couldn't bring himself to change it, to write his only child out. Anyway, I assure you that Mother and I are delighted with the house and the way things have worked out. She has a lady lodger from the Harris, now, a classics teacher, Miss Davis. Can you imagine if we'd had the boarding house when we were at the Harris?'

'You could have had old Smelly Socks to board. You'd have got one hundred percent in everything,' laughed Elsie.

'If we hadn't been closed as a health hazard.'

Tensions were forgotten for a moment as they laughed like young girls instead of the sophisticated young ladies they now were.

'And I hear Dr Currie boards with you as well. Now there is someone I admire, Victoria, and would love to meet sometime, if it could be arranged. What integrity. A woman in a man's job and she carries on with such courage when mud is thrown.'

'There's no dirt would stick to our Dr Flora,' responded Victoria, ready to fly to Dr Currie's defence, but Elsie was totally on her side.

'I'm so jealous of your life, Victoria,' she said. 'I have been no farther than Glasgow, and you have sailed all the way to India and lived there.'

'Your bairnie's greetin,' said a wee voice at her elbow and there stood Jimmy Sinclair. 'We're gettin another yin, are we no, Mammy?'

Victoria laughed and so did Tam, who had come up with his wife to claim their son. 'There's Mammy's wee surprise ruined.'

Victoria introduced them to Elsie, who seemed rather surprised at the obviously intimate terms between Camerons and Sinclairs.

'I'll away and get Andrew. He's heard the fiddles and is furious at being shut away from the fun,' said Victoria. 'I'm so thrilled at your news, Nellie, and I'll hear—'

What she expected to hear was cut off by an excited cry from Catriona. 'Victoria, Victoria. Look who's here.'

Victoria looked past her mother to the door. There stood a beaming Davie, Dr Currie and . . . Victoria jumped up from her chair and ran.

'Eddie, oh, Eddie,' she said, her heart in her eyes and, oblivious to the crowds around them, Eddie folded her in his arms.

He did not seem to be in the slightest bit embarrassed by the loud cheer that went up as he kissed her vigorously.

'Come on,' he said, grabbing her by the hand and pulling her to the door. They went out into the starlight, accompanied by a great many catcalls, whistles and cheers. 'These farmers are just like the ones at home. They'll be telling me what to say next.'

'You're so sunburned, Eddie,' said Victoria, suddenly overcome by the actual presence of someone she had been dreaming about for so long. Dreams are usually easier to deal with than real live human beings. 'I've got some marvellous ointment Mother makes from elderflowers.'

'My mother makes wine from elderflowers,' said Eddie. 'They can swap recipes.'

They did not notice that the barn had gone quiet behind them and that more than one person was making an excuse to take a little fresh air.

'I didn't take a train from Tilbury to talk about flowers, Victoria. It's all clear in my mind now. I was a good soldier while there was a war on, but I'm not cut out for army life, not as an officer anyway, and working in an office would bore me to distraction. I'm a farmer and I can't change that. I want a farm of my own – just a wee place would be fine, a place where a man can breathe, where he's not falling over his neighbours all the time, like in India. God, but that's a soul-destroying place, Victoria. I've travelled as much as I ever want to travel. I know you enjoyed it, but the road from Scotland to England is about all the distance I want to travel now. Now, you got my letter, I know, and I wrote everything but the actual words. But you know what I was trying to say. I've talked to your mother and to Mr Menmuir, and now I'm asking you. Victoria Cameron, will you marry me?'

In later years Victoria was to tease Eddie that she had never really accepted his proposal. If she did answer, then her reply was lost in the cry of joy from the host of well-oiled folk standing in the doorway. The fiddlers began to play for the young couple, enabling them to waltz as they had waltzed on the night they had first met.

Elsie sat watching them and, although she had decided that marriage was not the only fulfilment available to women in the twentieth century, she had to admit that they did indeed look very right together and she sighed. Dr Currie watched them with tears in her eyes. Were the tears for her own situation, or were they tears of happiness for Victoria? Catriona's were tears of joy. 'He's such a fine-looking boy,' she told Davie for the tenth time. 'What a pity he has to go all the way to England for a farm. You master that car, Davie, and we won't have to rely on the bus.' She sighed with happiness at the thought of all the pleasurable preparations she would be called upon to make. 'Davie, do you mind old Jock? Do you mind what he would have said about this party?'

'I know fine what he is saying, Catriona Menmuir. He's saying, "What a lovely walnut shell day!" '

20

IT WAS DAVIE WHO BROUGHT Catriona the letter. He had looked at the stamp but could not decipher the smudged writing. He didn't think it was an Indian stamp; he had got used to those while Victoria was abroad. He stood in the garden, where he had been when the postie had given him the fragile letter with its blue and red markings and its strange stamp, and he almost wished that it had not come. Why, he could not understand.

Catriona was making something special to try to tempt Dr Currie's never robust appetite. 'This'll bring a gleam to her eyes, will it not, Davie?' she asked. 'She never did much mind what was set in front of her, not like Miss Davis now, who likes her food. Still, these days I feel I could put old rope on Flora's plate and she wouldn't notice. That letter must be for her,' she added, rejecting the envelope that Davie held out. 'Or maybe it's for Miss Davis. Who would send me an airmail letter?'

'It's got your name on it.'

Catriona took the letter and looked at it suspiciously. 'Mistress Cameron,' she read. 'How very old-fashioned. Goodness, Davie, haven't I been *Mistress* Menmuir for near two years. Who would be writing to Catriona Cameron and not know that she was Mrs Menmuir?'

Davie laughed as he watched her study the writing. He had had a few letters from his parents during the war and he had ripped them open within seconds of receiving them into his dirty, muddy hands. How could she stand there and look and question, and never ever think to open the envelope to unravel the mystery? 'Better open it, love, and find out.'

Since the unopened letter would certainly yield up no secrets, Catriona took a sharp knife from the kitchen drawer and slit the tissue, like paper. She read it carefully for a few minutes, then she gasped and Davie, to his horror, saw the colour literally drain from her face. He ran to her and helped her into a chair.

'What is it, love? Bad news?'

'Yes. No. Oh, Davie, it's John. There have been times when I did not wish him well, but this . . . He's dead.' She gestured with the flimsy paper to Davie, but he shook his head. He wanted to read nothing about John Cameron. Catriona took a strengthening breath and went on. 'There was a terrible accident.' She looked at the letter again and then in anguish at her husband. 'Near a year ago now, Davie. You would think they would have sent one of them Marconigrams, but well, maybe John didn't tell them about us. It doesn't say how they knew to write to me. He'd never have me still down as his next-of-kin, do you think, Davie?' Poor Davie was becoming so frustrated by his wife's dallying that she bent her head again and finished the letter. 'He was staying with friends in Mexico. Mexico? This is from their lawyers. Why didn't they write themselves? The guest rooms – what a fancy house, Davie, to have special rooms for guests, not just a spare bed, but a separate room. Anyway, they are far away from the family living area of the house and John was alone in his bedroom. It was a rattlesnake, Davie. Somehow it got into the house and he must have surprised it, they think. He was bitten several times and no one heard him. The man of the house, someone called the padron, went upstairs when John did not appear for some kind of late party they were holding, some celebration or other, maybe to do with the end of the war. They were all waiting for him downstairs. This man, the padron, shot the snake, but it was too late to help John. What kind of a country is Mexico, Davie, where a man walks around his own house with a gun? Oh dear God, Davie, what a dreadful way to die.'

Catriona began to cry for John, her once-loving husband; for old Jock, who had died at odds with his only child; for Victoria, who had never really known her father and whose memories of him were unhappy ones. Like Davie, Catriona had quite forgotten that wee Andrew was also John's child.

Davie held her and let her weep. She should mourn. It was natural, but as he held her a feeling almost of exaltation filled him. He too could have prayed for an easier death for his enemy, but John was dead and his heir was Victoria.

Catriona was too stunned to realize what John's death meant, but Davie and his father had talked of old Jock's real wishes many times. And the old man's wishes were finally, in this dreadful way, being carried out. The realization could only cheer Catriona.

'Sweetheart,' Davie whispered into her hair. 'Do you see what this means? The Priory belongs to Victoria. Your daughter won't have to leave you after all.'

At his words Catriona began to wail.

Arbuthnott Boatman was a contented man. He poured coffee from his mother's second-best Georgian silver teapot into one of her second-best Minton coffee cups and handed the cup, resting on its equally lovely saucer, to his newest client.

'Your grandfather would have been very happy to see you at the Priory, Victoria. He always meant to make a will in your favour. I reminded him several times, but I don't think he could bring himself to face the fact that John was a waster.' Suddenly conscious of the fact that he was talking about his client's late father, the lawyer coughed as if needing to clear his throat. 'Too bad about John. Perhaps if his mother had lived . . .' He changed the subject. 'I do hope your mother is well. It's been so difficult for her.'

'She has Davie and wee Andrew, Mr Boatman. No one could have wished . . . my . . . father such a death. The Mexican family was so sorry; they did and said everything right – through their lawyers, of course. Perhaps they speak no English. I would like to have known more: what my father was doing in that strange country, for instance. Still, they explained the circumstances of his death. He surprised the snake, which was nesting in an unused guest room. It's an arid country and sometimes snakes do come inside, as in India.'

Mr Boatman coughed. He led the topic of conversation away from the horror and sadness. 'You do understand that the farm and the trust fund are solely yours, Victoria. Your brother is—'

'To have half of everything, Mr Boatman,' said Victoria firmly. She had had plenty of time to think since her mother had broken the news of John's death. 'Andrew is not to blame for the circumstances of his birth. But that will be between us. My mother and stepfather love Andrew and think of him as their child. I have written to my fiancé. Naturally I am hoping that we will make our home here: he is a farmer too, and it would be good for the Priory to have an owner-occupier who loves the place. Edward could certainly come to love this area. But he is a proud man and may prefer a tenancy in England to living on my land.'

My land. Oh, what beautiful words. Until the lawyer had actually spoken, Victoria had not really let herself think about her new status. She owned outright every stick and stone of the Priory – every flower, every tree – and she loved everything about it: the burns that rippled through the meadows, even the very leaves that fell from the trees in autumn. Edward had to be prepared to love it too. Edward, however, did have some initial doubts.

* * *

'Come on, Eddie lad.' It was his father who convinced him. 'It's the twentieth century. Marriage is a partnership, you know, and you're a farmer born and raised. You'll be equal partners with Victoria. She may own the land but it's your brain and your sweat as will make a living from it. From what you tell us, your lass hasn't lived on the farm for years, and even then she did no labour . . .'

In his tiny room under the eaves Eddie read and re-read the letter from Victoria.

I can't mourn him, Eddie, although I hate to think of anyone dying such an awful death.

The farm is mine, because Andrew is illegitimate, but I have to share it with him. I know you will understand. There's room too for my mother and Davie and the bairn, but they want to stay in Blackness Road and make a go of the boarding house. Mother thinks newlyweds should be on their own. Besides, she has come to enjoy being self-supporting, and now with Davie as a partner . . .

I have thought and thought and prayed too for guidance and I can see that a proud man might not want to start married life in his wife's home. I cannot sell the farm, but I am prepared to leave a manager in it and to go with you wherever you want. In India I realized that I can only be happy on the land, but I will be blissfully happy wherever you are.

Eddie sighed with sheer happiness. What a woman! She was prepared to give up her beloved home for him. No. When they were married, he would work all the hours God gave him to make her farm the best in the county. On that first visit to Angus, when he had asked Victoria to marry him, they had wandered hand-in-hand around Priory Farm and his trained eye had seen areas that could be improved, low hills where nothing was growing, which would be ideal for sheep-grazing. He knew nothing of soft fruits, but Victoria had told him there was a great summer trade and plenty of workers from nearby Dundee to help with the abundance of raspberries, strawberries and redcurrants, which hung like rubies from the bushes every harvest. And Eddie would learn. He rolled off his bed and went to the table in the window to write to his Victoria. He was much more romantic, or perhaps more expressive, in his writing than she.

My dearest wife-to-be, he began and filled a page with sweet nothings that Victoria carried close to her heart until the next letter arrived.

Victoria had, of course, given in her notice to Mr Smart and had spoken to him about the advisability of having her train her own replacement. But although he said that he would advertise for a new assistant, he seemed reluctant.

'He hates change,' pronounced Miss Jessop. 'It's a shame you are to marry, Victoria, although I don't mean that in a nasty way, because I had hoped to see you in my place. Goodness knows what he will do when we both leave him. Men are such useless creatures, you know. They may talk about widening the Empire, but that's all it is, talk. Your Eddie will be the same, you'll see. Just start the way you mean to go on. Tell him what to do, congratulate him when he's done it and let him believe he thought of it for himself.'

'How that dried-up old stick, who's never got near a man except the two of us in all the time I've known her, can pass herself off as an expert on holy matrimony, I can't imagine,' sniffed Mr Gordon, once Miss Jessop was safely installed in Mr Smart's office.

Victoria smiled as Euan proceeded to tell her how to make her marriage a success. That was what she had heard everywhere since her engagement had been announced. The only two people who had not spoken to her of the dos and don'ts were the two people to whom she would have listened, her mother and Dr Currie. Both seemed strangely reluctant to offer advice.

'It's a meal on the table, clean clothes, and a bit of peace and quiet to read the paper, Victoria. That's all a man needs, and as for women, get your Eddie to take you to the pictures every Saturday night without fail. A bit of a canoodle in the one-and-nines and a choc-ice at the interval, maybe fish and chips on the way home.'

'Thanks, Mr Gordon. You can tell him yourself at the wedding.'

'And well I may, my girl. Forty-two years I've been married, man and boy.'

Catriona prepared for the wedding with a joy that knew no bounds. Victoria was to marry a young man whom she loved, and who loved her, and she was to live in the home that her beloved grandfather had always wanted her to have. *I always meant to put it in the lassie's name.*

How often those words had come back across the years to disturb Catriona's rest. But everything was going to be wonderful. John was gone and the farm belonged to Victoria. Everything had turned out well. She had Davie – dear, kind, hard-working Davie. A few weeks before the wedding, when she should have been deep in preparations and thank-you notes, and possibly even pre-wedding nerves, Victoria, with the aid of Dr Currie, had taken Catriona and Davie into Dundee. And there Victoria had presented them with a motor car.

'It's a second anniversary present, or a gift to celebrate my wedding. Call it what you like.'

Catriona and Davie had stared in fascination at the little black car.

'Lassie, lassie, brides don't give presents, they get them,' said Davie, as he wiped away a tear.

'The look on your face is my wedding present, Davie Menmuir,' laughed Victoria. 'No, seriously, it's to say thank you to the two of you for everything.'

'This is not the way to begin married life, Victoria Cameron,' said Catriona sternly, but her gloved hand was already protectively rubbing imaginary dust off the mirror. 'You shouldn't be spending your trust fund on presents.'

'I have only bought one present, Mother, and if you're going to mention Eddie, he knows and he thinks it's a great idea.'

'And I shall give you driving lessons, Davie, and you too, if you'd like, Catriona,' volunteered Dr Currie.

Catriona managed not to shudder at that terrifying prospect, but privately vowed that Davie should learn to drive properly, in spite of dear Dr Flora's efforts to help. He was already talking of hiring himself out as a private taxi service. So much quicker than the horse buses or those draughty, uncomfortable motor buses that now clanked their way up and down Reform Street and the High Street. They would keep the telephone when, and if, Dr Flora left – she had said nothing about Lord Inchmarnock for some time, but Catriona had noticed the new watch and the long telephone calls. The telephone machine would be very convenient for her other lady guests and for those who needed a private hire car.

Wedding gifts for Victoria were pouring in from all sides. Mr Smart had given her a chest of sterling silverwear, each piece engraved with a flamboyant W. Dr Currie had given them a Crown Derby dinner service. Davie's mother had hand-embroidered an Irish linen tablecloth and twelve napkins. Where had she ever found the time, and how had those hands that could milk cows, cut wheat, clean brasses and sort potatoes ever been able to do do such delicate work? The stitches, Catriona admitted, for she was always honest, were better than her own. There were humbler gifts aplenty too, but each one would be treasured. Thank-you notes were being written as the gifts arrived and posted back to the generous givers.

'We'll not need to buy a thing, Mother,' said Victoria as she unpacked a second copper jelly pan. 'That means that what's left of the fund can be used to improve the farm. Oh, Eddie is so clever and has such plans. If only Mr Smart . . .'

She stopped talking, but Catriona pressed her. 'Mr Smart what, dear?'

Victoria looked perplexed. 'He hasn't been himself since we came back from India and he hasn't done a thing about replacing me. I'm worried about him. I hope he didn't pick up some germ there.'

Catriona could imagine just what illness ailed Mr Smart. She had seen his eyes as he watched her daughter, and she ached for the man, but that was the way of the world. Victoria was far too young for Alistair Smart, and Catriona hoped he would soon realize it and put his foolishness behind him. He had been so generous and always so unfailingly courteous. Well, the young ones would soon be married and busy on their farm with their new life. An advertisement for secretarial assistance should go into the pages of the *Courier* soon, and the sooner the better, thought Catriona, giving her already scrupulously clean sink another wipe.

And Elsie had taken Victoria to a meeting in the Caird Hall. This votes business was another nonsense that Catriona could well do without. The sooner Victoria was married and away from the sphere of Elsie's influence, the better. Elsie had taken to popping in once or twice a week during the school dinner hour, and Victoria was certainly enjoying having a friend to talk with again. Better when they were discussing dresses and petticoats, though, rather than women's rights. Catriona rubbed her kettle until she could see her face in it. This war had done no good to anyone and had merely, as far as she could see, turned the world on its head.

'And when you're standing on your head,' said Catriona as she attacked the dust that had dared settle on her clean floor, 'you're no use to man nor beast.'

'Who is standing on his head?' It was Davie at the door, looking for his dinner.

Catriona laughed. 'There's nothing like getting angry for getting brasses clean. Away and lift the bairn, Davie, and we'll maybe have peace to eat our dinner. I'm glad Elsie has classes this afternoon, for Victoria has another fitting at Draffen's and, according to Miss Morrison, yours truly has no eye for the latest fashion. She'd have Victoria walking up the aisle like a dressmaker's dummy, if I wasn't there to say No. Victoria's mooning over Eddie's letters all the time: I don't think she knows what she's doing half the time.'

'Don't underestimate my lassie, Catriona Menmuir. Remember she's been all the way to India and back again, and run a big office full of men that say "Yes, Miss Cameron" and "What do you think of this, Miss Cameron?" She'll let Elsie talk, but I've yet to see her pay attention to anything she's said.'

'Except this suffrage nonsense.'

Davie took his undisputed courage in both hands. 'Maybe the lassies are in the right of it, Mistress Menmuir,' said he and ran off up the stairs to fetch Andrew.

21

Las Estrellas, Mexico

AFTER THE CRUEL TWIST OF fate that had left her a widow, Lucia Alcantarilla Cameron had passed the long, hot days in prayer. At least, she had tried to pray, but for what? Mother Mercedes told her that she should pray for the repose of the soul of her husband, so cruelly killed on their very wedding day, but Lucia did not want to pray for a dead man. She wanted to pray that it was all a horrible mistake and that the accident had not happened and the snake had not killed Juan. She wanted to pray that one day, perhaps today or surely tomorrow, her father would come to the convent and he would say, 'Ninita, you are forgiven. I have come to take you home, so that you may have your baby in the luxury and comfort into which an Alcantarilla-Medina-Cameron should be born. As far as we can, we will put these awful months behind us.'

But he had not come.

Sitting under the jacaranda trees, Lucia had remembered the discussions between her father and her brothers, when it became obvious that the child-widow was about to become a child-mother.

'We will take her to Mexico City. Surely a doctor can be found there who will abort this child.' That was Alvaro.

And then the shocked tones of José Luis. 'Cut out your tongue in shame, Brother. To abort a child is a sin against God's law.'

Abortion was, to the religious José Luis, a sin. Those who whispered, therefore, that he had known of the snake in the unused guest chamber were wrong. For surely if to kill an unwanted baby was murder, then conniving at the death of a man who had seriously embarrassed one's family must also be murder and just as much against the laws of God.

'No reputable doctor will do it.' This from Jaime. 'We should take her to the United States, Papa. There you can pay for anything.'

But to *el padrón* also, abortion was a sin. He would have none of it. 'My daughter will return to the convent of the good sisters. When this child is born, they can find a home for it and my little girl will come home and be herself again. We will find her a suitable husband and she will forget this madness.'

But no one asked the girl, who could never again be as she had been before. She had loved a man and she agreed with her father and brothers that she had sinned, but she was a married woman with her mother's ring upon her slender fingers and there was no need to hide her away in shame. The baby was her compensation for the loss of all her dreams, and so she would change those dreams. Papa would see the baby, his first grandchild, and he would love him. But Don Alejandro did not even say *adios* to his daughter, as she left to hide her mistake away in the cloisters. Lucia did not understand that it broke his heart to banish his treasure, and that he did it only because, after hours of prayer and thought, he had come to the conclusion that what he was doing was best for her.

José Luis had accompanied her. 'Everything is going to be all right, Ninita. This man took advantage of you, but the sisters will never tell and no one, except your future husband, need ever know. It is a bad dream, Lucia, but all dreams, good and bad, come to an end. See, I have bought for you some dream-stealers.'

He handed her the jeweller's box and, when she would not take it, he opened the box. As if she were a child who could be humoured into taking her present, he showed her the beautiful silver earrings shaped like delicate spider's webs, from which dangled a tiny silver eagle's feather. In the centre of each fragile web hung a small turquoise.

The indigenous peoples of the Americas believed that if they hung a representation of a spider's web above their baby's cradle, any bad dream flying through the air would become trapped in the web and would not disturb the child's slumbers. Clever jewellers had taken the legend and turned it into money.

José Luis had bought her the pretty baubles because he loved her, and he was sorry that he had had to make her cry. The old Lucia would have delighted in them, and would have thrown her loving arms around her brother's neck and kissed him. The new, mature Lucia had turned her head away and looked out of the dusty windows of the car.

'Lucia,' pleaded José Luis, 'try to understand. The blood of hundreds of years of Spanish history flows in your veins. It must not be mixed and weakened. You have had a shock and, unfortunately, you are to have a child. But you will never see the baby and therefore will not love it. It will be as if this year had never happened. Papa talks of taking you to Europe. Think, Lucia. Paris, Rome, Seville, the city of your ancestors. You will come home and there will be celebrations and a real marriage, to someone who is worthy of alliance with you. There will be other babies. Wear your earrings, Ninita, and let the bad dream go away.'

But Lucia did not wear her dream-stealers and she did not answer her brother.

And she did not speak much to Sister Mercedes, who loved Lucia and who did not judge and wonder how it could be that there was to be a baby and there had been no wedding night.

They walked in the convent gardens and the nun described the great cities of Europe, which another young Mexican girl of good family had seen years before.

'It is strange, Lucia – and you must write to me and tell me if it is the same with you – but everywhere in Seville I saw and heard Beethoven, who was not of course a Spaniard.'

But the nun looked at the stricken face of the child beside her and stopped speaking of Beethoven, who had written so powerfully of the rights of man. What, she wondered, of the rights of women and of this unborn baby, condemned even before his birth by the very people who should have loved him most?

'Mozart, too, set operatic work in Seville, Lucia.' The nun tried again, but she fell quiet at the realization that perhaps *Don Giovanni* was not the best opera to discuss with a girl who, according to her father, had been violated.

Lucia saw her difficulties and smiled politely. 'I prefer Beethoven, *Madre*,' was all she said.

For the months of her confinement Lucia was biddable. She rose each morning and went to the chapel and seemed to pray. She ate a little of everything that was presented to her, but only smiled when coaxed to eat and reminded that she was eating for two. Every day she walked in the shade of the gardens and sat reading in the cool of the evening. Twice Don Alvaro arrived in secret and she awoke to his presence like a flower to the sun.

'Don't let them take my baby away, Alvaro,' she begged.

'I don't know how to defy our father, Lucia. If he knew I was here . . . We must pray for time, little sister. Papa loves you.'

Her delicate hands gestured that thought away.

'He does, Lucia, but I think perhaps he does not know how to love. He mourns for you as if you were dead. He truly believes that this is the right thing to do, and maybe it *is* best.'

She stood up imperiously. 'Leave me, Alvaro.'

'Please, Lucia, listen. To deal with Papa you must be as devious as he. Wait. The Sisters have been asked to give your baby away. I will know where he is, Sister, and I will keep my eye on him and his well-being until we can convince Papa that he should return to his family.'

She would not ask the only question she wanted to ask: Did my father murder my husband? She smiled at her brother. Poor Alvaro. He knew how to love.

'I hope you find someone worthy of your love one day, *mi hermano*,' she said.

'I love you, Lucia, and Papa too when I am not afraid of him, and even José Luis.'

'He is a cruel man, Alvaro.'

'No. He is, as he sees it, just, Lucia. How unfortunate to be born the oldest son of Don Alejandro. I am forgiven much, because no life or death decisions depend on my competence.'

'There must be more than competence. There must be feeling.'

'Papa feels, Little Sister, and so too does our brother.'

'So they banish me with my sin to the convent and they will take my child away, an Alcantarilla Medina to be raised by some peasant.'

'You will change them. Papa can deny you nothing. How he missed you during the civil war. "Is she safer with the sisters than with me?" he would ask. "The war rages close. Should I bring the rose of the Alcantarillas here, where I can defend her honour with my blood?" And, yet, despite his care, it was in his house that . . . well, you know, Lucia. And he blames himself.'

'Was it so great a sin to love a man who is not of our people?'

Alvaro thought of the man, John Cameron, but he could not say to her, 'Only that man, Lucia, for he knew you were only a child.' So he took his sister's hand and wondered that the hand of a pregnant woman should grow so thin. And he promised that he would help her and he walked with her in the garden.

Then Alvaro went home and dared his father's wrath by admitting that he had visited his sister. And his father smiled sadly. 'Do you think one blade of grass grows on my acres that I do not know about, Alvaro? I am doing what is right, *ninito*, for all of you. I am arranging a great alliance in Spain for your sister. She will thank me when she sits at her table with many fine sons around her. But not the child of Cameron, Alvaro. The man was a cheat and a liar and he seduced a sixteen-year-old child. The snake was too good for him. Visit your sister when you must, but do not come whining and confessing your trangressions to me. And, for the sake of peace in my unhappy home, keep out of your brother's way, for he does not have my forbearance.'

A few months later Alvaro stood by the altar as his oldest brother took a wife. And when José Luis was safely on his wedding journey, Alvaro went back to the convent and what he saw there made him send his groom back immediately for Don Alejandro.

The child comes before its time and my sister does not try to help. You must come and tell Lucia that she is loved and that you will bring her and her baby home.

And Don Alejandro drove through the night to the convent and found the door to his daughter's rooms barred to him.

Inside the room, the girl lay on the narrow white bed and held in her hand the jewelled crucifix she had held on her wedding day. The pains gripped her tired body, and at last she could bear no more and cried out. The old nun who sat by her bed stood up and went to the door.

'It is time, *padrón*,' she said to the tall man who knelt at the prie-dieu in the corridor.

'If I could suffer her pain for her, I would,' said Don Alejandro. 'Do your best for her, Sister.'

'You should not have put her here, Father,' whispered Don Alvaro. 'She is a flower, and flowers die without sun. There was no sun for my sister without the love of her family.'

Don Alejandro stared blankly at his youngest son and wondered why he did not strike him for his insolence. Sun! There had been no sun for him either, for the last nine months, but soon it would be over and Lucia would come home and forget all her troubles. New clothes, jewels, travel, new friends – the girl whom José Luis had just married would be a perfect companion for his beloved daughter. Soon the baby that had ruined Lucia's life would be born and she could come home and be his little girl again. He willed it to be so.

Three hours later the sobbing nuns held out the squalling baby to him. 'She did not try, *padrón*,' they wailed. 'Her heart was broken.'

He ignored the wailing child: he felt no love, no pity, for it. He ignored his youngest son, who wept quietly by the bed. He knelt and kissed his daughter's clasped hands. Gently he removed the heavy emerald-encrusted wedding band and the jewelled crucifix. They had been his wife's jewels and then, for so short a time, his Lucia's. He handed them to the nun who held the baby.

'Get rid of it,' he said coldly. 'I never want to hear from you again. Go outside until you can behave like a man, Alvaro,' he ordered, as he pulled the young man to his feet and thrust him into the corridor.

He waited until they had gone, sobbing, from the room and then Don Alejandro knelt down on the bare floor beside the body of his child and began, very quietly, to weep.

22

LORD INCHMARNOCK TOO WAS A man who was having to adjust to circumstances. He had been taken by complete surprise when his Flora had told him that she would find it difficult to choose between him and medicine. His upbringing had not really prepared him for a strong, capable and yet intensely feminine woman. Everything he had been brought up to believe in was as much under fire as the men in the trenches during the war.

'I love you dearly, Sandy,' she had said and he could not doubt the sincerity in her voice, 'but I have accustomed myself to living without your love. I am a doctor, and I find that I cannot give that up while I am still useful. Don't make me choose between you.' She had stood up then and moved away from him, and Sandy had looked at Flora and seen that she had never been more beautiful, or more desirable, and he had wondered at this mysterious chemistry, for to most she would have looked tired and even gaunt. She had turned back to him and put out her arms, as if to hold him, then she had dropped her hands by her sides. And she had spoken eloquently about her calling and her patients.

He cast his mind back all those years and saw the young Flora – Flora, whose every unexpressed wish had been answered by an army of faithful servants. She tore a flounce on her dress and somehow it was mended. She soiled her gloves and they were returned to her clean. She was hungry and every dish that could tempt her appetite was prepared in case Miss Flora should prefer ... That dratted war had changed things – and not all of them for the better. Women who had been brought up to expect that there would always be servants to do things for them had dirtied their hands for the first time, and had enjoyed the experience, and his Flora more than most. He had jilted her for the flighty Julia, and Flora had squared her delicate shoulders and become a doctor: she had been present at births, at deaths and at every human condition in between. Now he wanted to take her away from it all and make life as sheltered and charmed as it had once been, but she did not want that. She wanted him, but she wanted her life of service too.

Was Britain ready for them both yet? He could no longer stay in Scotland, because in that beautiful country he had been too happy and then too sad. Perhaps after several years had passed he would not see Robert everywhere, would not turn with a start because the set of the shoulders of a young man who had just entered the room made him think, 'Robert'. One day he would surrender to the knowledge that Robert would not return.

England, then? No, not yet.

Australia. That was the place. As soon as the divorce was final he would go to Australia and buy some land. He and Flora would marry and no one there would care that he was divorced. Flora could practise medicine. From what the ambassador had told him, she would be welcomed with open arms. Pity he didn't know a thing about sheep – but he could learn, *would* learn. If that laddie Sinclair could step out of a jute mill in Dundee and take to farming like the proverbial duck to water, then how much easier for him, who had grown up on the land. With Flora beside him, he could do anything.

Again the searing pain of his loss tore through him.

'Oh, Robert, laddie, how can I even begin to think that I might get over losing you. But, oh dear God, I pray to be able to think of you without pain.'

Sandy sat down to write to his love and, like Eddie Welborn, he had no trouble saying what was in his heart.

Dr Currie laughed and cried when she read the letter. Australia. If they went there, it was tantamount to saying goodbye to everything and everyone she held dear: Catriona, Victoria, wee Andrew, Davie, her colleagues, her patients. And here was Victoria in the middle of preparations for a summer wedding, and Flora did not want to miss that. And did she even want to go to Australia? She looked into her heart and answered the question herself. If she had Sandy Fotheringham and her work, she would go anywhere – even to the other side of the world, away from everyone and everything she knew.

Darling Sandy,

Of course I will go with you to Australia. I would walk beside you and, with you, brave any hardship. It's going to be such an adventure, but we must go together.

I shall begin to wind up my affairs here, but there are one or two patients who still need me and who will need me for the next few months. After that, your Flora will go anywhere with you.

Victoria and her Eddie are to marry and to live at the farm. He is a very sensible young man and it is obvious that he is deeply in love with Victoria. She, of course, is walking around deliriously happy and getting in Catriona's way. The wedding is to be at Priory Farm and I should like to be here for that. Then there is Nellie's second confinement.

Wee Jimmy arrived with the help of his granny, but Jimmy's sibling is to have all 'modern conveni-ences'. You see, I am as welcome as the latest in plumbing. No doubt I will be valued in like fashion in the great outdoors.

And do you really intend to become a sheep farmer? Since your wife-to-be is determined to work, are you determined to labour too? Thank you for understanding my needs.

The next part made her write and tear up the first few drafts. She was, after all, forty-two years old and had, many years before (the year in fact that Julia had drifted down the aisle to marry Sandy Inchmarnock) given up all thought of having a child of her own. But, maybe, just maybe she was not too old. Should she say something that might raise hopes of a bereaved father? Yes. No. She wrote and discarded, then took refuge in being enigmatic.

And remember, my dearest, that my health has always been good. Perhaps one day I shall have other things to occupy me – and I do not mean 'good works', like Victoria's friend, Elsie. I shall miss day-to-day knowledge of Elsie's career, but I am sure even Australia shall one day hear of her. She has determined that the vote is not

enough and that women are also entitled to representation. A female member of parliament!
Can you think what my dear father would have
had to say about that? Perhaps it is as well that
you propose to take me halfway across the world,
for the notion of joining the martial Elsie has
occurred to me, and I fear I have already blotted
my family copybook enough. I see that Julia is to
be a member of a committee that will raise funds
for war relief. It is an excellent way for her to begin
to reinstate herself in her circle. I could not be
happy, Sandy, at the expense of her suffering. She
sent me a sweet note to wish us well, and I pray
that she too will eventually find some happiness.

Can you come north for the wedding? Then we
too can be married quietly and make that incredible
journey to the Antipodes together. See how bold
the modern woman has become!

I wear your watch every day and take comfort
from its inscription.

Dr Currie delivered Miss Mary (after her majesty
the queen) Flora (after the lady doctor) Bains-Sinclair
two days before Miss Victoria Cameron married Mr
Edward Welborn at the wee church at Liff, where both
Miss Cameron and Mrs Sinclair had been christened.

Miss Cameron was given in marriage by her stepfather, Mr David Menmuir. And since her chosen attendant was necessarily unavailable, she was attended rather amusingly by Master James Sinclair, who ate the flowers in his posy all the way down the aisle, and by her brother Andrew, who abandoned both sister and posy in the middle of the aisle, when he discovered his Menmuir grampa trying to hide from him in a side pew. Miss Elsie Morrison was heard to mutter that she could hardly wait to get both little boys to the Harris Academy for 'sorting', but even she was seen to wipe a tear from her eye at the look in Eddie Welborn's face when he turned and saw the ethereal figure of his bride coming down the aisle on the proud arm of Davie Menmuir. Neither wee boy would stand still for the obligatory wedding picture, so Victoria held one and Eddie the other. But even the stiff result of modern photography could not hide the happiness in the eyes of the new Mr and Mrs Edward Welborn. The young couple, who had both travelled extensively, went off for a week's holiday to Pitlochry, where Eddie began to teach Victoria to play golf and Victoria taught Eddie the new dance steps learned from Elsie, that arbiter of fashion, in the days before the wedding. Then they had a week in the Lake District with Eddie's parents and, during lovely long walks, began to think seriously about the changes they might make at their own farm.

'I can still hardly believe that the Priory is ours, Eddie,' said Victoria, as she sat very decorously beside her new husband on the train journey back to Dundee.

Boldly Eddie took her hand with the shiny new gold ring and held it in his. 'Yours and Andie's, Victoria.'

'We're partners, Eddie, in everything,' smiled Victoria. Then she blushed furiously at the thought that Eddie might think her remark bold.

Davie met them at the station and, after a quick visit to Catriona at Blackness Road, he drove the Welborns to their own home.

'We're having a telephone put in, Davie,' said Eddie, 'and as soon as my wife is ready, she will ring you two and invite you to dinner.'

Davie was delighted. He had never before been formally invited to 'Take yer dinner with us, Davie', and he drove off happily to tell Catriona of the delights in store. But it was three weeks later before Victoria felt confident enough in her housewifely abilities to contemplate having guests for dinner. Nellie Sinclair was anxious to get back to work and seemed to see no problem at all in working for her old school friend. Still, Victoria wanted to tidy her new house all by herself and to cook her very first dinner for company without any help. Because Catriona had always washed the best dishes before and after every use, Victoria spent a lovely day washing her new china and setting the table in her grandfather's panelled dining room. She looked at the beautifully embroidered cloth, the fine silverware and the exquisite china, and she smiled with brand-new house-wifely pride.

'The food won't be as good as Mother's,' she whispered to whatever happy spirits hovered around her, as she went about her self-appointed tasks, 'but there's a surprise after dinner and it's especially for you, Grampa.'

The Scotch broth was a little too salty, the roast beef rather well done, and the sherry for the trifle had been poured with rather too liberal a hand. But the errors were all ones that would mend, and the guests, Catriona, Davie and wee Andrew, were lavish with their compliments, although Andrew made a terrible face when he tried his trifle and demanded to get down, in a tone that brooked no argument.

'Don't let him outside, Davie,' whispered Victoria. 'We don't want him falling in our hole.'

At last the time had come for her surprise. Davie captured Andrew and kept him happy rolling nuts along the table, while Victoria told Eddie about walnut shell days.

'And because we are so happy, darling Eddie, and our life is going to be full of walnut shell days, we are going to have our very own walnut tree. Outside, everyone.'

They went outside to the small lawn that ran from the house down to the brook. A few days before the party Tam and Davie had dug a fine hole in the middle of the lawn, and sitting lopsidedly beside it was a small sapling.

'That's our walnut tree, Eddie, for our tomorrows are going to be full of walnut shell days, just like today.'

She stood still suddenly as from the past a well-loved voice came to her. *It's a day that's beautiful because you are with the person you love most in all the world* . . . Victoria listened to the beloved voice and smiled mistily at her husband. 'Now, Eddie, if you and Davie lift it and put it in, Mother and I will finish planting it.'

Catriona said nothing, but her eyes were wet with tears as she watched her husband, her son and her new son-in-law manoeuvre the walnut tree into its new home. The men walked off to the brook to sail leaf boats for Andrew, and Victoria and her mother were left alone.

'This is for Grampa, Mother, and for you, and for dear Davie who has brought so much happiness into our lives.' And Victoria knelt down on the grass and firmed the soil around the tree's roots with her hands. She laughed as the good Angus earth dulled her tiny diamond, and she brushed her ring clean on her skirt.

Catriona knelt beside her and took handfuls of soil which she patted into place around the base of the sapling. 'And it's for dear Flora, who will soon be the new Lady Inchmarnock, and for Nellie and her family, and for your Eddie, Victoria, and for all the people who will belong here after us, and especially for you. I couldn't have wished for a better daughter.'

They were Angus farm folk. They were unused to the kisses on the cheeks that other people used, often with little meaning, but their hearts were full. And there on the ground they leaned towards one another and Catriona held her daughter in her arms, as she had done when she was a child, and Victoria held her mother, and together they thought of all the people they had mentioned.

'And it's for all the others who mean so much to us, Mother. Mr Smart and all the Menmuirs, and even Arbuthnott Boatman and Lord Inchmarnock. Do you think they're too grand to want to be in a walnut shell?'

'Och, lassie,' said Catriona, getting up rather stiffly from the ground. 'Is there a person in the world who doesn't need the memory of a walnut shell day? Be happy here, lassie, with your Eddie, all the days of your life.'

Welcome to the world of *Eileen Ramsay*!

Keep reading for more from Eileen Ramsay, including a recipe that features in this novel and a sneak peek at Eileen's next book, *A Pinch of Salt* . . .

We'd also like to introduce you to MEMORY LANE, our special community for the very best of saga writing from authors you know and love and new ones we simply can't wait for you to meet. Read on and join our club!

www.MemoryLane.club

Dear Friends,

Twenty years or so ago, *My Weekly* ran a competition for a serial. I wanted to enter and so I sat down to think about what I could write. What did I know that readers might find interesting and, what was I prepared to write about which I did not know but was prepared to find out? I remembered that in Teacher Training College I had had to dress a doll in the costume of its, supposed, native land and collect as much information about said country as possible. This was part of every teaching student's life; in order to be a good teacher one had to show some skills in Art, Music, sewing and knitting. I could sing and play the piano – 'well enough for infants' according to the music teacher – and 'tried to be neat', according to the art teacher. I decided that the only way for me to pass this step to graduation was to find a country that no one else, including the teachers, knew much about. I struggled with this one and then remembered that one of the lovely air force wives at the nearby US base was Mexican/American.

Mexico. I canvassed friends, even rather clever ones. Few were sure where Mexico was. Perfect.

Dress a doll? Me? No. In one of Margarita Rosa's magazines I found a picture of an Olmec head. Not a doll, but very Mexican. The art department gave me a ball of clay which I squeezed here and there and voila – Olmec head. I put him on a board I had painted yellow – the desert – and on which a friend, much against her will, had painted a Saguaro cactus. I was halfway to a pass. I learned some songs in Spanish. Then Margarita suggested that I write to 'el regente' or mayor of her hometown.

Eventually I did, explaining that I could find little information about Mexico in the local libraries and travel agents. Time passed and the art room was full of Spanish senoritas, Irish Colleens, Welsh ladies holding daffodils, an Eskimo and a very heavy, incredibly ugly Olmec head. Then one day the postman arrived with a large parcel – for me. It was packed full of books – geography books, maps and even music, art and history books and they were written in three of Mexico's languages; Spanish, French and English. The mayor had never had a letter from a foreign student and invited me to visit. Unfortunately I never managed but after my husband and I moved to California, I studied Spanish and Mexican music and culture in Cuernavaca and Mexico City. Therefore I knew I would try to share some of my love of this 'beloved country' in a story.

I also wanted to set the story in Angus where we live, looking across fields to the sea. Not our fields but belonging to farmers who made us welcome from the start, even though we had very large dogs and gave our sons Jacob sheep and hens as pets. Our hens laid eggs everywhere and the ones I couldn't find always hatched and became chickens that scratched up our neighbour's seeds. The Jacobs could jump everything but the paddock wall and often we had phone calls from patient neighbours who never berated us when they found one or two really lovely Jacobs eating their flowers.

So, *The Farm Girl's Dream* was born.

Our sons are now grown and their children love to visit us – we no longer have sheep or hens and the children are content to note the miracles of the changing seasons, 'From **Granny's window.**'

And, by the way, I won the competition.

Best wishes,

Eileen

Walnut shell day picnic griddle scones

These scones are delicious with any topping but I love them served warm with proper butter and a cup of tea.

You will need:

200g (8oz) self-raising flour
25g (1oz) caster sugar
25g (1oz) butter
1 medium egg
75ml (3 fl oz) milk

How to make the griddle scones:

1. Combine flour and sugar. Rub in butter.
2. Mix to a soft dough with egg and milk.
3. Knead lightly, divide into ten pieces, and roll each scone into a 5mm– (¼inch) thick circle.
4. Cook over a greased griddle for about 2 minutes on each side or until golden.
5. Serve hot with butter or honey.

MEMORY LANE

Victoria's vegetable soup

Be 'pioneers' like Victoria and her mother and use up whatever is in your cupboards to make a warming soup. Or follow this simple recipe.

You will need:

1 knob butter
1 onion (chopped finely)
1 stick celery (diced)
1 leek (sliced)
1 large carrot (diced)
1 large swede (diced)
1 potato
300ml (10 fl oz) vegetable stock
salt and pepper, to taste

All you have to do is:

1. Sauté onion, celery and leek in butter until softened.
2. Add carrot, swede and potato and cook for two minutes.
3. Pour in vegetable stock and simmer for twenty minutes. Season to taste.

Enjoy this sneak peek at Eileen's new novel
A Pinch of Salt

IT SEEMED AS if she had been running for hours; there was a stitch in her side that was almost unbearable but she knew that if she stopped, if she fell to the ground and sobbed as every fibre of her small being implored her to do, she would never find the strength to get up and so she kept going. She had to keep going or Mam would die, it was as simple as that.

You haven't run that far, she told herself. *It's no even a mile tae the doctor's and no a mile frae his house tae the pit.*

'Doctor's at the accident,' had said Dr Hyslop's very superior housekeeper, 'and certainly will have no time for the likes of you tonight, Kate.' Her sniff implied that he would never have time for the likes of Kate Kennedy, but Kate knew better. Doctor Hyslop always had a smile or a word even though she sometimes found it hard to understand what he was saying.

'Speaks wi' bools in his mooth', was how the mining fraternity described the cultured tones of the village doctor, and then, of course, there was the terrible speech impediment that – so rumour had it – had prevented him from becoming a rich and famous surgeon in a place called Harley Street.

Kate ran on, her breath coming in laboured gasps. She *could* not go on but she did, proving, not for the first time in her short life that the will is stronger than mere bone and muscle. One leg followed the other, her breath was ripped painfully from her throat and tears, of which she was completely unaware, ran down her cheeks. They were tears of frustration and impotence and naked fear. Why was the doctor not at home when she got there? Why did there have to be an accident down the pit, that loathsome open jaw that gaped open farther and farther under the ground; for months it stayed quiet, almost acquiescing in the rape and plunder of its precious fruit and then, when they were lulled into a false sense of security – it roared, demanding sacrifice – but why tonight of all nights?

At last she was at the pithead. There were makeshift lights swinging from hastily erected structures and men running around as if they had no idea at all about what they were supposed to be doing. Women were standing huddled together for warmth or comfort more likely, and she recognized one of them. 'Mrs Brown, it's me mam; she needs the doctor.'

The woman looked at the girl and the effort to wrench her mind away from the horror of the coalface to the exhausted child was clearly written on her face. For a moment she seemed not to know her; she had a man and two lads down there. 'Yer mam?' she managed at last. 'Och Kate, the bairn's no comin', she said impatiently. 'Look round ye, lassie. We're dealin' in death here. Away home, yer father'll hae tae manage himself. He got her pregnant easy enough, let him be in at the end o' it.' She turned back to her vigil and then, conscious of the child still at her side, she relented. 'Away and chap up Mrs Breen. She'll no be here and she's birthed more bairns than oor braw doctor.'

Kate stood for a moment looking at the woman's back. She felt tears welling up again and desired nothing more than to submit to the luxury of being thirteen years old and to cry for her mammy, to be held in soft, warm arms, certainly not to have to face that three miles of dark fields and woods between the pit and her tumbledown home. Mam, she sobbed quietly and started once more to run – to run like a frightened hare back across the ground she had just covered so painfully. Her mother was in labour for the sixth time in thirteen years – not counting the miscarriages – and something was wrong. Kate was used to childbirth, the newspapers collected furtively for weeks and then spread on the old stained mattress, the neighbour women crowding in, glad that they were not lying in agony in that uncomfortable bed, ready to do what little they could to bring this new life into the world as easily as possible. They never sent for the doctor. His fee was minimal; but there was usually no way that Liam Kennedy could pay it – and why should he pay for something so natural as a woman's Godgiven function; this act of giving birth. Kate remembered huddling in the big box bed with her brothers and sisters, trying to block out the sounds of her mother's screams, soothing the frightened babies, telling them stories, crooning little songs. Tonight they were alone, well, Da was there, but he would be of little use what with Mam so bad and all the little ones there. When Kate had left, Da had been walking the floor with little Colm sobbing himself to sleep in his arms.

Mrs Breen. Mrs Breen. Kate turned and ran, her pains and fatigue forgotten. Behind her the desperate rescue work went on but she was already divorced from that tragedy and would never in the years to come be able to remember clearly anything at all about it.

Kate stumbled down the hill that led from the mine, reached what passed for a main street and turned left towards the miners' rows. The road ran along the river and usually she stood stock still and let the sound of running water seduce her but tonight she hardly noticed it at all; past the doctor's fancy big house with its beautiful garden – so much time, I've wasted so much time – and on to the foot of the village. Number six, that was Mrs Breen's house and it looked deserted, drawn in on itself like a tortoise. Everywhere else there were open doors and light spilling out. Of course, Mrs Breen had lost all her family long ago, no need to alert her to the trouble at the pit. Kate leant on the door for a moment to get her breath; she had been running for ever and only the door stopped her legs from going on and on. Don't sleep, she admonished herself and battered on the door as hard as she was able. What a puny battering the door received; there was no strength left in her tired little body.

I can't wake her. Mammy will die for I'm useless. She picked up a stone that lay on the path and thumped it – with the strength of a dying moth – against the door, screaming and crying 'Mrs Breen, Mrs Breen,' and not hearing a sound except the silence from inside the house. And then the door opened and the old woman stood there like a witch, her black shawl pulled round her voluminous flannel nightgown.

'Lassie, lassie, ye'll hae the house doon aboot ma ears. What's wrong?'

She bustled the slight, undernourished little girl into the kitchen assuring her that she could easily listen while she pulled on her drawers and her shoes. Kate poured out her story, be grudging every second that the old woman took; it was years before she fully appreciated how fast Mrs Breen had actually been.

*

'Where is the doctor, lass? Did I not send you for the doctor?' Liam Kennedy's natural courtesy surfaced. 'Sorry, Mrs Breen, but I've had to send for the doctor, Mary Kate's been took terrible bad.'

Mary Kate was in labour – this looked to be the hardest yet – and he was almost out of his mind with worry but he would struggle to be polite to this neighbour, however Mrs Breen seemed not to hear him. Already she was over at the box bed where the slight figure with its huge distended stomach was struggling desperately to bring her child into the world.

Mary Kate gripped the old woman's hand with desperate strength. 'My Katie, Mrs Breen,' she whispered through cracked bleeding lips, 'send her to bed; 'tis not a place for a wee lass.'

Mrs Breen smiled at her reassuringly but said nothing. She threw her shawls over the dilapidated old armchair and began issuing orders. 'Liam, boil water' – useless occupation but would keep him busy – 'Kate, hen, ye'll need tae help me wi' Mammy. Where have ye put the cloots, Mary Kate?' For weeks, Mary Kate would have been boiling and cutting up old sheets. 'Kate, get the cloots frae ben the wardrobe, that's a good lass.'

The labour went on for hours. The echoes of her mother's screams never left Kate although on that awful night she was so numbed by fear and fatigue that she paid little attention to them. After a while she was completely anaesthetized, and although, for most of the night, her body did as it was bid, when her mother died she had dropped asleep by the bed. They left her there while Liam ran, at the old woman's bidding, for the priest. Mary Kate would have wanted a priest.

Liam didn't. All his life he had lived by the dictates of the Roman Catholic Church; he ate fish on a Friday when he could afford fish, he fasted before receiving

Holy Communion on Sundays and holy days, he gave up everything he could think of – including the comforts of a sexual relationship – during Lent; in every way possible he tried to be a good Catholic. He had accepted every misfortune fate handed him, believing that his 'reward would be great in heaven', but this . . . this . . . Mary Kate lying there dead at the age of thirty-three . . .

'Get away from her,' he yelled at the boy, for that was really all the young priest was; 'don't prate about eternal life with me Mary Kate lying there in her own blood and me left with these babbies and Kate only thirteen . . .' he choked on his tears and visibly tried to control himself, his hands clenched and shaking.

'Now, now, my son,' began the young priest, desperately trying to say and do the right thing; he could not allow this child of the church to lose his immortal soul, 'you should have fetched me earlier but I have given her the last sacrament, Extreme Unction; Mary Kate is sleeping with the Lord.'

Liam, distraught, turned on him in a rage. 'Get out of my house and take your extremes and your unctions with you. Eternal life; damn you and your kind for ever – it's now she wants life. Now.' His voice broke and he turned away from the priest, brushing aside the younger man's arm as if he scarcely noticed it.

The old woman soothed the priest. 'Away home with you, Father, and say your prayers. He'll get over it, sure he will and be back to beg your pardon in a day or two.' Gently but relentlessly she pushed the young man, who spent what was left of the night prostrate on the concrete floor of his little chapel begging for help, out of the door. Then she returned to work that she had had to do far too often in her life. Forgetting her seventy-five years she issued orders and instructions to the young man who stood bowed and helplessly weeping beside the bed and when he was incapable of responding she carried them out herself.

'Ye'll need tae shift the bairn, Liam. I cannae manage her.' For a moment she could not interpret the loathing on his face and then she understood. 'Naw, it's wee Kate. The undertaker'll need tae get in, that's if he finds time with an accident at the pit. Ye'll have tae get him and the doctor; ye cannae bury her withoot seein' the doctor.'

Liam eventually got the doctor and the equally over-worked village undertaker. One hundred and nine men and boys had died in the pit, many others had been hide-ously injured and so, on the day that Mary Kate Kennedy was buried, mourners got mixed up and merely went from one grave to the next. What did it matter whether it was a boy born and bred in Dumfriesshire and his father and his father before him – fodder for the mines – or the wife of one of those Irish Catholics? Her man was a miner and miners all gave their wives far too many bairns, especially the Catholic ones. With any luck there would be some sister or auntie or grannie to come and help with the bairns for the women of the village who would normally have pitched in were all too busy mourning or nursing boys who would never walk again or husbands who would lie in the big box beds coughing their lives away.

Most of the vilage changed in the next few months for the miners' rows needed working miners and if the workers were dead, well then their widows would have to throw themselves on the mercy of relatives for the but n' bens were needed for able bodied men. More Irish flooded in but Liam did not hold out the hand of fellowship. His spirit had died with Mary Kate and he rose and went to work and he returned and sat in his chair staring into the fire until he fell asleep.

There were no relatives and so at thirteen Kate became the mother of the family. On the day her mother died she had been at school and the teacher had mentioned a writer called Charles Dickens and a book called *A Tale of Two Cities*. Oh, how Kate hungered to read that book. Reading was for school children or the leisured classes and Kate belonged to neither. She could have asked Pat to borrow the book for her but when could she have read it? Without a qualm she forgot all about Sydney Carton, until years later she was introduced to the wonders of motion pictures and fell in love with a young actor called Dirk Bogarde.

For now, Kate set herself to rising every morning at half past three. She would rinse the sleep from her eyes with the ice-cold water she had left out the night before, pull on some clothes and then, while everyone was still asleep, she would rake the coals in the grate and throw on some kindling, hoping desperately that the fire would catch and that she would not have to start it all over again. Next the kettle would be set on the hotplate, and the pan of porridge that she had also prepared before going to bed. Only then would she wake Da from the exhausted sleep that never seemed to refresh him. Almost as soon as he pulled on his moleskin trousers she would pass a mug of hot sweet tea into his hand which was still grimy from yesterday's coal dust, and then set before him a heaping bowl of porridge. Liam would wolf it down without a word while she spread dripping over four thick slices of her own crusty bread and put them into the tin box carried down the pit every day. Falls of coal and rock were quite common, if not always dangerous, and it was the miners' tins that bore the brunt of them. Liam Kennedy's tin was bashed, as were his fingers, fingers that had once, long ago, teased such sweet music from his granda's fiddle. It was doubtful that he had any idea of that same fiddle's whereabouts and even more doubtful that he would have cared. Music belonged to his childhood in Limerick.

Did he ever look at Kate's childhood? Could he have borne it if he had? He would smile when he took his dented tin from her small hands – the smile for which a stronger woman than Mary Kate Kennedy would have left her home in Limerick.

'Thank you, Allanah,' he would whisper softly and she would watch him on his long walk to the pithead until his thin figure disappeared from view. Then, at the beginning of the day, she would have her moment of peace and quiet. She would set water on to boil for the washing – Mary Kate had been fanatical about cleanliness, mouthing all the old platitudes as if she had invented them; 'Sure isn't cleanliness nearest to Godliness' – and while Kate waited she would pour herself a mug of the thick, black tea, add three lumps of sugar, and sit down in Da's chair to enjoy both the tea and the solitude. If she was very lucky she might sit long enough to enjoy the morning song of the birds, but she would never ever waste time. There were always the baby's cloots to wash, and the other bairns' clothes, and once a week the pit clothes that never got clean no matter how hard she scrubbed them on the scrubbing board. Then there were her own underclothes. She had made herself two pairs of knickers, one to wear and one to wash. As soon as she could manage, she would make a third pair for emergencies. She remembered her mother talking about a young woman who had died suddenly in the Main Street.

'Her underclothes was as clean as if she had just come out of a shop; you be sure, Kate Kennedy, that if you're ever hit by a cart, which God forbid, you need never be ashamed of your knickers.'

As well as keeping her underwear clean, Kate had a hip-bath every Saturday night and it was then that she washed her long, blue-black hair with carbolic soap. Her hair was truly a crowning glory but no one ever said so, and Kate had neither the time nor the inclination to admire it herself. Perhaps if she had, she would have stolen a few more moments for herself, to brush and curl it. As it was, she washed it every Saturday and for the rest of the week, was content to drag a comb through it every morning.